Lee Hunter
Private Detective

I0668205

The Devil Calls Twice.

The third book in the
Lee Hunter Crime files.

This book is a work of fiction, except in the case of historical fact. Any resemblance to actual persons, living or dead, is purely coincidental. All names, characters and incidents are either the product of the authors imagination or are used fictitiously and their resemblance, if any, to real life counterparts is entirely coincidental.

Contact - Olmi Publishing© -
Olmipublishing@yahoo.com

Many thanks to:

Richard and Stephen. *(Yes, they really do exist!)*
Andy Rymer.
Chris Davis.
The Prince of Wales pub, Steeple Claydon.

A word about the author.

I live in breath-taking Abruzzo, halfway up a mountain in an old farmhouse. The views of the magnificent mountains, rolling countryside and the Adriatic Sea are a great inspiration for my work.

I have been here for several years now enjoying the atmosphere, the people and the wonderful traditions of this little-known Region of Italy.

I would normally write adult fiction, of which the Beyondness series is one, although I do occasionally write for children. My latest children's book are about "Popysan the Green Dragon".

My latest works are the Lee Hunter Crime Files, the intention is to develop this series into several books, most of which will be available as paperbacks, Kindle and Audiobooks.

Check out my Facebook page, Russell.B.Smith Author, this contains my newest releases and information.

Books by Russell B Smith.

The Peter Parker Series.
The Beyondness of Things.

The Beyondness of Fear.

The Beyondness of War.

The Beyondness of Peace.

Children's books.
Popysan The Green Dragon.
The Mystery of the Stone Eggs.
Also available as an audiobook from Audible, Apple eBooks and Amazon.

Popysan The Green Dragon.
The Legend of the Golden Unicorns.

The Lee Hunter Crime Files.
Five Murders and Counting.
Also available as an audiobook from Audible, Apple eBooks and Amazon.

Bodies on the Ninth.

The Devil Calls Twice.

Tomorrow you die. (Spring 2025)
Vectis. (Autumn 2025)

Characters in the book.

Lee Hunter.
Private Detective, Ex-Metropolitan Police Force.

Chris Davis.
Ex-cop, now working for Lee Hunter.

Lennard Post.
Convicted murderer, now released from prison.

Detective Inspector Deborah Smith.
Murder Squad, Merseyside Police.
Detective Sergeant Sharron Shacklady.
Murder Squad, Merseyside Police.

Inspector Marcus Cooke.
Thames Valley Police, C.I.D.

Detective Sergeant Nick Walker.
Inspector Marcus Cooke's deputy.
Thames Valley Police, C.I.D.

Smelly Ken.
Drug addict and informant for Lee Hunter.

Tony Bianchi.
Local gangster and friend of Lee Hunter.

Richard and Stephen.
Local gangsters helping Lee Hunter.

Victoria and Emma.
Lee Hunters daughters.

Olivia Cranfield.
Ex-girlfriend of Post.

Peter Dexter.
Ex Detective Chief Inspector, person originally in charge of the case.

Paul Willow.
Ex Detective Inspector and partner of Peter Dexter.

Twenty-two years ago.
The Royal Courts of Justice. London.

Court number 1 was packed, reporters, members of the public and families of the victims watched in silence. The atmosphere was electric but hushed, the trial had come to a head and the judge was ready to pass her sentence. The accused stood behind the brass balustrade of the dock, escorted on both sides by a prison officer. The judge, resplendent in her red robes and wig looked up from her papers, took a deep breath and began to speak.

"Lennard Post, you have been found guilty of the murder of your wife, Julia Post. During this trial you have shown no remorse or sorrow relating to the events of some eighteen months ago. You strangled and then stabbed Julia nineteen times in a strangely ritualistic manner. Following that, you dumped her naked body in a lay-by, in plain sight of passers-by.

Despite the overwhelming evidence and supporting statements, you continue to plead your innocence. You seem unable or perhaps unwilling to accept any blame or responsibility for this crime, that is, the brutal murder of your wife.

You have shown yourself to be both callous and lacking in any remorse. In fact, you seem willing and indeed insistent in blaming others for this crime, which you clearly committed and have been found guilty of by the jury. In addition, you have continuously called into question the integrity and professionalism of the Police force and the detectives involved in this case.

I consider you to be both extremely dangerous, and according to the psychologist's report, someone with an antisocial personality disorder, sometimes called sociopathy. There are also reports stating that you present a high level of risk to members of the public due to your sociopathic tendencies.

Therefore, I have no choice in sentencing you to the maximum term permitted under the law, that is, life imprisonment. I shall be recommending to the Home Secretary a term of no less than twenty years be served before you are considered for release.

Dock Officers, take this man down"

Thank goodness for summer.

I hate the cold, I guess I am not alone in that feeling, but summer is here, and I am nice and warm at last......well most of the time. I had an unexpected invite from Tony Bianchi, he is importing a new line of Scotch whiskey, never before sold in England, it's only £500 a bottle! I have decided to go along to the launch party, at least the free samples might be fun.

I rang Jan Talbot, see if she wanted to come. Since the last case she has not been able to return to work, or any part of normality to be honest. She is certainly on the mend but it's going to take time, a lot of time. Jan is a strong woman, much stronger than myself, not sure if I could have ever recovered from what she has been through. Anyway, she is getting the best treatment and support, her job is here for her when she feels the time is right, absolutely no pressure there.

So, what am I up to? I think I might take a short break, go and visit my daughters in London. Oh yes, I have hired Chris Davis to help run the business. Like me he is an ex-cop, some 30 years in the job, mainly violent crime, murder and a spell with the drug squad. Without Jan the book keeping is a bit.....well, behind schedule. We muddle through the paperwork and accounts, try and keep on top of the admin but it's not easy, we are both rubbish at it, so we end up going to the pub, that's never going to work.

Still, it's nice to have someone in the office, I don't like working alone, I am too easily distracted. Chris is a great help, hardworking and very conscientious, and being from around these parts, has lots of good contacts. I hope he will be here for a long while, the trouble is, he is 60, has a great Police pension, and no mortgage. So, what's keeping him from just going off and doing something more interesting? Well, he says he enjoys the work, hates golf and gets bored sat at home, long may that last!

So, I need to ring my girls, arrange a convenient time to drive down and stay for a long weekend. It's been ages since I spent any time with them, I guess work has a habit of getting in the way, if you let it that is! Right, turn on my 'out of office' reply for my emails and call the girls.

As I gazed at the screen there was just the one email I hadn't responded to, some rambling nonsense from a Lennard Post. It's been sitting in my inbox for a few days, I really couldn't be bothered answering it to be honest. He had just got out of prison and wants me to help clear his name. The trouble is, he was sentenced twenty-two years ago, it might be just a tad too late to do anything about that now. Also, after reading the transcript of the case, including the judges summing up. I am afraid poor mister Post has absolutely no hope of ever clearing his name, he is as guilty as sin I am afraid, and there will be no changing that.

So, I archived the email, pushed back from my desk and began to think of my two girls. I can't wait to see them; it's been too long.

As I stood up, I reached out for the phone, pressed the 'speed dial' button for my eldest daughter Victoria, and waited for her to pick up.

"Hi dad, what's up, how's work, anyone tried to kill you recently?"

She did make me smile, but I guess she did have a point.

"Nope, still here, but there is plenty of time yet. I was thinking about driving down, spending some time with you two. We could go for something to eat, catch a movie"

"Hey dad, that would be great. Can't make this weekend though, I have a job interview Saturday morning. Nothing special but it will help pay my university fees. Not sure about Emma, I think she might be off to some muddy field to watch a band and drink lots of warm beer"

I felt a crushing wave of disappointment wash over me. It was my fault of course, I should have checked first, they have lives to live, just like me. Lives that I had neglected for far too long, one day that might well jump up and bite me.

"Oh, ok well what about next weekend?"

"Yeah dad, that will be fantastic. Emma and I were planning a catch-up weekend of girlie movies, wine and Chinese food. Having you over would be really cool, when will you arrive?"

"Saturday, late morning, can I stay at yours?"

"No prob's dad, I will tell Emma, she will be stoked, we will have a laugh"

We chatted for a while, it was so nice to hear her voice, she made me feel young again, well just a little bit younger. We talked about life, her university degree, we even got around to boyfriends. Emma seemed to be doing just fine, still living with her mum, living life to the full. It seemed like months since we last caught up, to be honest it was, and it did strike me just how quickly life moves on.

Anyway, that left me late on a Friday afternoon, standing in front of my computer, with an empty weekend and next week in front of me. Chris had already gone home, so I had nothing and no one to worry about, apart from me. Nevertheless, I had something to look forward to, just get through next week in one piece and then off to see my girls, what could possibly go wrong!

It was at that precise moment when the phone rang. Part of me said, 'leave it Lee, it's late Friday', whilst the other half somehow commanded my right arm to extend and pick the phone up. That turned out to be one unholy bloody mistake, what the hell was I thinking!

"Lee Hunter, can I help?"

There was a short pause, I could hear someone breathing on the other end of the line, so I knew it wasn't a missed call.

"Lee Hunter, private detective, can I help?"

"Mister Hunter, my name is Lennard Post. I sent you an email a couple of days ago, I wonder if you have had time to consider my request?"

It took me a moment or two to recall his details. When you get a dozen requests for help each day, it can get a little confusing.

"Mister Post, if I recall, you wanted my help in clearing your name in connection to a murder charge, for which you served over twenty years in prison, is that correct?"

"That's correct mister Hunter, you see I was fitted up by the police, I didn't do what they accused me of"

I felt this sinking feeling, why the hell did I pick the bloody phone up? I had some loser on the other end wanting to stick it to the police and make a name for himself in the local press. That certainly wasn't the first time I had heard that load of crap. It will probably turn out that he wants to sue them and get lots of cash, some hope of that. I took a deep breath, no need to appear rude, but I needed to get rid of him, quickly!

"Mister Post, it's not really my area of expertise, you might be better going to see a lawyer who specialises in wrongful conviction cases, you can find plenty of names on the internet, I am sure. I am more suited to much more boring stuff. Watching errant husbands get off with their mistresses, and fraud cases with the department of work and pensions"

"If I may mister Hunter, you are exactly the person I need. I have read your 'bio', you are an ex-cop, lots of knowledge, and a desire to do the right thing. After all, you managed to crack that case with those three bent cops. No mister Hunter, you are perfect for what I need to get done"

This was very strange, a lawyer would be able to sort this in minutes, either you have a case of wrongful conviction or not. Why hadn't he gone to see some specialist law firm? Maybe he already had, and they had sent him packing. I didn't want to get involved, there would be very little I could achieve, and these things can get very drawn out. If I was being completely honest, I couldn't really be bothered.

"Listen mister Post, thanks for the compliments and for contacting me but I have read the paperwork pertaining to your case, and it seems absolutely watertight.

They found your wife dumped naked in a lay bye. She had been stabbed and strangled. The knife used in the murder was found nearby, with your fingerprints on it. The police found your T shirt in your house, covered in her blood stains. You had been seen by several people engaged in a violent confrontation with your wife, in the carpark of a local pub two nights previous. Also, mister Post, you had recently found out she'd been having an affair with someone at work. To cap it all, your semen was found all over your wife's body, mixed in with her blood, how do you explain that?

It's possible that some of these things may be purely coincidental or not overly significant. It maybe that the local police wanted to get this case sorted as soon as possible and took a few short cuts. It might be that they have some sort of vendetta against you, all those things are possible.

As you say, I spent many a long year in the police and I know mistakes can and are made, but not this many mister Post. They can't fake your fingerprints on the murder weapon, or your wife's blood on your T shirt. They can't magically mix your sperm with the blood of your wife and smear it all over her body.

Yes, many people do find out that their partner is having an affair, and they don't go and stab them to death. I accept that people have too much to drink and end up in a confrontation with their wife outside the local pub, but don't go home and strangle them.

You have to look at all these things in their entirety mister Post, there are too many coincidences, way too much evidence. There isn't a court in the land who will overturn your conviction. Maybe mistakes were made, but this case is not filled with blunders or incompetence mister Post, it's what it seems, cut and dried"

There was an understandable silence, whatever this man had in mind had now surely been shot to pieces. I know that convictions are overturned, guilty men found innocent sometimes years after the event, but I didn't see that here, this was what you might call a cast iron case and that was never going to change.

"Forgive me mister Hunter, but I knew you would say that. To be honest, I would say the same thing if I were in your position. No, I will not give up on this mister Hunter, I will not go and talk to some shiny suited lawyer who will take my money and just laugh in my face. This needs a keen and clear mind, someone with years of experience in investigating crimes. I need a person who won't give up, no matter how difficult things become. That's why I have contacted you mister Hunter, you are the only person who can help me"

"But mister Post, you have spent the last twenty-two years in jail, why haven't you done anything about this before, why now?"

"Oh, believe me mister Hunter I have tried, but no one really wants to talk to a convicted murderer rotting in jail, there is no money in that! Anyone who might consider taking on such a case, simply runs for the hills once they read the court papers, they are damming I have to admit. It's as you say mister Hunter, an open and shut case, plainly obvious who did it, a very safe conviction. The trouble is, that's not the case, I didn't do it, it wasn't me, but I am the man who has been sitting in a stinking jail cell for the best part of a quarter of a century, for absolutely nothing at all. No one wants to help me, no one wants to see justice done"

I wanted to place the phone back onto its cradle, I simply didn't have the patience or the appetite for this kind of thing. Running around tracing witnesses, talking to the now retired cops, even if they were still alive, which they probably weren't. Then there was reading volumes of court papers, drowning in legalese and lawyer talk. No, I wasn't going to run down this particular blind alley, the answer would be no, it would be completely pointless.

"Before you say no mister Hunter, can I just outline a few things. I do have money, plenty of that since my parents recently died, not much to spend your inheritance on in prison. I have a lot of supporting evidence to back up my case, it's just no one wants to look at it. All I will ask for is one week, say until next Friday at noon. If you haven't found anything out by then, I will pay your bill, plus twenty-five percent bonus"

I still wasn't convinced but my fee plus twenty-five percent sounded cool. Also, most of the people involved in this case might well be dead, so there wouldn't be too much work involved in trying to find and talk to them. The guy had spent twenty-two years in prison, his time was done, no way of getting those years back.

This proposal was beginning to make more sense. A week poking about in a very cold case, no chance of overturning any conviction or changing anything at all to be honest. Only a few people would be left alive from the case, most of which wouldn't be able to remember anything to do with Post, so nothing new would emerge from that. All expenses paid plus twenty-five percent! What could be the harm I guess; it would fill in some time before I went to see my daughters and help pay the rent at the end of the month, seemed like a plan.

"Right mister Post, I will give it until noon next Friday and not a minute longer, I have a weekend with my daughters planned. I have to be open from the start though, I hold absolutely no hope of helping you. There is no way the police will look again at the case. Any witnesses may well be dead and buried and it's very likely that most of the evidence will have been lost or destroyed. The effort needed to get courts to look again at old convictions is unbelievable, judges don't like to be told they were wrong.

It is very likely, perhaps even certain that this will turn out to be a total waste of time mister Post. So long as you are aware of this, then I will proceed on my normal terms plus full expenses. Forgive me for asking, I will need your credit card details, I am sure your parents left you a very comfortable inheritance, but mine didn't and I need to pay the bills"

"That's fantastic mister Hunter, I am sure you will be able to help. I am staying at the Red Rose Hotel, just outside Southport. I can buy you dinner this evening, we can talk about the case"

"You are in Southport mister Post; I thought this case happened in Buckingham"

"It did mister Hunter. You see I knew you would help me, so I booked myself into this very nice five-star hotel, better me coming to you, saves on your expenses"

Friday evening.
The Red Rose Hotel.

Well, here I am just outside the Red Rose Hotel. A very posh looking fake neo-Georgian kind of place, made to look old but probably built within the last ten years. It had a semi fake, corporate look, set as a semi-circle around a large ornamental fishpond, with a very noisy fountain. Still, it looked very nice, and it was certainly better than braving a three-hour drive to Buckingham where this murder took place.

So, what the hell was this conversation going to be like. "I didn't do it mister Hunter; I am an innocent man". Well I have heard that story a thousand times over, and so has every other cop and Judge in the land. Trouble is, it doesn't change the fact that he was found guilty and sentenced, and by the looks of the court papers he was bang to rights.

The summers evening was gloriously warm, the sun was still radiating it's magic as it sunk towards the western horizon. I parked my car in the ample customer parking and made my way towards the main entrance. I wasn't expecting much from tonight or any part of the case but hey, it was full expenses, plus twenty five percent, what's not to like.

The gold framed doors swished open, and I stepped forth into a deep carpet sea. There was light oak furniture everywhere with serious looking business people seated, studying their MacBooks and phones. A dizzying array of signs guided to the lecture theatre, guest accommodation, bar and many more. No sooner had I crossed the threshold, than I was greeted by a very smartly dressed gentleman in a dark grey suit. I caught sight of his gold name badge with black letters, 'mister Simon Barnett, Evening Manager'.

"Good evening sir, welcome to the Red Rose Hotel, can I help?"

He had one of those winning smiles, well-practiced and perfect for putting people at their ease.

"Yes, I am here to meet one of your residents, a mister Lennard Post"

"Ah yes, mister Post, I believe he is in the restaurant, please follow me sir"

Mister Simon Barnett, Evening Manager turned at set off into the restaurant with alarming alacrity. I stumble slightly as I turned to follow him into the warm and not too busy room. In one corner sat a man, possibly in his sixties, tall, slightly built and with a shock of short completely white hair and beard. He looked very distinguished, not someone who had served the best part of a quarter of a century in jail. As I approached, he looked up, smiled and stood, holding out his right hand.

"Mister Hunter, I am so pleased you could come, please take a seat, drink?"

I sat, easing myself into the chair opposte Lennard Post.

"Pleased to meet you mister Post, or can I call you Lennard?"

"Oh Lee, Lennard will do just fine"

"Thank you, well I will have a pint of bitter please, must make it last, don't want to be caught drinking and driving by the local plod"

We ordered out food and sat back. The room had a pleasant atmosphere, there was ambient music gently playing, and the staff seemed friendly and efficient.

"Lennard, thanks for the invitation, it seems very nice here, and looks to be a very expensive place. Also, thank you for contacting the agency, but I must be both honest and come straight to the point regarding this case.

I have thirty years' experience in the police force and have dealt with similar cases during that time. The evidence is overwhelming and the chance of overturning your conviction is close to zero. Unless you can furnish me with some new and very convincing evidence, then the chance of any success on my part is extremely low.

I would like to discuss some salient points relating to the case. To be honest, if we can't satisfactorily explain these, I can't see how I could progress the investigation.

I would like to start with the forensic evidence. For example, your semen was found on your wife's body and her blood on your T shirt. Please tell me you have a reasonable explanation for this, and not just "I have no idea how that got there".

Also, the relationship with your wife. There are some witness statements regarding a violent confrontation in a pub carpark. There is also the issue regarding the affair with a man from work.

These are all very important areas Lennard, we need to be able to present new evidence, explain things away or at least prove the police wrong"

He sat back and took a sip from his whiskey. He looked around the room, perhaps seeing if anyone was listening, before turning back to me.

"Ok Lee, here it is. The violent confrontation was not what it first seemed to be. My wife and I were lovers, and moments later, we hated each other, that was our relationship. There was overwhelming passion between us, but we were incompatible, doomed from the beginning, never meant to be. To be honest Lee, you could call our relationship poisonous, very toxic, but it's what we had.

If you ask any one of our friends, they will tell you the same. That 'violent confrontation' was no more than a physical urge, a self-destructive rage, it's what we were, it's what we did. There was never any real malice, it never went beyond what happened in the car park that night, ask anyone who knew us Lee, it's the truth"

"That sounds reasonable, but why didn't that come up at the trial?"

"Because I am a bad man Lee, I do have a criminal record, some petty crime, a couple of drunk and disorderly charges, and most importantly, an assault on two bent cops. The police called me a bloody nuisance, and they said I needed to be put away. That's exactly what they did, they stitched me up and sent me down. This pub car park incident was never fully explained, the cops simply wouldn't let anyone else give a statement. They wanted me Lee and they fucking got me, cost me twenty-two years"

"Wait a minute, two bent cops?"

"Yep, on the take from local businesses, they were well known for it. They tried to extort money from my dads engineering firm. They came around one afternoon, threatening him, saying they would make sure he was shut down. Sorry Lee, but what son would put up with that, certainly not this one.

So, I waited for them, the next time they came to my dad's place they said they were going to beat him up. I jumped them, put one in hospital, they deserved everything Lee. I might not be big, but I can take care of myself. That's when it all started to go badly wrong, trumped-up charges, harassment, all kinds of shit, they wanted yours truly and they got me in the end, I guess it was inevitable. That's why the trial went so badly, they closed ranks Lee, they prevented me from getting a fair trial. They put the frighteners on witnesses, tampered with evidence, and the rest you know"

"So, you are trying to tell me that the whole force in that area is bent?"

"No Lee, just a couple of senior cops. They fixed me up, destroyed evidence, changed statements and fabricated all kinds of things. That's why I contacted you, your first big case involved bent cops, so you know what to look for"

"Hang on a minute Lennard, that was an extreme example of what can go wrong. Don't for one minute think that's normal. There was a very big criminal gang at the centre of that case, headed up by a mister Brau, with millions of pounds at their disposal.

That's nothing like your case, it takes a whole network to do what you are accusing them of, not just a couple of bad apples. They couldn't have managed what you are saying they did with your trial, sorry but I don't accept that argument.

Also, what about the forensics, how the hell did they mix your semen with your wife's blood. Then there is the knife with your bloody fingerprints on it, and your T Shirt with her blood stains all over it.

I might accept some witness intimidation, maybe even tampering with evidence but that forensic stuff, no chance, they couldn't do that. Sorry Lennard but you are going to have to try harder than that, a lot harder. And another thing, what about this affair your wife had, there are statements alleging you threatened to kill her"

"Look Lee, have you ever used those exact words, 'I am going to kill you', I have. I don't deny it, I was very angry, but it doesn't prove I killed her, they are just words"

"Lennard, I have to be honest, I don't see any way of undoing any of this, there is no way you can simply explain away a lot of the evidence. You asked for my help because I have experience as a cop, that experience tells me to walk away. I have to be truthful with you, there is nothing I can do to help. The evidence is simply overwhelming.

Added to that, the case is over twenty years old, some of the people involved will no longer be around. You can't get back the time you were locked away, even if you manage to overturn the conviction. My advice would be to look forward, make a new life and start again. You have your freedom and money, go and live your life, make new friends, visit exciting places, enjoy what you have"

He sat back once again, I knew he wasn't going to give up, I could tell that by the look on his face. Don't get me wrong, I am more than happy to take a customer's money, even if I know not much is going to come of my investigation. This however was far more than that, it was clear, this case was going nowhere.

"Lee, listen. I am paying you for your time, plus a bonus. You have been clear about the likelihood of things changing, and I thank you for that. I need you to do this for me, even if you don't hold out any hope. You said you would give it until next Friday at noon, humour me, at least until then"

Maybe it was the effects of the beer, or the wonderful food, but I could feel myself moving towards his wish. After all, a week down south, what could be the harm? I could book into a nice hotel, find some swanky restaurants, maybe even pop down to London and see some old colleagues. In fact, I could complete the job and go straight to my daughter's next Friday. My daughters place couldn't be more than an hour from Buckingham, better than the four-hour drive from Southport. I am sure Chris could manage the office for a week, it might be a nice change of scenery.

"Ok Lennard, here is the deal. I will give it until Friday at noon, my normal rates plus expenses and that twenty five percent bonus. I won't be able to change anything, I am sure of that. Perhaps I might unearth some additional evidence, but I doubt it. I will talk to whomever I can find who had any connection to the case. If you furnish me with a list of your acquaintances, I will go and have a chat to them as well. At the end of the week, I will write a report and email it to you. If there are any further leads generated from the report, I will follow them up, normal rates apply"

He smiled and extended his hand. "Thank you Lee, I need to clear my name, and I am sure you are the man to help. I am looking forward to working with you, I am sure we will have a very successful partnership"

Saturday afternoon.
A meeting with and old friend.

I had started the drive down south, the M40 was chaotic, much as I recalled from my days living in these parts. Nose to tail cars formed a river of humanity stretching as far as I could see. Welcome to the southeast corner of England, this certainly wasn't sunny Southport, that's for sure. Fortunately, I had remembered about Inspector Marcus Cooke, he's the partner of DI Deborah Smith. We had worked together in the five murders case. He is actually based with Thames Valley Police whose jurisdiction I was now in and might be able to help with any records relating to the investigation that I was now undertaking. He had agreed to meet me and share what he had discovered. I was more than happy with that; he could probably save me days in trying to find people and searching for non-existent evidence.

I drove straight to the Prince of Wales pub in a little village called Steeple Claydon. Marcus had suggested that place, it was supposed to be nice and quiet, and out of the way. I don't suppose this will take long, I am sure Marcus will confirm everything I already suspected and that will be the end of that. The area seemed pleasant enough, HS2 had certainly had an impact but I guess that was the same for many places in this part of the world.

I pulled up in the carpark behind the pub and made my way inside. Marcus was already here, sitting in the corner, two pints of bitter and a large packet of crisps at the ready. He smiled that warm and friendly smile, stood and greeted me with a friendly handshake.

"Lee, how the hell are you? I hope this isn't going to involve a load of murders and a major gangland operation. The last time I worked with you, Deborah was nearly killed, and three cops got sent down. Please tell me this is something simple, very simple!"

"Don't worry Marcus, this won't take long and there is no suggestion of anything like that"

We both laughed and sat down. The pub was reasonably quiet, warm and with a friendly atmosphere. I took a large drink of my beer, it had been a long drive from Southport, but at least I was here in one piece.

"Right Lee, let's get down to business. You asked about a case involving Lennard Post. He was convicted of murdering his wife around twenty-two years ago. It was a cut and dried case, no doubt about the perpetrator, plenty of cast iron evidence to back it up. However, I bet he didn't tell you about the other cases he was suspected of being involved in though"

"He did actually Marcus, some petty crime and an assault on a couple of local police"

Marcus laughed, "Oh no, no, no Lee, not that. Lennard Post is a very bad man indeed, much more than you think. Lee, you need to be careful about your dealings with him, he is a fucking nut case of the highest degree"

"I am not sure what you mean Marcus, he seemed ok to me"

"Well, he's not ok Lee, far from it. The local police were convinced he was involved in some very serious crimes indeed, in fact they were absolutely certain he was! Around twenty-five years ago there was a string of serious sexual offences. It all started with women being approached late at night. They were touched up, groped before the perpetrator made off into the dark.

These attacks escalated into more serious assaults, including one woman being knocked unconscious, dragged into an alleyway, stripped and seriously assaulted. It didn't end there, they were followed by three murders, all women in their early twenties. Before you ask, none of them were sex workers, just girls on their way home from a night out"

"So, what's this got to do with Post, he murdered his wife, not three young women, that's not why he went to jail"

"No Lee, there is more to this. Did he tell you about the way he killed his wife? There were many similarities between her murder and those of the three young women Lee. It only went to reinforce the beliefs of the detectives at the time, that Post was the killer, in fact was a real bonafide serial killer!

"No, he didn't mention that, there wasn't anything in the court papers either, why?"

"No, there wouldn't be, there was never enough direct evidence, they could never actually pin these other killings on anyone, let alone Post.

Just remember though that his wife was very slowly strangled with a silk scarf, a red silk scarf. Also, she was stabbed nineteen times, several in each breast and to finish, several in her crotch. She was strangled after, yes after the stabbings, he really enjoyed torturing her before he finally murdered the poor woman. The coroner recons it could have taken hours before she finally choked or bled to death, she must have been in agony and terrified for her life. This guy is a piece of shit, stay clear Lee"

"Yes, but what's this got to do with the other attacks?"

"Because the three women were tortured and murdered in a very similar way as his wife. Nineteen stab wounds, same parts of their bodies, before being strangled with a red silk scarf. Ok, these women also had other wounds, including stab injuries to the eyes and throat. Most of these details were never released to the public Lee, only the perpetrator would have known them. Considering Post was suspected of these murders, then he goes and kills his wife in a very similar way, you can guess why he was the prime suspect"

I sat back in shock, I couldn't quite get a grip on what Marcus was telling me. Lennard Post was a serial killer, and they let him go! What the hell was going on, surely this guy should be locked up in a deep dungeon somewhere.

"Hang on a minute Marcus, so why the hell didn't they charge him with the other murders and assaults?"

"Because he had rock solid alibis every time Lee. There was even some indication that he was in police custody on one occasion. However, no one could find the records, they had gone missing, but the suggestion was, he was locked up in the cells of the police station here in Buckingham. As for all the other cases, the slimy little tosser simply denied everything and pointed to where he was at the time, and no one could prove otherwise"

"But surely they could connect him with the other murders, after all, he had killed his wife in a similar way"

"Trouble was, there was no evidence at all, no fingerprints, no DNA, no witnesses, nothing to connect him with the previous murders. You can't convict someone because you 'think' they did it. He also denied everything to do with his wife's murder, I guess that's what every murderer says though. His defence lawyers maintained the real murderer of his wife was the person who carried out the previous murders and sexual offences, not Lennard Post"

"So why did he end up getting convicted of his wife's murder only?"

"Because of the fingerprints on the knife and the DNA on her body. Post and his lawyers tried to argue she was the fourth victim of the Devil, not of Post"

"The Devil Marcus, what bloody Devil, what's that all about?"

"Sorry Lee, it was a mask the perpetrator wore on each of the assaults, and as seen by one witness shortly before the second murder. That's how he came to be known as the Devil Killer"

"So, I understand that Post was not initially charged with the other crimes because there was no actual hard evidence. Also, there were no witnesses and he had strong alibis? But the crimes were very similar Marcus"

"Yep, that's what the detectives tried to argue at the time, but there was doubt you see. Perhaps he wasn't the killer of the other women after all, there was no direct evidence and Post had concrete alibis, you can't argue against that Lee as much as you might believe he is lying. The murders were very similar but weren't exactly the same! The detectives were certain it was him though, they found rope and knives in the boot of his car. Witnesses say they saw a devil's mask at his house, but that's not a crime, even if the mask was similar, and certainly not at Halloween. There was lots of circumstantial stuff, but nothing concrete, and the judges want 'concrete' when dealing with cases like this one.

He was certainly the killer of his wife, the DNA proved that, even though he denied it. The resemblance to the previous murders was purely coincidental, or at least a copycat killing, that's what his lawyers argued before the trial, so he was never charged with the other murders.

In the end, it was only a majority guilty verdict for the killing of his wife Lee. The Judge sent him down for as long as she could in the hope that more evidence would come to light to connect him to the other killings. Evidence that would allow the other cases to go to trial, but it never did. Despite the detectives' best efforts, nothing could be found.

It's really strange Lee, there is always something, no matter how remote the connection or how complicated the case, but not this time. No one is that careful Lee, it's as if things just disappeared, like he managed to get rid of the evidence, it's really odd"

"Hang on a minute Marcus. The murder of his wife, that was sloppy, DNA evidence everywhere, fingerprints on the murder weapon, but nothing at all from the other murders? To kill three women and assault goodness knows how many more without leaving any evidence at all. Then go and kill you wife and leave your calling card at every turn, that doesn't make sense"

"That was something else his defence team argued Lee. If he was the serial killer, how come he left no trace at the original crime sites or on the victims. The Crown Prosecution Service explained it by saying it was uncontrolled fury and rage when he killed his wife, that why he left so much evidence, he had lost control.

That of course just added to his lawyer's argument that the crimes were not committed by the same person. Anger and fury with his wife, cold controlled hate at the others. Serial killers like Post kill for pleasure. They enjoy the hate and the rage, they become aroused by the terror and the fear, it overwhelms them, that never changes. If he applied so much hatred to his wife's killing, he would almost certainly have done so with the other murders. That all helped Post's case, they weren't the same, it all adds up to reasonable doubt, and that's all the lawyers and judges need to throw out a prosecution.

Anyway, the case was not pursued for the three murders and assaults. Once the psychologists had made extensive reports on what serial killers are really like, and the lack of specific evidence, the Crown Prosecution Service thought it would be thrown out before it went to trial. Therefore, it was not in the public interest to chase Lennard Post for the previous crimes. At least Post would be prosecuted for his wife's murder and that would be a good start"

"That's incredible Marcus, if what you are saying is right, Post got away with several assaults and three murders"

"That's exactly what happened Lee, and nothing more could have been done at the time. Another thing though, since his incarceration twenty-two years ago, there has been no more incidents of this kind, strange that given the regularity and savagery of the original murders. Serial killers don't operate like that, there are only two reasons why they stop, because they are dead, or they get caught and thrown into jail.

Now if it's not Post, the real perpetrator may well be dead and gone, that's not beyond the bounds of possibility. However, if it is him, well the killing stopped exactly when he was banged up. A bit of a coincidence to be sure, and not one that I particularly believe. However, maybe there is something we could do now"

"Go on"

"Well, you are working for him, perhaps you might be able to get him to admit to something. He might let something slip, confirm he was near one of the crimes, not where is alibi put him. It worth trying to get something out of this Lee, let's try and put this bastard away. One thing is certain in my mind, if we don't, he will start killing again, we have to stop him Lee, before more women die"

Saturday evening.
The Travel Lodge. Buckingham.

I sat eating my Chinese and staring at my can of Coke trying to figure out what the hell I could do to flush Lennard Post out. Marcus seemed certain that Post was the serial killer and that was good enough for me. I had until next Friday to come up with something, this wasn't going to be easy. I had been involved in cases like this before, we knew who it was, but could never get enough evidence to prosecute. I had to try to get something on Post, if Marcus was right, things were going to turn deadly and very soon.

So, where do I start? My first thought was to go back to Southport and confront Post, see what he had to say about the allegations. The thing is, all these crimes happened in this part of the world, where all the witnesses would still be. No, I would stay here for a couple of days, talk to the locals, see what gossip was around, people love to gossip.

Also, Post must have family around here somewhere, had he any brothers or sisters, what about ex-girlfriends? I doubt if any of them would talk to me, but you never know, it's surprising what people will tell you on the quiet.

Of course, there was one huge problem with this case and that was time. All this happened a quarter of a century ago. Would anyone still be around who remembered the case, what kind of recall would they have? Time fades memories, distorts the facts, things can take on a whole different life, especially given twenty-five years of time.

Right, I needed a pint, this Chinese was making me thirsty. Marcus had mentioned Post was a local in the pub we met in this afternoon, The Prince of Wales. Surely someone would remember him, let's get out there and see.

As I drove up Addison Road, it was clear that the pub was a lot busier than it had been this afternoon. In fact, the car park was full, so I ended up parking on the street. I stood on the pavement looking at the little country pub. It was clearly the heart of the village in which it stood, Steeple Claydon. Ok, straight in, up to the bar and start a conversation with the landlord, he's bound to know someone who remembers what happened.

I bold straight in, no point in looking like the nervous outsider. There were a few gazes, a couple stop chatting to watch me walk over to the bar, but that reaction soon faded away.

The man behind the bar looked over and smiled.

"Evening sir, what can I get you?"

"Pint of bitter would do nicely, Lee Hunter's the name"

"Hi Lee, I am Frank"

"Worked here long Frank"

"Kind of, I am the Landlord"

Well, that was a good start, and he looked to be the right age to remember the crimes. He gently placed my drink on the bar, "anything else Lee?"

"There is actually. I am working for a client, up in the northwest, I wonder if you or anyone here might be able to help with some information"

"Oh yes, a real detective case. Go for it, I love things like this"

"Thanks, do you or anyone you know remember someone called Lennard Post?"

"Erm, not sure, how long ago was this guy about?"

"I am afraid it was almost twenty-five years ago. I am sure someone will remember him"

He looked up, scanning the customers for anyone who might be of help. I was beginning to get that sinking feeling when the expression on his face changed. He stood up on his tip toes and shouted a name across the bar.

"Simo', got a minute?"

A large rotund man, possibly in his late fifties started to make his way through the customers. He had a strong build, thinning blond hair and a ruddy complexion.

"Yeah Frank, what's up?"

"This is Lee Hunter, he is after some information about......, what was his name?"

"Lennard Post, anything you know might be helpful"

Simo' rocked back and started to laugh, his ruddy complexion glowed in the subdued light of the bar.

"Oh, the fuckin devil killer, what the hells he done now, I thought he was in jail for life?"

"Well Simo', I have some questions about things he might have done in the past. I know he was charged with the murder of his wife, but what about the other crimes he was linked with, do you recall any details. Also, did you know him, what kind of person was he? Anything you might know will be useful, I am sure"

"Know him, I went to school with the twat, lived three doors down from his family. Never did like him, my mum used to say he had a creepy feel. Not sure what that meant but she wouldn't let me out when he was around. No one liked him, he didn't have any friends. Terrible temper as well, if you messed about with Post, you were asking for trouble.

As for the devil killings, people around here were certain it was him, but that was just hearsay of course"

"Why were people so convinced it was him Simo', why did they think that?"

"Partly because he was a loner, never had any real acquaintances. He used to go around talking to himself a lot of the time, real strange. The most important thing though was his attitude to women. He had a couple of girlfriends, they told terrible tales about him. He was rough with them, he enjoyed hurting them, lots of really strange requests. He also liked to play some fuckin weird sadomasochistic games, odd man was Post, that's for certain. Every girlfriend he had ran for the hills as soon as they found out what he was like.

Everybody knows each other in these parts Lee, word soon gets around. He was the one, there was never any doubt about that, no one else even came close. Thing was, he was very careful, never left any evidence, planned his attacks when no one was around to see him"

I thanked Simo' for his help, bought him another drink and went to sit down in a quiet corner. The evidence, albeit gossip, was beginning to mount up, especially when you added it to the material Marcus had on him, but it would never be enough. I guess the cops at the time were right, they just couldn't prove it.

So where does that leave me and this case? I can ring Post, tell him I don't want the job. That's the easy way out, just forget it and drive down to see my girls and enjoy a long weekend.

I guess I could try and find some new evidence that might help catch Post for the other crimes, but I am certain that would be a non-starter and hardly worth my time. Probably the best idea would simply to walk away altogether, this cold case was stone cold, trying to unearth anything new now would be next to impossible.

I was just about to leave when a woman approached me, seemingly out of nowhere.

"Sorry to disturb you, but I couldn't help but overhear your conversation with Simo'. I need to tell you something"

I turned to my right, there was a diminutive woman, late fifties, dark hair, quite attractive. She stood only a foot or so away from me. She had a tired, almost weary look in her eyes, perhaps borne from years of pain and anguish. She looked around suspiciously before turning back to speak.

"Are you a cop or something, are you investigating that Lennard Post?"

She was clearly agitated, I wondered if she would simply stop talking and walk away before saying anything further.

"Listen, whatever your name is, if it's any easier, we could go outside into the carpark and talk there"

She looked back at me and smiled, "Actually, I could do with a cigarette so that's a good idea, let's go"

I looked about the place as we made our way to the rear exit. There weren't any obvious signs of people watching us, but the place was very busy. I couldn't help wondering why this woman was so very nervous, I guess that would come to light soon.

The evening was relatively warm, so I was somewhat surprised to see her shaking uncontrollably as she pulled a packet of cigarettes and a lighter out of her shoulder bag. Whatever she wanted to tell me was obviously making her very anxious indeed.

"Cigarette, sorry what's your name?"

"My name is Lee, no I don't smoke but thanks anyway"

"Ok, my name is Olivia, but people call me Olly. Let's go around the back, less people there, and most of the regulars stay out to the side of the pub"

Without another word she spun and disappeared into the night. This was turning into some cheap spy novel; I followed as quickly as I could before I lost her altogether in the darkness. Eventually she came to a stop, in a corner between the back of the pub and a tall wooden fence. She had chosen this place well; I could hardly make out her features in the overwhelming gloom.

"Ok Olly, what's this all about then?"

"Firstly Lee, what have you got to do with all of this, are you from the police in Buckingham?"

"No Olly, I am a private detective, investigating any links Lennard Post might have to crimes committed in these parts, at least twenty-five years ago. Anything you tell me will of course be treated in the strictest confidence; you have my word on that"

"Listen Lee, I will simply deny anything I tell you, don't doubt that for a moment. What I have to say is for your ears only. There is no way I would write this down in any statement, even if you held a gun to my head, is that clear?"

Still with shaking hands, Olly pushed a cigarette into her mouth, and lit it with a cheap lighter. She almost needed two hands to get the little yellow flame to the end of the cigarette. She inhaled a large lungful of smoke, blew it out to one side and stared directly into my eyes.

"In the late nineties me and Post had a thing, you know, boy and girlfriend. I was around twenty-five at the time and very naive. He was my first proper boyfriend, my friends told me to walk away, but Post was charming, he seemed ok to me. I thought they were just jealous; you have to remember how inexperienced I was all those years ago. Anyway, for the first couple of weeks things seemed to be normal, I was very happy. We came in here for a drink a couple of times a week, at weekends we went into Buckingham for something to eat or into Aylesbury to the cinema or a nightclub.

Then he started to ask me to do things, get tied up, rough stuff. I went along with it at first, but it escalated. I was fucking frightened I can tell you; Post really scared me; I didn't know what to do. I tried to break it off with him, but he wouldn't leave me alone. Then he wanted me to join in with other people, become part of a group doing this kind of shit, well that was enough for me. I ran away to my sisters in Aylesbury, he would never find me there, I would be safe.

Eventually I got a job in Aylesbury and then my own place, I had a new life and was enjoying my freedom. That was the last I heard of Post, until his arrest for the murder of his wife. To be honest I wasn't really surprised at all, I thought he would end up doing something like that. Anyway, I eventually moved back here, married, divorced and married again, life was as normal as it gets, I guess. That was until I overheard you talking to Simo' about Lennard Post. Is he coming back here Lee, is he coming back to Steeple Claydon?"

"That's a very disturbing story Olly, I can see why you were very frightened of him. As for his movements, I can't comment on them, to be honest I don't really know what he has planned. If he does have something to do with these other crimes people accuse him of, I aim to find out and pass that information onto the local cops, be assured of that"

"You have to sort this man out Lee, he needs to be locked up for ever, no question about that. If he is out, then women will die, I promise you. They will die like last time, with terror raging in their minds, humiliated, stabbed and strangled"

She was shaking uncontrollably, Post had certainly screwed this woman up, and probably still had a hold on her. How many others had the same story to tell.

"Listen, this is my number Olly, when you get a minute, give me a ring, I would like to talk to you some more"

"Thanks, but I won't be talking to you any further Lee, it's way too dangerous even to mention his name. This man is too evil to be anywhere near or have anything to do with, trust me. If I even suspect he is coming back here, I will be leaving as fast as I can, and I won't stop running.

I suggest you do the same Lee, if you mess with him, he will find you, and then you will die, don't doubt me Lee, he will fuckin kill you just for the pleasure of it. Please take my advice, walk away, far away, unless you want to stare into the face of the devil killer as so many women already have"

Late Saturday night.
Back at the Travel Lodge.

Olly disappeared back towards the pub side entrance. I tried to find her again, but she had already left. How bad was Post to have affected a person like this, how many other victims were still out there?

That got me thinking, surely Olly wasn't his only girlfriend, I needed to find any more that might still be alive, and willing to talk. Serial killers escalate, their crimes become worse as time passes bye, the violence and hate increases. I was certain that there would be other women just like her, with a story to tell, with more information and evidence to help lock Post away for ever. The trouble was, how the hell did I find them, and even if I did, would they want to recall the trauma imparted on them?

I picked up my phone and called the only person who might have some information. Well at least I hoped he did, otherwise this investigation was already dead in the water.

"Inspector Cooke, how can I help?"

"Hi Marcus, Lee here, listen I need some help. I need to talk to anyone who might have been connected to Post, in particular, ex-girlfriends. I have spoken to one such woman this evening, it wasn't a pleasant conversation I can tell you. She was terrified, could hardly string two words together without shaking. She confirmed what Post was like, especially with her, there was no doubt in her mind that he was your man"

"Ok Lee, but you might want to look at the clock, it's half past midnight and I want to go to bed. You are going to have to wait until the morning mate, I will have a look when I get into the office and give you a call"

I felt somewhat embarrassed at my oversight, and I apologised immediately, cases like this have a habit of taking over, consuming your thoughts and the time. It seemed that this investigation had burrowed deeply into my mind. If Post was some psychopathic killer, and it seemed likely, he needed to be locked away as soon as possible before another innocent woman lost her life.

My sleep that night was troubled, broken and filled with images of the devil, evil practices, people begging for their lives. I woke several times, fear running through me, cold sweats about my body. At the middle of all of this was Lennard Post, hiding away in the shadows, laughing at the forces of good, murdering for fun and to satisfy some perverted lust for pain and humiliation.

As I lay there in the early morning, it struck me just how difficult this job might be. The police couldn't crack this case, so what the hell was I supposed to do. I wondered if I had already spoken to the only person who would talk about Post. What if all the others were too terrified of the man to even say they knew him. Olly had been on the edge of terror last night and had finally vanished into the darkness. This man had really frightened people, that was for sure, I couldn't think of what to do next.

I rolled reluctantly out of bed, plodded into the bathroom and turned on the shower. The water was gloriously hot, and my shampoo smelled of summer fresh days, or at least that's what it said on the side of the bottle.

Post seemed to be a loner, but Olly said they used to go out during the week and the weekends. Perhaps he wasn't as detached as some people had come to think of him. Maybe there was another side to Post, another life, a different person.

This wouldn't be unusual for someone with a dissociative identity disorder. That made me smile, it's strange how you remember things. I had been on a course years ago in the Met, all about people with multiple and distinct personalities. Perhaps Post was one such person, that might also account for Olly's explanation of how their relationship changed from normality to vicious sadomasochism. If that was the case, it would complicate things greatly. One person might know Post as a friendly easy-going guy, whilst the next might see him as a killer, depending on who spoke to. That's how people like this survive, they are chameleons, able to camouflage themselves, change to suit the circumstances and become someone else altogether. One thing I was certain of though, he was a manipulator, a controlling maniac and I had to be very careful that he didn't begin to control me.

Added to this was the probability of some kind of sociopathy, in other words, a person who consistently shows no regard for right and wrong and ignores the rights and feelings of others. Post was one screwed up puppy, goodness knows how many people he had actually killed and maimed, I don't think we will ever know.

I ran the fluffy white towel through my thinning hair, got dressed and made my way down to my car. There was a café not far from the Travel Lodge, breakfast was next on the 'to do' list.

The morning was crisp and bright, a classic summers day was just around the corner. It immediately put me at my ease, a smile appeared on my face, today was going to be a good day. I hadn't got more than fifty yards from the hotel carpark when my handsfree phone rang. I looked over at the cars colour display, but the number was listed as 'withheld'

"Lee Hunter, can I help?"

"Hello mister Hunter, my name is Peter Dexter, Marcus contacted me this morning and asked me to give you a ring"

"Hi Peter, what's it in relation to?"

"The Lennard Post case, I was the principal officer in charge of the investigation, one of the two detectives trying to catch the slimeball. The other died a few years ago, so I am here to help if you need anything. Marcus said you wanted as much info' as possible. I retired from the force fifteen years ago, but the investigation is still fresh in my mind. Most cops never come across a case like that, thank goodness! We can't have Post running amok again, so whatever you need to know I will gladly help you with"

That short conversation really made my morning. This was the first big break, one of the actual detectives involved in the original case.

"Great Peter, please can we arrange a meeting as soon as. I need to get things moving, I don't want Post getting suspicious of me and running for the hills"

"Yeah, no problem, thing is, I am over in our holiday apartment in Marbella. Got the wife with me, so I won't be back for a week"

"Dam, that's a shame, I was hoping to meet you, go through a few things"

"Listen Lee, I will call you as soon as I get back. We can meet up, chat for as long as you like. I will even bring my notes and reports over, they will be helpful I am sure"

That was a slap across the face, I must admit. Just when I thought I had a great lead, and then to find he won't be around until next week. Well at least that meeting will be very helpful I am sure, and I don't have long to wait. We chatted for a short while, but I could hear someone calling his name in the background. We said our goodbyes and promised to meet up as soon as he returned.

A room somewhere.

It had been twenty-two years since the suitcase was last opened. There was a layer of dust covering the light blue plastic outer casing. Memories started to flood back. Excitement, domination, pain and fear, the smell of fresh blood, the thrill of the chase and the deep satisfaction following the climax of the hunt.

A gloved hand reached out, clad in a blue surgical nitrile rubber. It swept the layer of dust from the cheap plastic cover, causing grey particles to curl into the air. The zip slid back, the metal teeth sliding effortlessly, slowly opening the join in the two halves of the suitcase.

A hot rush surged through distended veins and arteries, pulses pounded in the temple. The mouth was dry, "slowly, slowly, take your time, there is plenty to enjoy"

Unhurriedly the lid of the case was opened, flashing images exploded, screams from hapless victims rang in the ears. There was intense pleasure here, it had been over two decades since the contents last saw the light of day. It had been a long wait but now the time had come, the time to start the hunt once more, a time to kill.

Now the contents were open to the light, gloves, a rope, a pair of handcuffs. The small block of knives and a pack of scalpels. There were two bottles of chemicals, one contained acid, the other chloroform.

The most important article was right in the middle of the case, the face itself, red, orange and black. It glared back, back from the day it was locked away, back from time and darkness. Its power was overwhelming, the fear it engendered was irresistible, delicious and all encompassing.

Once it has stalked these parts, assaulting, torturing and murdering. It was outside capture, it ruled the night, it went beyond terror and fear. Now it was at large once again, free to hunt, free to kill. It was the face of the devil, and it would take its revenge for the lost years.

Gently the mask was lifted from the case, treated with extreme reverence. It was gazed upon, softly dusted and finally positioned on the face. It gave the feeling of power, absolute control, unimaginable evil. Tonight, it would be used once again in the hunt. Its power would transform the wearer, elevate them to the status of a god, empower them beyond the comprehension of any mortal being.

"Tonight, I will range once more, but to kill or torture, to mutilate or extinguish life, what should it be? I will sit and consider, ponder the fate of that person whom I will meet. They know not of their destiny, of the meeting they will have with the devil, of the pleasure they will impart. However, they will soon know of the power I command and regret with bitter tears, the path which took them to their meeting with me, the devil killer"

Sunday morning.
Hill Sands Walk Aylesbury.

The overnight chill had caused a thick mist to form just before dawn. However, the light was becoming stronger, filled with the power of the sun. There were still dark and menacing shadows though, deep and black, untouched by the rays of the sun. The scene was quiet, occasional birds singing in a far-off tree, an early commuter driving past. The place had a peaceful air about it, the day had yet to come to life.

Simon had not been able to sleep well, not since his return from the Gulf. Fear and insecurity filled his dreams, he never felt stable, always wandering, unable to settle. The war had taken its toll, turning him from young soldier to an old, ruined soul, a shadow of his former self.

He had taken great pride in his appearance, enormous fitness and a sharp mind. Things were very different now though. He shuffled along, shattered both mentally and physically. His wife had long since left, crushed by the mood swings, alcoholism and hate.

He had one friend left though, his rescued Jack Russell dog, Jake. The dog asked nothing of him, and willingly gave so much in return. Jake seemed to understand the pain of his master, recognised his anguish, so forgave his moods swings without question. Together they lived apart from society, in a symbiotic relationship, one party a victim of war, the other of neglect and abandonment. The bond they shared was unbreakable and lifelong, it was special and permanent.

Every morning they left the flat, started out, whatever the weather and went on a long walk. Sometimes they left the town and ventured into the countryside, often they stayed within the confines of the centre. Just before dawn was the perfect time for them, they would meet no one, there would be no need to interact. They could just walk, breath in the cold morning air, bring some calm to tormented minds.

This morning was just like so many others, cool, quiet and peaceful. They were on the outskirts of town, in the boundary between suburban normality, and the green disorder of the countryside. Jake ran ahead, no need for a lead at this time, he ran free, bouncing from hedge to tree, enjoying his freedom.

It was at one large and overgrown bush that he stopped. Simon saw him back up, look around to his master and bark. He then moved once more, nervously, barking, sniffing.

"What's up Jake, what you found, a dead badger I bet?"

Simon advanced towards Jake, cautiously peering under the bush, scared that whatever

Jake had found might not be dead. The last thing he wanted was some demented fox attacking them, causing mayhem in the early morning. As he closed the distance though, he caught site of something he had seen so many times before in his earlier life. It was a hand, darkened by death, the blood pooling in its lower extremities. Closer and closer, his racing heart pounding so hard he thought it would surely burst.

"Shit, it's a fucking body, right, back off, get the dog, put him on his leash before he runs amok. The cops won't want me walking anywhere near this, fucking up the crime scene, destroying evidence"

He reached for his tatty old mobile, took a deep breath and dialled 999. Simons quiet inconspicuous existence had just fallen apart. Soon there would be questions, conversations, intrusions into his and Jake's private world. He wanted to run but knew he couldn't, the discipline of a soldier kicked in.

Sunday morning.
The office of Inspector Marcus Cooke. Thames Valley Police HQ, Bicester.

Marcus sat back and looked at his coffee steaming away on the desk. His early morning run had gone well, charging his batteries for whatever the day would bring. He disliked working weekends, it interfered with his life, but he had little choice, they were short on staff and the job never took a rest. At least he had a few days off this week, he would drive up to Southport and meet up with Deborah, he couldn't wait.

Suddenly his desktop phone burst into life, shaking him from his early morning dream. He reached out and snatched it from its cradle.

"Inspector Cooke, what's up?"

"Sorry to screw up your weekend boss, DS Walker here. I am on the outskirts of Aylesbury, some walker with his dog has found a body. The local plod's out here with me helping to secure the scene. It's a bloody mess boss, stab wounds all over, some kind of sicko by the sounds of things, stabbed in both eyes"

"What did you just say?"

"Stab wounds everywhere, eyes, throat, breasts and crotch. Some drugged up smack head gone off on one no doubt. Anyway, best get out here, you are in charge by the looks of things"

"Just to be clear Sergeant, a dead woman, stab wounds in the crotch, breasts, throat and eyes, both eyes?"

"Yep, SOCO are on their way, should know more soon. I will ring you when I have spoken to them"

Inspector Cooke dropped the phone back on its cradle and lurched back in his seat.

"No, this isn't him again surely. He's not that fucking stupid to start killing again, twenty-two years after being banged up. Dam it all, I need to phone Deborah, last I heard he was on her patch, she needs to know"

With trepidation raging through him, Marcus picked up the phone and made the call.

"Morning Marcus, why the hell are you phoning me at this time in the morning, we don't all have to work Sundays you know"

"Deborah, you need to clear your head, what I am going to tell you will blow your mind……………it's Post and he's killing again"

"Surely not Marcus, not right after getting out if jail, it's a bit obvious. What makes you think this nutter is at it again, what makes you think that?"

"You are going to laugh when I tell you"

"Go on"

"It's your best mate Lee Hunter again, he's got tangled up in all of this. He was hired by Post to try and clear his name, wrongful conviction and all that. However, we had a chat and I set Hunter right on the original case and what the cops back then knew Post had done. Thankfully he saw the light, now he's trying to find any new leads or information, let's see what he turns up, hopefully we can bang Post up again, this time for ever.

In the meantime, we want Post in a cell soonest, this man is killing again, and we need him off the streets. He won't stop Deborah, the only thing that stopped him last time was getting arrested for killing his wife.

Go see if you can grab him but be bloody careful, the last time Hunter saw him was at the Red Rose Hotel just outside Southport. He is a nutcase of the highest order Debs; he will kill just for the pleasure of it. If he's not at the hotel, then maybe he is on his way back here. Look, just see what you can find out, we need to know exactly where he is"

"How did I know Hunter had something to do with this Marcus, that man is a bloody curse. Ok, I am on it, I will get back to you soonest, if not before and don't worry, I will be very careful indeed"

The morning had turned out warm and sunny. By the time Inspector Cooke arrived at the murder scene, the early mist had cleared, and the day was looking much brighter.

The whole area had been cordoned off, yellow 'crime scene' tape flapped about in the breeze. Several uniformed officers stood guard at various points and a large white tent had been erected over the sight of the murdered woman.

Marcus parked his car some distance away, he liked to survey such scenes, walk slowly, try to get into the mind of the perpetrator. There was little doubt who had committed this murder though, it was Lennard Post. He was at large again after twenty-two years, and the murders had started again.

He was greeted by a fresh-looking WPC, clip board in hand, standing at the only entrance to the area. She looked up, perhaps she recognised Marcus, but was determined to follow protocol. She needed to ask for his ID and take his details for the crime scene record.

"Good morning sir, can I see your ID please"

Marcus smiled; it wasn't that long ago since he had stood guard over his first incident. A local alcoholic by the name of Tommy who had finally drunk himself to death. He was lying in a bus stop, empty bottle of white lightning cider in one hand, and a cheap bottle of vodka by his side. Perhaps he had decided to end his life rather than facing another day of squalor, addiction and mental pain. The inquest noted a verdict of 'misadventure', but Marcus always believed it should have read, 'because no one fucking cared'.

"Good morning, Inspector Marcus Cooke, this is my ID, I am the senior officer in charge. I see the scenes of crime people are already here, they were quick"

"Arrived about ten minutes ago sir, got straight to work"

"Ok, thanks, best go across and introduce myself"

Marcus walked through the narrow gap in the tape and straight towards DS Nick Walker. Walker was in his thirties, a strong broad chested man, light blond hair, ruddy complexion with a passion for playing rugby. He was standing a few feet from the scenes of crime tent, looking very tired.

"What's up Nick, late night again"

"Sorry boss, there was a party at the rugby club, one of the lads got engaged. I didn't need this murder scene this morning I can tell you"

"Serves you right Nick, one day you will learn, but I fear your liver will be shot to hell by then. Now, what can you tell me?"

"Ok, a female, I would estimate early to late twenties. She was naked, stabbed multiple times, as I described to you on the phone. There was a red silk scarf around her neck, we don't yet know if the stab wounds or the strangulation were the cause of death.

There are no possessions around her, no clothes, mobile phone, nothing. There is very little blood either, despite the extensive stab wounds.

So, I would guess she was killed somewhere else and just dumped here"

"Right, are there any missing persons reports, anything in the area?"

"No boss, to be honest it's a bit early. Maybe her parents, partner or friends aren't expecting her home until later today. I have the office on it though, as soon as something comes in, I will give you a shout"

"Fucking hell, what a mess, Post's lawyers are to blame for this, they argued for his innocence in the murders. Now he is out and at it again. If we don't find him soon, there will be more, a lot more, he has twenty-two years of catching up to do.

I need to make a phone call, I don't really want to, but Lee Hunter might have some additional information regarding the whereabouts of Post. I hate encouraging him, but to be honest, he does seem to come up with some good leads"

"He's not police though, is he?"

"No Nick, but he's right at the centre of this, and anything he knows will be useful"

Marcus Cooke reached for his mobile. This phone call shouldn't really happen, but Hunter was his one and only lead back to Post. He needed to establish Post's whereabouts before he killed again.

"Hello Marcus, what's up?"

"Lee, have you had any further contact with Post in the last couple of days?"

No, last time I spoke to him was Friday at the hotel in Southport. We had dinner and that was it. I said I would get back to him as soon as I had any further information, perhaps early this week, why?"

"I can't say anything at this time Lee, but I need to know where he is, and I need to know right now"

There was a short silence, Marcus could almost hear Lee Hunters brain whirling away. Hunter was an ex-cop with years of experience at the highest level, he would know exactly what this conversation was about.

"Ok Marcus, reading between the lines, I guess Post has done something, perhaps something really bad?"

"I can't say Lee, but I need to know where he is, I need to have a chat with him, right now, understand!"

"Ok, I will give him a ring. I will come up with some reason why we need to meet, perhaps set something up today. Trouble is, he might smell a rat Marcus, if he does, he will disappear into the bright blue yonder, never to be seen again"

"I will leave that to you Lee. Just get something sorted and soon"

"Right, I will get back to you soonest Marcus"

With that, the phone line went dead. I slipped my phone back into my pocket and made my way out of the hotel room.

I knew what that phone call had been about, or at least I was pretty certain. If my guess was right, Post was up to his murderous activities once again, and I had better do something about it. Shouldn't be a major problem, I would make up some story regarding evidence I had uncovered. What I mustn't do was scare him, if he did a runner, we might never find him again.

Right, dial his number and sound relaxed, he mustn't suspect a thing! I just needed to set up a meeting, I will leave the time and place to him. After pressing his saved number, I waited to see what happened.

"You have reached the voice mail of Lennard Post. Please leave a message after the tone and I will get back to you shortly"

Shit, that's not good, now what do I say? Just stick with the original plan, calls go to voicemail all the time, doesn't mean he has gone into hiding.

"Hi Lennard, listen, I have some new photographs of the crime scenes. A very helpful police archivist helped me out, with the assistance of a few quid. I need to discuss them with you. they might well help the case. Speak soon, Lee"

Right, phone Marcus back, at least keep him updated.

"Hi Lee, have you spoken to the psycho', what did he say?"

"Nothing Marcus, the call went to voicemail. I left a message for him to get back to me, I gave him some cock and bull story about some crime scene photos. I will keep you updated"

"Thanks Lee, I appreciate that. Oh, by the way, did Peter Dexter get back to you? He's a good guy and always willing to help, plus he was the lead detective on the original case"

"He did, thanks Marcus. He's away at his place, somewhere in Spain, I think he said Marbella. Anyway, he will give me a call when he gets back next week"

"Marbella, I think you must be getting him mixed up with someone else Lee. I met him in Bicester Rugby Club a couple of nights ago"

"No Marcus he definitely said Marbella, with his wife"

"No, no Lee, Peter isn't married and to the best of my knowledge, he hasn't got a place in Marbella or anywhere else for that matter. I think the local whiskey has got a few things mixed up in that head of yours. Anyway, my boss has just rolled up, speak later"

The phone went dead. What the hell was all that about? I distinctly remember Dexter saying that he was in his, "holiday apartment in Marbella, got the wife with me, so I won't be back for a week"

Odd, maybe he was trying to cover something up. Maybe he was having a secret affair with some married woman, but why say he was in Marbella?

I couldn't fathom it, if he was trying to be shifty about something, why go to the Rugby Club, where everyone will see you? Maybe there was nothing in it, just my mind working overtime, as usual! Most likely he was busy and couldn't get to see me until next week. He was an important contact, the lead detective in the murder cases. He would know everything there was to know. Ok, he might be trying to cover up an affair with some friend's wife, or something not exactly kosher, but he was a very important contact indeed.

I looked at my watch, ten thirty a.m., I was hungry and thirsty, so time to revisit that café again. I turned, picked my coat up off the bed and made for the door. I hadn't taken more than two steps when my phone started to ring. I reached into my jean's pocket and looked at the screen. Much to my amazement, it said 'Lennard Post'.

"Morning Lee, sorry I missed your call, but I've had a bit of an accident"

"Accident Lennard, what the hells happened?"

"It's alcohol related I am afraid to say. I had a bit, well quite a lot to drink on Friday night after our meeting at the Red Rose hotel. I decided to go for a walk to try and clear my head. Trouble was, I kind of missed the top step leading out of the hotel. Next thing I knew I was in an ambulance and on my way to hospital. Seems I had a bad concussion, must have smacked my head on the way down. So, I spent Friday and last night in the local A&E department. They told me I couldn't go until Sunday morning, so here I am, standing in the hospital carpark. Don't suppose they can take chances with head injuries"

I couldn't think of what to say. If what he was saying was the truth, and I had no cause to doubt him, then Marcus needed to think again. Lennard Post could not be in two places at once, if he was in the local A&E department on the night of the murder, that would put him in the clear. I quickly pulled myself together. I needed to confirm his story, that would be easy enough.

"Hell Lennard, you need to be careful, maybe drink a little more coke and not as much whiskey"

We both laughed, "listen, this was just a quick catch up, I have nothing much to report other that a few crime scene photos that I have managed to acquire. I am meeting the lead detective in the case in a few days, that might well throw up some more interesting clues as to why they stitched you up. Are you still at the Red Rose hotel?"

"Yep, I might as well stay here for the rest of the week. That's sound interesting Lee, the more evidence we have the better. I am too sore to go driving my car, I need to relax for a few days. I guess you will be heading back to Southport before visiting your daughters"

"I will Lennard, I need to get some stuff before I go and see them. Right, well take care and I will phone you in a day or so, we can meet at the hotel at the end of the week"

"That sounds like a good plan Lee. Listen, you need to get everything you can, these bastards sent me to prison for nothing at all. I have to get to the bottom of this, I know I can't get the years back, but I can get to the truth. They owe me an explanation. We need to ensure that the real perpetrators are brought to justice and punished for what they did, including the murder of my wife"

"Don't worry Lennard, if I can sort this out, I will"

We said our goodbyes and ended the call. It was strange, I know you can never go on 'gut' instincts, but he seemed genuine. I know people are convicted of crimes they didn't commit. Some, when the death penalty was in existence, paid for that with their lives. I did wonder if Post was the victim of a miscarriage of justice, but I guess Inspector Marcus Cooke would disagree with me on that point.

Right, look up the number for Southport Hospital, I needed to know if Post had been admitted. If he had, then there was no way he could have committed the murder down south, and we would all need to think again.

A room somewhere.

It had taken some time to clean the blood off the mask and the equipment. Many years had passed since the last killing, the process needed to become more efficient. If it didn't, clues would be left behind, and that would lead to arrest and conviction.

It had been a magnificent night though. The first of many, the devil was back, and the feelings of excitement were immeasurable.

The victim's screams had sounded primeval, she howled into the night, whilst choking on her own blood. The end of her life was so perfect, as she convulsed with pain, the look of fear and panic in her eyes was a delight to behold as the red silk scarf tightened around her neck.

The next sacrifice would be selected very soon, the lust for more blood and dread was uncontrollable. This time the devil would not be stopped, this time the number of victims would be countless. They would all come to respect and fear the devil, they would eventually bow low and welcome such power into their miserable lives.

Now the cleaning was done, the selection would begin, a lone person, unsuspecting, innocent. Their life would end tonight and then tomorrow there would be another, and then another, until the end of time.

There would be no stopping the devil this time, no twenty-two-year break. The devil's evil would prevail, casting a dark and morbid shadow across the world.

The murder scene, the outskirts of Aylesbury.

Inspector Marcus Cooke looked into the scenes of crime tent for the last time. He had spoken to the scenes of crime people and the dog walker, ex-serviceman Simon. He stood just a few feet away, holding onto his Jack Russell dog with all his strength, he kept whispering its name, Jake, Jake. His hands trembled, his voice broken and quiet, beads of sweat rolled down his temples, despite the cool afternoon air.

Uniformed police had conducted a fingertip search of the area and the police dogs had ranged a little further, with nothing to report. This confirmed to Marcus that the woman had not been murdered here or anywhere around or about.

There was an unsettling quiet about the place, traffic had been re-routed and pedestrians kept well back from the scene. The police helicopter had long since departed the area, called to a major traffic incident somewhere south of the city.

There was something more though, something very disconcerting. Marcus was an experienced police officer; he had attended several murder scenes before. As they go, this one was by no means the worst. However, there was something in the air, a feeling of evil about the scene. He couldn't shake that sensation off, and there didn't seem to be any cause for it. His deputy, Detective Sergeant Nick Walker seemed to come out of nowhere, taking Marcus by surprise.

"What's up boss, you look lost?"

"Sorry Nick, I was well away there, what's the latest?"

"I don't think we both need to be here boss. SOCO's have got this lot under control, the undertakers are on the way, and the uniforms are changing shift as we speak. As you know, the dog section has finished their search and the chopper didn't find anything of note. I have a team going door to door, you never know, someone might have seen something"

"Well done Nick. I am off back to the office; I need to get the paperwork underway. You stay here, if anything crops up, give me a call. And look, here is twenty quid for Simon and his dog, call it a donation to the ex-servicemen's appeal. Go slip it into his pocket, they look half starved. At least they can have something hot to eat tonight"

DS Walker didn't get chance to reply before Marcus's phone began to ring. He pulled it from his jacket pocket, smiled at Walker and began to walk away.

"Hi Lee, what you up to?"

"Hi Marcus, you asked me to check up on the movements of our friend Lennard Post"

"Sorry Lee, I was just thinking about things here, so what's the latest then?"

"Well, he was in the local accident and emergency department last night and the night before. He was only released this morning, and that's from the admissions department, not from Post. So, I am afraid to say whatever you think he has been up to, is a no go. He has an absolute cast iron alibi, no doubt on that front"

There was a long silence before Marcus replied.

"That can't be, I was counting on Post for this Lee, you say there is no doubt at all"

"None Marcus, I spoke to the guy in the hospital's admissions department myself. Post was brought in by ambulance on Friday evening. He had been drinking heavily and had a bad head injury. The doctors decided to keep him in for forty-eight hours, just to be safe. Apparently, that type of impact in that area of the skull can be very serious indeed, often fatal. So, he was in the hospital Marcus, he's not your man I am afraid, can I ask what you thought he had done. I don't suppose there would be any harm in me knowing now"

"I guess not Lee, anyway, it will be all over the news tonight, so all you need to do is wait. There was a murder here last night. A dog walker found the body this morning. It had the identical, and I mean identical wounds to those of Post first killings. There was even a red silk scarf, it was uncanny, but I guess Post was not responsible"

"Sounds like a copycat case Marcus, some nut case wanting to relive the acts of his hero"

"Not a chance Lee. There were several details deliberately left out of the press reports at the time. We kept some specifics secret, like the total number of stab wounds to the crotch. I spoke to the SOCO's, they counted the same number of stab wounds to this victim. There was something else, the red silk scarves. The ones found on the three original victims, and Post's wife, had all been made by the same manufacturer, William Q of Paris"

"Well, that's a slip up on the killer's part, just find out who bought them. Then you have your man, job done"

"Yeah, we tried that one Lee. William Q of Paris went out of business just after World War two. Seems like the survivors of Europe had better things to spend their money on in 1945. We think it was a warehouse or garage find, probably a job lot sold privately years ago, something later discovered in a dusty basement. There were certainly no records from the Paris company, their offices closed perhaps seventy plus years ago. We couldn't find anything, there were no more scarves being sold, not a bloody thing"

"That's odd, if Post was in hospital last night, and the scarf found on the victim was the same as the previous murders, that puts our friend in the clear for the whole lot, including his wife's killing. If you kept that info' back, no one could possibly have known it, and would have simply used any old silk scarf, or no scarf at all"

"That's the short and tall of it Lee, I guess we need to start again, it looks like Post is not our man"

I stood motionless for several moments. How come two experienced detectives had got this so wrong and had Post down as the perpetrator? Also, there was the issue concerning the murder of his wife. Maybe Post was telling the truth after all, had he really been stitched up all that time ago, I still had my doubts. Was he simply an easy conviction, someone to blame and then get a quick verdict and close the case.

Don't get me wrong, I have been in similar situations myself. The powers upon high wanting to throw someone into prison and put an end to the bad publicity. Pressure from the press, families, the local mayor. The clamour can become deafening when all kinds of people and groups are demanding a conviction, and you are told to give them one, it's never easy. Sometimes it would be simpler to blame the first person you came across. After all, who is going to take the word of the local scum bag over that of the police?

At least in this regard I can hold my head up high, and state that I never folded under such circumstances. I have suspected people of doing it though, an innocent man thrown under the bus just to make people shut up. If that was the case with Post, why wasn't he prosecuted for all the murders? After reading the case papers, it would have been relatively simple to do, after all, he was sentenced for the murder of his wife in very similar circumstances.

This didn't quite fit, it seemed that everyone was sure Post was the murderer, or at least they wanted him locked up for the crimes, not only of his wife, but the other three women. Post was certain the police stitched him up for his wife's murder, so why didn't they go all the way and prosecute him for the other killings?

Then there was the question of the red silk scarves. If Post did kill his wife, he must have had access to these, she was found with one twisted around her neck. Then there was last night, one of these French red silk scarves was used, but Post was in hospital?

"Marcus, I know you believed Post was the previous killer but surely you can't think that now?"

"To be honest Lee, I don't know what I believe. I think it's time to clean the board and start again. Have a fresh look at the incident papers, see who might have been overlooked. Look Lee, I need to get back to the office, I will be in touch soon"

The line went dead, Marcus sounded very tired, it had been a long day for him, and it wasn't over yet. When his boss found out about the red scarf and Post having a cast iron alibi, that would also add to his woes.

This case was just about to get big, and very quickly. For my part, I had to pursue the issues relating to Post. After all, he was my client and I had to try and clear his name..........so why didn't I feel comfortable about that, what was troubling me?

Sunday evening.
The cloak of darkness.

Despite the warm sun of the day, the evening had turned cooler, a mist gently sweeping in from the fields around the town. It was time, the hunt had begun, and the quarry needed to be identified and subdued. There were no feelings of pity in this process, no thought of mercy. It was pure lust, an overwhelming need for the smell of blood, and a must to quench the cravings once again.

It was quiet on the streets, perhaps a little early to be hunting. It sometimes took a while, there was no rush, after all, there would be plenty of prey to find. Tonight, the devil would kill, the silk scarf would strangle the life from her. The blood would run over the ground, her screams would be loud but never heeded.

The cold air was drawn into the lungs, it filled every capillary, explored into every space and void. Heart pounding, the devil walked the streets, the unsuspecting populous unconcerned. Was that a suitable victim ahead, no too old. Did she fit the bill, was it safe, no wait she is on her mobile.

Eventually, the quarry was identified. She was out alone, in a narrow alleyway between two places, no one to look out for her. She walked confidently on her high heels, skirt not too short. The victim must be respectable, the devil didn't want common trash. The devil desired respectable women, ones that would feel the terror, the humiliation to the full.

She was approached, stealthily, no warning must be given. The devil looked around, the area was quiet, no cars, no people. Now was the time, it was so easy, taking victims was simple, so long as planning and care was taken.

The syringe was full, he pushed gently on the plunger to ensure no air was present. He would drive it into her buttocks, the effect would be almost instantaneous. She would fall backwards, gently into the devils embrace, the deed would be done, the nights pleasure would commence.

Her night ended with the streetlights fading into a blurred haze. She felt a sharp pain as the needle broke her skin, someone's arms around her shoulders. The was a broken whisper, a terrifying message.

"Relax my darling, tonight you are mine. I will indulge my inner most perversions upon you. Your agony and dread will be felt by the spirits of the night, and they will be rapturous. The suffering and torment will not be short lived, it will take many hours. You will beg for your life, but I will simply grin and enjoy the fear in your voice.

Just before your torn flesh surrenders the last of your life's blood, I will wrap a red silk scarf around your throat and pull it tightly. The panic in your eyes will be my final thrill as you slowly die. I will dump your naked body for all to see, your final humiliation before retiring to dream of my nights work.

Monday morning.
Breakfast in the café.

The place was jammed, not a seat or table available. The guy behind the counter busily wrote out people's orders, and two young girls delivered cooked breakfasts', large pots of tea and mugs of coffee.

I was glad I arrived early, at least I had a little round two seat table in the corner. The man sitting opposite me had spent more time on his phone that eating his toast and marmalade. Beats me why he didn't just make that at home, but when I pieced together who he was talking to, it started to make some sense. He was clearly deep in conversation with his girlfriend, his face was animated, he lauched and made jokes. The thing was, his wedding ring gave away the complete picture, as to why he rushed out and didn't make his breakfast at home!

On my part, I sat there wondering why I had these feelings of unease with the events of yesterday. Not the murder of the young woman, but the fact of Post being innocent. It still didn't feel right, I had spent some time with him, and then there were conversations with Marcus. It didn't add up, but then it did. The facts were the facts, Post was in hospital and couldn't have been in Aylesbury, but it still troubled me, what a conundrum. I just needed to put my instincts back in their box and get on with the job in hand. I needed to find something, anything to help Lennard Post prove his innocence.

The thing was, where do I start. Peter Dexter, the ex-detective and person originally in charge of the case, was supposed to be in Marbella. This despite Marcus saying he met him in the rugby club. I decided to give him a ring, see if he was back, if he had actually ever been away, that would be a good start. At the same time, I could try and find out why he lied to me in the first place.

Ok, find Dexter's number and set up a meeting. Right, here it is, press call.

"The number you have dialled is unavailable, please check with your service provider"

I ended the call and pressed 'call' again. I was met with the same bland response. Perhaps the number I had was corrupted somehow, it wouldn't have been the first time. I would call Marcus later and check.

I paid for my breakfast, sausages, eggs and bacon, large black coffee, one sugar. As I left the café, I was surprised to see the change in the weather. It had started to rain, that fine drizzle, it blew about on the breeze like a manic mist. That's the great English summer I guess, portents of what was to come perhaps?

The fine rain soon began to soak everything it touched, it was time to get to my car and out of the weather. I pressed the remote unlock well before reaching the vehicle, pulled open the door and slid inside. No sooner as it closed, my phone started to ring.

Pulling it out of my pocket I looked at the screen to see who was calling, 'number withheld'. Ok, let's see what insurance scam they are trying this time, should be fun.

"Lee Hunter, private detective"

"Ah, mister Hunter, forgive my brevity, but It's concerning the case you are now investigating, the one involving Lennard Post. I determined your number from your business website, it was very helpful"

"Very well caller. how can I help? Before I do, I must inform you of the upmost importance of client confidentiality, in this or any other case that I am involved in"

"I fully respect that mister Hunter, but I won't be asking for information, I will be giving it. You see, I was involved in the case all those years ago. There are things pertaining to the investigation that I think you should know"

That was a bit of a shock. I thought the other detective in the case was dead, well at least that's what Peter Dexter had told me. Maybe this was someone from forensics, or the local press.

"Very well, go on"

"No mister Hunter, not over the phone. I think we should meet, it's safer that way, no chance of others listening to what you are saying"

"No problem, as long as you feel more comfortable. Where and when would you like this meeting to take place?"

"Time is short mister Hunter, very short. We need to meet this evening, but it can't be local, I mustn't be seen with you. There is a large Tesco supermarket in a place called Winsor, I will send you the address. There is a car park to the front, side and rear. I will meet you by the 'Park and Ride' bus stop at the back of the store, you can't miss it. I will be there at seven pm, this will be your one and only chance mister Hunter, so don't be late"

I didn't get chance to speak again, the phone clicked, and the line went dead. That was bloody odd, what did he say, "time is short mister Hunter, very short". Strange thing to say, peculiar conversation altogether, very James Bond. Why the need for such a clandestine meeting? As it happened, I knew Winsor, he was right, it certainly wasn't local, it was miles away.

You need to be vigilant in my profession, these 'out of the way' meetings can be a trap. Better meeting in a pub, somewhere public, but I didn't get a chance to do anything about that this time. Still, I would go and see what this man wanted, maybe it would be worth the journey. Chances were, it would be an individual with an axe to grind concerning someone connected to the case, or someone with aspirations to be an amateur sleuth. In all probability, it was just an opportunity to create trouble, and perhaps gain some degree of retribution for some wrongdoing in the past.

Anyway, that was for later. In the meantime, I had a favour to ask Tony Bianchi. I just hoped he would agree, before he got all caught up in his whiskey launch. I searched for his number, and yes it was listed under 'Fat Tony', don't tell my daughter. I tapped the 'call' button and sat back.

"Lee, how's it going my friend, not got yourself into another fix I hope"

"Tony, you know me, getting in a fix is part of what I do"

We both laughed, but to be honest, that witticism was probably not far from the truth!

"Tony, I need a quick favour and I wonder if one of your guys could help?"

"No problems Lee, all you need to do is ask"

"Thanks Tony, I need someone checking out. His name is Lennard Post, he is currently staying at the Red Rose Hotel, Southport. He was staying there, I am sure of that, I met him in the restaurant, and the Manager definitely referred to him as a guest. I just want to know if he is still there and if not, when did he leave.

I am sure you can slip someone twenty quid and find out, I will pay you back when I get home"

"You won't pay me anything Lee Hunter, this one is on the house. What does he look like Lee?"

"He is in his sixties, tall, slightly built and with a shock of short completely white hair and beard. He may also have some kind of dressing to his head, he says he had a fall and knocked himself out. He did attend A&E, I checked that myself"

"What's this all about my friend?"

"Long story Tony. Sufficed to say, I am not completely certain that all is as it seems, or at least that's what my guts are telling me"

"Trust your instincts, that's what I say Lee, more often than not, they are right"

"Yeah, I agree Tony, but in this instance, I can't be certain, it's more than likely he is genuine. If you can sort this out though, it would confirm his story.

He is supposed to have been at the Hotel for several days, except during Friday and Saturday night, which he spent in the local A&E. He was discharged Sunday morning, that's when I spoke to him"

"Didn't you confirm that with the hospital Lee?"

"I did Tony, and his story checks out. But it's those instincts, they are bugging me, and I need you to confirm what he said"

"Consider it done Lee, I will get back to you soonest"

We passed some pleasantries and ended the call. Tony was right of course, sometimes it's worth going with your instincts, even if they don't always make sense.

It was almost seven pm and the night had turned into a real stinker. The fine drizzle had by now developed into a steady and heavy rain. Streetlights reflected in the puddles and wet roads, their yellow and orange glow colouring the night. The temperature had plummeted to, it was a night to spend at home or in a cozy bar with someone you loved.

I was parked as instructed, right by the 'Park and Ride'. Several small buses had come and gone, taking people to Winsor city centre and bringing office workers back to their vehicles, ready for the drive home. It seemed eerily quiet in between these little white busses coming and going. The picture outside had turned to one of slick shiny grey. The rain hammered on the roof of my car, tapping out a rhythm all of its own. Bright white LED lights illuminated the area, keeping people safe, ensuring the CCTV cameras could see into every shadowy corner.

I kept scanning about, but no one seemed to be coming my way, perhaps he had lost confidence, maybe it was just a silly joke from the start. I turned on my car radio, might as well stay entertained. It was tuned to Smooth FM, "The Smooth Sanctuary with Gary Vincent, playing the Detroit Spinners, making my way back to you"

Dam, now that tune will be playing in my head all bloody night. I settled back into the seat and started to hum along. I couldn't sing and I certainly couldn't remember the lyrics, but it was nice to just relax.

The last couple of days had been hectic to say the least, and very confusing. One moment I was chasing evidence to try and prove Lennard's Post innocence, the next Marcus was telling me he was a mass murderer.

There had also been another murder, and it would seem Post, or someone who knew the details or the previous murders, was responsible.

Then there was Peter Dexter. He was the lead detective on the case all those years ago. He told me he was in Spain with his wife. I have since been told that he is not married and not actually in Spain at all!

Then there was Olivia, Posts ex-girlfriend. She was so shit scared, she ran away into the night after talking to me. Had she described a man with multiple personalities? Was Post actually two or even three distinct people all wrapped up in one disturbed mind? That was certainly possible and wouldn't be the first time a psycho' serial killer had some kind of multiple personality disorder.

Now some mystery guy wanted to tell me something, I think I needed to start taking notes, this was getting bloody complicated. I wasn't holding out much hope of anything of consequence with regard to this mystery man, it just sounded a bit too convenient, like someone wanting a bit of attention. All he said was time was short, time for what I wonder. So, I will just sit here and try and relax my mind. If this guy doesn't turn up, I will go to the local Indian restaurant and enjoy the rest of the evening.

The gentle music and the cars climate control must have ushered me into a gentle and easy nap. I have no idea just how long I was asleep, but something jarred me awake. I blinked several times and looked about, there was a man standing at the passenger door, softly tapping on the glass.

I rolled the window down, the rain splashed in, and a cold damp air permeated into the vehicle, it washed over me like a cold shower. A tall man stooped to look into the gap, he was cast in shadow by the streetlights, and had a menacing air.

"Mister Hunter, I presume"

"Indeed, and your name is?"

"My name is not important, please may I get in?"

"Certainly, but why all the secrecy?"

The man slid into the passenger's seat. It was difficult to guess his age, perhaps fifty or even sixty or older. He had unkept greasy grey streaked hair, two- or three-days stubble growth and an aroma not dissimilar to smelly Ken. He was dressed in an anonymous grimy grey overcoat with shiny black buttons that had a golden edge, one of which was missing. He had on dark trousers and black leather shoes.

"So, what is this information you want to impart, why all the secrecy?"

"Mister Hunter, if I may. I will tell you what I need to, but I won't be answering any questions. If this is not agreeable, I will leave now and not bother you any further"

This guy won't be winning any charm contests any time soon, that's for sure. I guess I could have sent him on his way, but we were here now, so best let him have his say.

"Very well, whatever your name is. Tell me what you need to and then we can move on"

He looked out of the front window, then the side before finally looking out of the rear window. He was nervous, this wasn't an act, this guy seemed scared.

"Right mister Hunter, here is what I need to say, please take note because I won't say it again. Twenty-two years ago, I was involved in the case of the so called, 'devil killer' murders. The investigation was headed up by one Detective Chief Inspector Peter Dexter. He was a 'results' driven detective mister Hunter, all he was ever interested in was getting the job done and taking all the credit and the occasional promotion along the way.

Consequently, like most of his cases, the end result was one of incompetence, rushed inquiries and at times, botched decisions. There was even some talk of corruption and coercion, although I didn't witness any of this first hand.

It's fair to say mister Hunter that Detective Chief Inspector Peter Dexter, was not one of Thames Valley police finest officers. In fact, I don't think I would be far off by stating he was probably one of the worst"

"Then how did he rise to the rank of Chief Inspector, that's a very senior rank, not common in any force"

"That's a good question mister Hunter. He seemed to have a degree of control over some very senior officers. You see, he was the perfect tool for high-ranking managers to get things done and not to ask any questions. He was the man to pervert the true course of justice, in order to get people locked away, to reduce the crime statistics for the bosses in their ivory towers.

The thing is mister Hunter, he was more than happy to see innocent men thrown into jail, and not to ask any awkward questions. He was prepared to intimidate some witnesses and pay money to others, bribery and exploitation where just tools to be used when required. No degree of corruption was beyond Dexter and the top brass knew it and in fact, condoned it.

However, this kind of 'arrangement' is a two-edged sword, and Dexter was more than happy to exploit that. That's where his power came from mister Hunter, he must have kept records of corrupt practices tolerated by senior managers. He will have made recordings of conversations with superiors. In the end, he must have had enough information on enough of them, to dictate the terms, not their terms, but his mister Hunter. You see, in the end, Peter Dexter was managing them, not the other way around.

So, Dexter became in time the proverbial loose cannon. A senior detective, out of control, beyond management, doing as he wanted. That mister Hunter is a very, very dangerous position for any police force to be in.

One casualty of Detective Chief Inspector Peter Dexter was his partner, Inspector Paul Willow. They had joined the force together and risen through the ranks, the best of friends, although Dexter had always been senior. Eventually Willow became suspicious of Dexter and tried to stop him. It was clear what Dexter was up to but suffice to say his complaints fell on deaf ears, I wonder why mister Hunter?

As time went by, Willow's attempts to bring Dexter to justice landed him in hot water. Willow found himself on a number of trumped-up discipline charges. He was faced with a decision, either withdrawing his complaints or leaving the force.

The thing is, Paul Willow was a principled man mister Hunter, he simply couldn't turn a blind eye, that would have made him no better than Dexter you see. In any case, even if he had withdrawn his complaints, he would have been hounded out. Dexter would not have tolerated such a threat as Willow, he was way too dangerous to have around, and Dexter knew it. He applied pressure upon pressure, accusation followed accusation. So, eventually Paul Willow handed in his notice, he wanted no part of a corrupt department and being controlled by Detective Chief Inspector Peter Dexter.

That's when Detective Inspector Paul Willow's life started to fall apart. The vacuum created when he left the force was impossible to fill. The camaraderie, the friends he had made during his time in the job, all went away, thanks of course to Dexter. There were rumours of a whole catalogue of affairs Willow had with a woman at work, all lies of course, promoted by Dexter.

Dexter had a network though, credible people, senior people, men and women, so it all sounded very convincing. Willow's wife found out about the non-existent affairs, she believed it, thanks to a lot of encouragement by Dexter's friends. A divorce followed, bankruptcy, a life in hell and it was all the fault of Dexter.

So, you see mister Hunter, when dealing with Peter Dexter, you need to be very careful indeed. Even though he has retired from the force, he is still a very dangerous man, with many contacts. I would encourage you to take extreme care, or face the consequences, and they will be severe, have no doubt about that.

"You seem to know a lot about Dexter and his corrupt practices"

"I do mister Hunter, you see, I am that Detective Inspector, Paul Willow"

I sat there for several moments, I had absolutely no idea who this guy was, other than what he had told me. If anything of what he was saying was true, then the whole devil killings case had been torn wide open. It would throw enough doubt over the conviction of Post to have him completely exonerated. Then a thought struck me, something that Dexter had said during our conversation.

"Paul Willow, if that is indeed your name, were you one of the two lead detectives in the case?"

"I was, and it is my name, yes Dexter was in charge, and I was his deputy"

"You see Paul, I have had a brief conversation with Dexter regarding Post, he told me one thing though. That is, his partner in the case, presumably you, had died several years ago, so there is something here that doesn't add up"

The man laughed uncontrollably, tears rolling down his rather grubby cheeks. It was two or three minutes before he finally managed to regain his self-control.

"That's a classic mister Hunter, don't you see, that's exactly how that bastard operates. He likes to control the narrative, leads people along, paints a picture of his making. He plants doubt, cast shadows and let's your mind do the rest. As you can see mister Hunter, I am far from dead. However, to Dexter I am a threat, just as I was all those years ago. If you believe him, he wins, and this investigation is lost. If you believe me, then things can start to be put right"

"Ok, but how do I know you aren't some ex-colleague of Willow, or just some crank masquerading as a dead Detective Inspector?"

"I knew you would ask me that question mister Hunter and I am glad you did. I have here my old police warrant card, my passport, a couple of photos of me with Dexter. Have a look, a good look, I think you will be satisfied"

The photos seemed genuine, having more than a passing resemblance to the man sitting in my car. I handed them back; his dirty hands snatched them off me and stuffed them into his coat pocket.

"Mister Hunter, please make a note of this mobile number. It is my number and a burner phone. As soon as this case is finished, I will be throwing it in the river Thames. This is the only way you will be able to contact me. I won't have this phone on all the time, just for a few minutes as I move around the countryside. Therefore, there is no point in trying to trace where I am. I know the score with tracing people via their mobiles mister Hunter, that won't work with me. Should you wish to contact me, simply leave a message and I will get back to you. Have you any further questions?"

I noted the number and said I would be in touch. He slid out of my car and into the cold and wet night. I watched him as he disappeared into the gloom, the rain and mist swallowing him up, like some ghost from another time.

Midnight Monday.

He looked at her flawlessly smooth skin, it glistened in the moonlight, slick with blood. It had been a most satisfying hunt and capture. Everything had gone to plan, nothing would be left behind to incriminate the devil, what a perfect night.

She had been the most arousing victim to date, begging for her life, screaming with the agony he inflicted upon her. She lay on the ground, looking up at him, her life was all but extinguished, and she knew it. Soon the red silk scarf would slide around her neck, its cool embrace tightening, strangling the breath from her lungs.

"You have been the most perfect subject my dear, I only wish our time together could have been longer. I have to move on though, soon the sun will be up and I need to be away. Safe in the mass of humanity, camouflaged by the seething bodies of people, where no one will know me, as I walk amongst their putrid and worthless civilisation.

There will be others to be sure, many more like yourself, I will kill, and they will know me once again. They will fear the devil as I stalk them, but they will not be able to stop me.

So, relax and let the final act unwind, as I pull this red silk scarf from my pocket. I will slide it around your neck and watch, as the life is choked from your worthless soul. I will place your naked body in a place where many people will see it, the final humiliation of your time here on earth. Goodbye my sweet darling, thank you for your participation, I only wish it could have lasted longer"

The devil knelt by her side and gently lifted her head. The scarf wrapped around her throat, like a gleaming red serpent. It tightened it coils, constricting the life from her. She thrashed around in the darkness, but her strength had long since drained away. There was laughter, somewhere off in the night. She gasped, choked and tried to fight but it was too late. A dark cloak of emptiness descended around her, a tear running down her skin, she felt no more pain, no more fear, and finally she faded away,

Tuesday Morning.
Inspector Marcus Cooke's home.

"You what? I am not even out of bed yet, what the hell's going on, is this Aylesbury or Dodge bloody city? Can't we just have a nice quiet start to the week for a change, or is that too much to ask"

"Sorry boss but I have just arrived here in the office. Walked in and the phone went off. It's a woman, perhaps in her twenties, naked and cut to ribbons. Before you ask, she has a red scarf around her neck. Two uniforms are there now, waiting for us to arrive"

"Ok, I am on my way, what's the address? Make sure you get the area sealed off, understood? No one within a thousand fucking miles of the scene, no one at all unless they are wearing a uniform or have a police ID card, and preferably both"

"Yeah boss, on it, I will see you there"

Marcus swung his legs out from under the quilt. His warm comfortable morning was beginning to turn into another nightmare, but one from which he will not awake. This was the second murder in as many days. It was just the thing to get the press and local act on groups baying for results, and his bosses' demanding arrests.

The first thought was for Lennard Post, where was he and why hadn't Deborah taken him into custody? He reached for his phone, he needed answers and needed them fast. He quickly found Detective Inspector Deborah Smith's number and pressed dial.

"Hi Marcus, I am just on my way to a meeting, can I phone you back?"

"No Debs, I need an answer on Post. Have you got him in custody, there has been another murder down here"

There was silence on the line.

"Sorry Marcus, that's my fault, it's been so busy recently and I have staff off with covid, I just forgot to get back to you. I sent Sharron out to see what that slime ball was up to, it's a no go I am afraid. He spent the weekend in the local A&E, she checked with the admissions desk. He was released at ten thirty-five Sunday morning. There is no way he could have been your way killing anyone. Sharron also phoned the hotel. He was staying there, they wouldn't give too many details but it all checks out, no doubt at all, sorry Marcus"

"Are you certain Debs, these killings are the same as last time"

"Killings Marcus, has there been another?"

"Yes, another one last night, I am on my way there now, are you sure Post was in hospital, are you certain Deb's?"

"Absolutely certain Marcus, Sharron even has a copy of the admissions report. If I remember rightly it said. 'Arrived via ambulance on Friday night, and according to the paramedics he was obviously under the influence of alcohol. Head injury and probable concussion'. Some stuff about x-rays, CT scan and further tests. He was admitted Friday through Saturday nights on doctors' instructions with regular checks. Sunday morning, upon doctors' instructions he was discharged, with advice, blah, blah, blah. Further appointments made……….something about medications, and not to drink any alcohol"

"That can't be right Debs, it's him, he is the murderer. He was twenty-five years ago, and he is now. There is no one else in the frame, these murders started up again soon after he got out. He's up to his old tricks, and if we don't stop him there will be another and then another"

"Sorry Marcus but that's as good an alibi as you will ever come across. It's not Post, it can't be, he was in Southport hospital, pissed and with a head injury. He was being x-rayed, CT scanned, and seen by doctors and nurses the whole time he was there. It doesn't get any better than that! It's not Post, it can't be, no chance, you need another candidate Marcus, it wasn't him"

Inspector Marcus Cooke stamped his right foot hard on the ground. He could feel his face turning red with anger and frustration. It had to be Post, he used a red silk scarf on his wife, a murder he was convicted of. All the other murders had the very same M.O. and the same red silk scarves made by William Q of Paris all those years ago.

If it wasn't Post, then they were as far away from an arrest as they could be. Who the hell was it, who could wait all this time to start killing again? Serial killers don't just stop, they die or are arrested. Also, who had access to the case, who knew the details of the murders and had the red silk scarves. It just didn't add up, it had to be him, no one else even came close to fitting all the clues.

The murder scene was wet with overnight rain, grey scudding clouds promised further downpours in the very near future. There was a gusting westerly wind which brought an unseasonal chill to the air.

By the time Marcus arrived the SOCO's had erected a small grey/white tent over the body of the young woman. As he made his way to the murder scene, the wet grass soaked his black leather shoes and the bottom of his grey suit trousers.

He was no more than ten feet from the tent when a Scenes of Crimes Officer slid from between the limp tent flaps. He waved at Marcus, pulled down his face mask and removed the nitrile rubber gloves.

"Hi Marcus, we have the tent up, but it's been raining all night, so I am not expecting much. Anything of note will have been washed down the gutters long ago"

"It's ok Jack, you can't be responsible for the weather. What do we have, is it the same as yesterday?"

"It is, same injuries, same red silk scarf. The body was posed and naked, here for everyone to see. This guy is a sicko Marcus, and one of the highest order. Her injuries are appalling, she suffered for a long time. She wasn't killed here though, no way, she was brought here after her death, no doubt about it"

"What makes you say that?"

"Given all her injuries, there is almost no blood here and there should be, even after all the rain. No Marcus, she was brought here, and seeing how she was posed, rigor mortis hadn't set in. That means she was killed no more than two hours before being dumped"

"Any idea of what time that might have been?"

"Don't know, given the cold night, the rain and the wind, could have been any time after midnight. Her body would have been super chilled by the prevailing weather conditions, it's going to be difficult to get any kind of accurate idea. It had to be the early hours though, it's an exposed site, someone would have seen what was going on if it were any later"

"It's not a commuter run around here. I bet there wouldn't have been a living soul within a hundred yards of the place, even after dawn"

"You might be right Marcus, but you never know your luck"

"I do Jack and the way it's going; I will never solve this case"

Marcus was shaken out of his melancholy by the buzzing and vibrating of his phone. His increasingly cold hands reached into his pocket, the screen read, 'Lee Hunter'. He started to laugh, and then shook his head, "today just keeps getting worse, I think I should go straight beck to bed"

"Lee bloody Hunter, what the hell do you want?"

"Hi Marcus, hope it's not a bad time"

"It's always a bad time Lee, what's up?"

"Can you remember the name of Dexter's partner in the original investigation?"

"Sorry Lee, Dexter did have a partner, can't remember his name though. I am sure he passed away a few years back. I did read the police file when I found out Post was being released, can't remember much about the team though, apart from Dexter.

Hang on a minute, just let me think. That's right I remember now, Dexter's partner committed suicide, swam out into the English Channel, his body was never found. There was a suicide note though"

"How about Paul Willow, was that the name of Dexter's partner?"

"That kind of rings a bell, can't be sure though, why do you ask?"

"I have been contacted by someone purporting to be Paul Willow, Dexter's partner and long-term friend. It all seems a bit far-fetched, he has photos of himself and a couple with Dexter, but those were taken a quarter of a century ago, people change. He has made some disturbing claims regarding Dexter, not sure what to believe if I am honest Marcus"

"I do remember reading a copy of his suicide note in the police file Lee. It gave mention to his failures in the case, and how Post got away with the other murders because of his incompetence.

I have to say Lee that those views were echoed by the upper management. The general consensus of opinion was Post was the killer of the three women, and the perpetrator of the other previous sexual assaults. It was also stated in the file that this Detective Paul Willow was directly responsible for Post evading prosecution due to his incompetence. If that was true, no wonder he killed himself.

The three murders and several assaults and Post getting away with it, and it's all your fault! I can't blame the guy for taking a long swim and not coming back. The thought of Post laughing behind your back and those families with no answers. The torment whirling around in his mind, must have been unbearable Lee"

"Then it sounds like this guy is a fake Marcus, either that or he has been swimming about in the channel for the last twenty-five years"

"Actually, there is something you could try Lee, to see if this guy is genuine. There is an infamous tale regarding Peter Dexter not many people would know about. I remember Dexter telling me this story about a pair of lady's pink knickers. We were pissed up one night in the rugby club, that's when all these stories seem to come out"

"Not sure how that's relevant Marcus?"

"Apparently, this Willow guy wasn't just his work partner, he was his best mate, in fact, he was the best man at Peter Dexter's first wedding. For a bet, Dexter wore a pair of pink knickers during the ceremony, and on his wedding night. There can't be many people who know that. Dexter would obviously know, also his first wife, perhaps a couple of us from the rugby club, and of course his best man, Willow.

If this guy is really his ex-partner, he would surely remember that. My guess is he won't, if that's the case, problem solved. I think Willow's remains will be resting somewhere at the bottom of the English Channel, not bothering you"

"Thanks for the info' Marcus, I will give it a try, see what he says. How's the investigation going re the body from yesterday?"

"I have just added another victim to the case Lee. We found a second young woman this morning. Same M.O., same everything, including the red scarf. Debs backs up your information about Post having a cast iron alibi, so I haven't a bloody clue what to do next"

"I agree with Deborah, he was in hospital over the weekend. I spoke to the admission people myself, they confirm his story. I have someone going out to check with the hotel staff to see if he is still there, but I think he is telling the truth"

"You will keep me updated won't you Lee"

"Yeah of course Marcus, that's a promise"

Inspector Marcus Cooke slid the phone back into his pocket. The rain had started again, slowly at first but gaining in intensity by the second. He looked up at the dark grey sky, it's gloom and lack of colour reflected not only the scene but his own mood. A deep sense of foreboding swept over him, there had been two murders in as many nights. What would tonight bring, how many more young women would die before the perpetrator was brought to justice?

Tuesday morning.
Sitting in my car.

Things had got very complicated since talking to Marcus. There had been a second murder, Marcus was still certain it was Post, but the guy had a great alibi, so it wasn't him.

Two murders in as many nights, it was clear that whoever was doing this was not ready to stop either. Perhaps a third tonight and a fourth tomorrow? This could turn into a long running serial case, and the truth was, no one was even close to being identified as the killer.

I had to concentrate on what I was doing, namely, getting Post's conviction overturned. That's how this had all started, and why I was being paid.

His ex-girlfriend Olivia had shone some light on Post and his mental state. Was that helpful for what I was trying to achieve? Well not really, it didn't explain why Post believed he was innocent, and it certainly didn't mean he was a murderer.

Then there was Dexter, the ex-lead in the original case, but he was not in Spain where he was supposed to be. So, he had already demonstrated his willingness to lie, just as Post had alleged. I guess I would get to talk to him sooner or later, now that could turn out to be a very interesting conversation indeed.

Just to add to the confusion, I had some guy trying to convince me he was Dexter's ex mate Paul Willow. I was not convinced, I guess the jury was still out on that one. Seems strange that the original Willow felt so disturbed by his alleged incompetence, that he took a swim in the channel, only to re-emerge twenty plus years later.

So, what the hell did all this mean, and where was I, in truth, no further on than when I started. I had got all tangled up with the notion that Post was not only the killer of his wife, but also of the three other women. Why, well Marcus had managed to convince me, and his ex-girlfriend had only reinforced that thinking, before telling me to run away, far away!

So, Lennard Post was living it up with a sore head in a very nice Southport hotel. He had a cast iron alibi for the two recent murders, but did that mean he wasn't responsible for the original crimes?

There were of course the red silk scarves. It could have been some blinding coincidence that Post had a bunch of those things twenty-five years ago, as had the recent killer, maybe! Perhaps they had purchased a part of the same bankrupt stock. But two separate killers, twenty-five years apart having the same M.O., stab wounds in the same places, strangled to death, I don't think so!

There was something not right about this sorry bloody mess. It seemed clear the only person who could have done this was Post, but he couldn't have committed the second two killings. I guess he could have an accomplice who was carrying on his homicidal streak on his behalf, but why?

If Post had anything to do with this, why would he put himself back in the frame by using the exact same M.O. That would only risk him being thrown back into jail until hell freezes over. It certainly wasn't going to help to clear his name for his wife's murder, far from it. So, I had a rat's nest sat on my lap and I had to try and untangle it, that wasn't going to be easy.

I had to come up with some kind of plan, but what? I think the first thing is to find and then talk to Peter Dexter, the original lead in the case. I needed to listen to his side of the story, not just the things he had already talked about, but what was going on between him and Paul Willow. Oh yes, and I had to try and ascertain if the guy I met in Winsor was actually Paul Willow. According to Marcus, this might be quite simple, just ask about the pink knickers.

So, back to Peter Dexter. Marcus said he had met him in the Bicester Rugby Club a few days previous. I think I might have a drive over to Bicester, and see if he was about, enjoy that look on his face when I introduce myself, and I bet he wouldn't have a suntan.

Right, I think I will ring Tony Bianchi, I wonder if he has any updates on Post in the hotel. I pulled my phone from my pocket, but as I did so, it began to ring. I looked at the screen, the familiar 'number withheld' was displayed, I wonder who the hell this could be?

"Hello, Lee Hunter, can I help?"

"Mister Hunter, you do know me, but we haven't met. I wonder if I could have a few minutes of your time?"

This sounded like one of those puzzle games. You can't identify someone, but you know them, who might that be? Well, I wasn't in the bloody mood for some pointless quiz, so let's get straight to the answer.

"I am rather busy caller, please can I have your name"

"All in good time mister Hunter, all in good time"

He had a quiet, controlled voice, staccato, subdued, almost a whisper. I guess it wasn't the bank trying to tell me I was eating into my agreed overdraft, that was a blessing at least.

"Ok, what is it you want to say?"

"Please listen mister Hunter, what I have to say is very important indeed. This mobile will be destroyed immediately after this call, so there is no point in trying to trace it. If you do, you will find the mast it used is located in Leeds, Yorkshire. I am telling you this because that will also be a pointless exercise. I have driven here to make the call, thus keeping my real location secret"

Well, someone was going to a load of bloody trouble, that's for sure. I had to be honest, this was very intriguing, but any minute now I expected Tony Bianchi to start laughing at the other end of the line.

"Very well, I am listening"

"Mister Hunter, up until now I have prayed upon single objects, this has been extremely arousing and indeed fulfilling, but I need to move on"

What the hell was this loony tune on, I guess some very illegal substance, smelly Ken would know and had probably used it several times himself! What did he mean by 'single objects', had he phoned me by mistake?

"Sorry caller, I am at a lost to know what you mean?"

"Mister Hunter, the 'objects' I refer to are those young women, acquired for my deeds and for my satisfaction and my glorification. You should have heard their screams mister Hunter, seen the blood pouring out onto the ground. It was wonderful, a true and magnificent sight"

I quickly realised what this call was about, it hit me like an out-of-control express train. This was the devil killer, and he was talking about the murders. My mouth went dry, I needed to speak but I couldn't think of what to say. It could be some crank call of course, I had to be professional, try and get some confirmation of who it was, was this actually the murderer himself?

"However, it's time to move on. You see I tire of this regime, just one kill per night, it is very limiting. I need to broaden my approach, develop and grow. So, mister Hunter I have given this some thought, and I have a plan.

Today is Tuesday, I will take another prey tonight, a second on Wednesday and a third Thursday. I will then indulge myself with all three on Friday night. I can't wait, imagine the terror, the blood, what do you think?"

I sat back in the seat, my head whirling with what I had just been told. Was this guy for real, he sounded genuine. If this was the devil killer, he had just given me a warning. Three more would be taken, and they would be killed on Friday night.

"How do I know you are the real devil killer?"

"You don't mister Hunter, isn't that fun. You can go and tell Detective Inspector Marcus Cooke, but you won't really know if I am that person, will you? You won't know until Friday, if there are three dead women, then I am, if not, I am a fake.

So, at least you know of my plan, the thing is, can you stop me, I bet you can't. You won't be able to because you don't know who I am, you don't know where I live, and you certainly don't know where I will strike next.

You are pathetic mister Hunter; Marcus Cooke is pathetic and the women who I will torture to death are all pitiful. You are all pawns, toys for me to play with. Perhaps when I have quenched my thirst on Friday, I will come after you mister Hunter, won't that be fun.

I will contact you again after Friday, just to gain your reaction with regard to the pleasure I will have with the three women. Please pass on my condolences to their families and assure them of the care I took when killing them. Please convey to them the great pleasure I had with them, and the fact that their deaths were long and painful.

Goodbye mister Hunter, please pass on my complements to Inspector Cooke, I do admire his work, notwithstanding the fact he is a failure at this time"

The line went dead with a sudden klick. Shit, if this guy was for real, things were going to get a lot worse. Fortunately, my phone records all my calls, so I needed to find Marcus and play this conversation back to him. I had no idea where he would start, I guess he wouldn't either. Safe to say, he had three days to prevent the killings, and the clock was ticking, very loudly indeed.

Tuesday afternoon.
The Red Rose Hotel, Southport.

Tony Bianchi gently closed the door on his Lexus LC500 Inspiration. It had cost him almost £108,000 but it was worth it. Business was thriving and the money was rolling in, so he had indulged himself, again, but as he always said, "no point in dying the richest man in the graveyard"

He stopped turned and looked at the gleaming black sportscar, it was certainly the most beautiful car he had ever owned, and he was very proud to be seen in it.

The gravel crunched gently underfoot as he approached the fake neo classic entrance to the hotel. It did look somewhat tacky, perhaps the architect was trying just a little too hard. "At least there is no doubt of the way in" he thought.

The day was bright, sunny, and very chilly. He buttoned up his Private White coat, another massive indulgence at over £1,000, but he liked to be warm, and of course he liked to look successful. Eventually he reached the automatic doors, they opened in a silent glide, the warmth of the interior and the bland none descript music wafted over him. Tony Bianchi made straight for the main reception desk. He had already identified someone who he could 'do business' with, or more likely somebody he could intimidate.

A young and very smartly dressed man, perhaps in his early twenties stood behind the desk. He looked up at the very well-dressed Tony Bianchi as he approached. The young man smiled, a brilliant white and slightly false grin, one performed perhaps a hundred times a day.

"Good afternoon sir, and welcome to the Red Rose Hotel, how may I help?"

"Good afternoon to you. I am looking for a Mister Lennard Post. I understand he is staying here. I wonder if you could confirm that for me"

"Oh, I am sorry sir, we never disclose who is staying with us, it's completely confidential you see"

"I understand that young man, but I really need to know, it's a matter of urgency you see"

"I am sorry sir, let me call the manager"

"Well, you can do that, but then you would miss out on the £500 I have in this envelope. Chances are, that manager will be more than happy to help, and to take this gift for himself"

Tony Bianchi pulled the envelope from his pocket and casually slid it across the desk.

"Also, I wonder if your manager will be angry at you, for the sexual advances you made towards me during our conversation"

The young man started to panic, his face flushed pink.

"Er, no sir, I have done no such thing"

"Are you sure, after all, I am a wealthy businessman, about to discuss a very lucrative contract with the hotel. I bet they will believe my side of the story, all day long. Especially when I disclose the amounts of money this new contract would involve.

Now, do you want that white envelope and the money it contains, or do you want the sack and a shit job reference, spelling out what you did to me? I promise you that particular document will follow you around like the blackest fucking nightmare, for the rest of your existence.

So, tell me what I want to know, or I will really fuck up the rest of your life, and don't doubt me for one second. I will screw you up to such an extent that the first thing you will think about every morning when you wake up is, "my life is shit and I don't want to live anymore"

The look on the young man's face was a picture, a cross between terror, and shock. Tony Bianchi was a hardened criminal, he was used to dealing with some very dangerous people. Once he started to come for you, he simply wouldn't stop. That overwhelming tidal wave of pressure and aggression would overcome the toughest of men, let alone an innocent young man working on the reception desk of a local hotel.

"Well young man, what's it to be, oblivion, no work and a life on the dole, or £500 in your back pocket and a nice quiet afternoon?"

Tony Bianchi slid back into the leather clad interior of his Lexus LC500 Inspiration. He couldn't help laughing to himself, the look on that young guy's face was perfect, he only wished he had a camera with him.

"The youth of today have absolutely no sense of humour, poor little boy. I bet that's the last time he will say no to me, but at least he has £500 for his trouble, I only hope he spends it wisely. Right, phone Hunter and give him the good news, I bet he doesn't laugh when I tell him though"

Bianchi pressed the voice call button on the steering wheel and spoke Lee Hunter's name.

"Hi Tony, how's it going?"

"It's going just fine Lee, albeit a young man in the hotel has £500 of my own money, but I guess he earned it and that look on his face was worth twice that amount!"

"What did you find out Tony, any news about Post?"

"Erm, well Lee, not sure if this is going to make a whole lot of sense"

"That sounds ominous Tony, give me the news"

"Well, Post was certainly a guest here, but only for the one night, the Friday you met with him. He checked out Saturday after breakfast, never to be seen again"

The was a long and silent pause. The news Bianchi had just imparted didn't seem to make any sense at all.

"What, I don't understand Tony, he fell down the steps and was carted off to hospital"

"Well, the desk clerk had no record of that call. He showed me the night log and there was nothing relating to any such incident. Post spent the night in the hotel and left very early Saturday morning, simple"

"Then what the hell is the hospital record all about?"

"I don't know Lee. Maybe the call was placed by someone outside the hotel. The ambulance turned up and carted him away. If that happened in the street, the hotel wouldn't have any record at all"

"Yes Tony, but the records say he was taken from the hotel after falling down the steps outside the front entrance"

"No Lee, Post told you that, not the hotel, they have no such record. He simply planted that seed in your mind, he suggested what happened and allowed you to fill in the gaps, you believed him, and the rest just fell into place"

"Yes Tony, but the hospital report said, 'brought in by ambulance on Friday evening', he had been drinking heavily and had a bad head injury"

"There you go again Lee, brought in from where, it doesn't say I bet. You are presuming from the hotel, but that's just what he led you to believe. The truth is, the only person to think that was you! Post is obviously a very clever man and able to influence the situation. He simply suggests events and then allows peoples imagination to do the rest.

Someone using his name, possibly someone he paid to impersonate him, was taken into Southport A&E with a head injury, that's for sure, but it wasn't Post. This was a set-up, just to throw you off the trail, give him just enough time to get away without you knowing. It also gave him a cast iron alibi, who the hell is going to question a hospital report, absolutely no one, including you. If you hadn't asked me to make enquiries at the hotel, no one would have ever known the real events, and he would have been in the clear. I have no idea where your man is now, but he isn't in the Red Rose hotel and hasn't been there since last Friday"

The enormity of what Tony had found out was overwhelming. This threw everything into reverse, perhaps Marcus had been right all along, Post was the killer. He was now on the run and could be absolutely anywhere.

This was my fault, how the hell did I fall for that pack of lies? I am a very experienced ex-cop, I have heard every possible story ever told, how did this one get past me? I had to ring Marcus and tell him about Post, things had changed and not for the better.

At least now we knew who we were looking for, and the police could circulate the correct description. With a bit of luck, Marcus could have Post in custody relatively quickly.

That reminded me, I had the telephone recording from the devil killer, or Post as we now knew. I needed to meet up with Marcus and give him a copy. The threats on that recording were real, I was sure of that. More young women would soon lose their lives, we had to stop him, and had to do it now.

Tuesday night.
A street in Aylesbury.

The night had descended like a silent cloak, a stillness covered the whole area, nothing seemed to stir. The devil killer sat in his van and surveyed the scene. This was the first night of the new strategy. The first woman would be taken tonight and imprisoned, ready for the festival of murder on Friday night.

The thought of what was to come made his pulse race, his mouth was dry, and a huge wave of arousal washed over him. This was the highpoint of the devil's calling, to be a taker of lives, a murderer supreme, and to spread terror throughout the community.

Tonight, the new chapter would begin, they would know his name and speak of his deeds for the rest of time. A sickly grin spread across his face, a guttural laugh sprang forth. He reached for the tools of his trade, a rope, a pair of handcuffs and a syringe full of sedative and of course, the disguise, the mask of the devil.

Without warning, the young woman appeared from a side street. She was tall, with blonde hair, dressed in jeans and wearing a long coat. She turned to walk towards the devil, but on the other side of the road.

"Tonight, you are mine my darling, you will start the collection. A collection that will be an example of purity and youth. I will take you and hold you, ready for the second and then the third. On Friday you will be sacrificed, your blood will be my cleansing bath, your flesh my meal of pleasure. The screams will be my balm, soothing my soul, assuaging the feelings I harbour for murder and pain.

I have no doubt that these thoughts will re-emerge in due course, but for the meantime, they will be silenced. When I gaze upon your naked bodies, all cut and bleeding, I will be happy again, like I used to be.

My mother always told me I was a special boy, that I would one day rise to greatness. She was right, my mother was always right. I can see her face now, smell her perfume, sense the softness of her skin. She loved me, like only a mother can. Everyone else hated what I was, they all wanted to hurt me, and some of them did. My mother was the only person to care for me, she would have adored me until the end of time, but she had to die.

In the end, even she hurt me, and wanted to lock me away. I didn't want to go and leave her loving protection. I didn't need to go away to a special school, I wasn't evil, why did she say those things? She had to die, it wasn't my fault, it was for the best.

So, one night I prevented that incarceration, saved her from the pain she would feel if she sent me there. I took her down to the canal, said I wanted to show her a puppy which had been tied up near a bridge. When there was no one about, I hit her on the head with the axe from the garden shed. She fell to the ground, but she wasn't dead. I hit her again and again. Her blood soaked me, it splashed into my mouth, it tasted good. It was warm, and thick, my mother's life force. It made me feel strong, aroused, keen, like the edge of the sharpest blade.

She coughed, choked for a few minutes and then died. I was so happy for her; she wouldn't feel the pain anymore because she wouldn't be sending me away. I knew she would be pleased at what I had done, her love would only increase for me. The policeman came, I said someone had attacked us, he believed me, I think he knew I had acted out of love for her. I wanted to be that policeman, his uniform and authority made me feel excited. Perhaps one day I would be like him, dressed in blue, with the power and influence over everyone.

"No one would ever know of your plan to send me away; I will no longer be destined for that place. I love you mother; you know I always will, I did this for you because I love you"

The devil killer slid out of the van and crossed the road. He was no more than ten feet from the young woman, but she was oblivious, texting on her phone. Closer and closer he got, looking around but no one was about. He drew the handcuffs from his back pocket and readied the syringe. His heart was pulsating, almost bursting with the excitement.

He closed the gap just as she turned, the woman tried to run but it was too late, he was upon her. The mobile fell to the ground, bouncing away into the gutter. She drew breath, started to scream but the midazolam was already surging through her system. A wave of disorientation broke over her, colours started to fade, fear drifted into the background. There was a strange taste in her mouth, her arms and legs had no strength. The world began to spin, she felt nauseous, there were words, but she was unable to comprehend what was being said.

"That's it sweetheart, just relax, I will take care of you now, you will be safe with me. Soon there will be others, then you will all be swept away in an orgy of pain and anguish. You are so lucky, I envy you, what a glorious end you will have, such screams, unimaginable agony.

My mother will be so proud of me for doing this, she will see that I am not evil. I do these things for her you know, so that she can rest in heaven, safe and warm"

Working as quickly as possible, he dragged the half-conscious woman back to the rear of the van. He opened the doors and pushed her inside. Looking quickly left and right, but there was no one about. He had chosen the location with great care, parkland to one side, a large block of flats hidden by a stand of trees. The street lighting was inadequate, and it was not on a route into town.

He had struck and had accomplished what he wanted to, he had taken his first victim, tomorrow there would be another and then a third. His plan was in place and soon it would come to its climax, and he couldn't wait.

Wednesday Morning.
Meeting room 1. Thames Valley Police HQ,
Bicester.

Inspector Marcus cook, DS Nick Walker and me were in the modern office in Thames Valley Police HQ, near to Bicester. There was a small coffee table in one corner of the room with four fabric covered chairs surrounding it. Nick Watkins had made the coffee, the three cups sat untouched in the middle of the table. The air handling system hummed quietly in the background; a CCTV camera watched anonymously over the proceedings.

I had played the recording of the telephone conversation with the devil killer three times. The room had long since fallen into complete silence, no one wanted to speak. If this man was genuine, three women would be captured and then murdered just three days from now. There seemed no way of stopping this, there was no clue as to where he might strike next or even at what time in the days leading up to Friday.

There was one more thing I needed to do, that was inform Marcus of the work Tony Bianchi had done for me. This would throw the whole investigation into complete turmoil. Up until now, Lennard Post had not been directly connected to the case. Yes, Marcus had been convinced that it was him all along. However, largely on my say so, he had been eliminated from the enquiry, languishing as he was in Southport Hospital, or so we thought.

"Before you speak Marcus, there is something else I need to tell you. A good friend of mine went to the Red Rose Hotel in Southport. It turns out that Post checked out Friday night. He wasn't taken from the hotel to the hospital, someone was, but I know not who.

"Hang on Lee, are you trying to tell me Post was at large, probably down here killing two young women?"

"I can't rule that out Marcus, it seems probable, in fact I would suggest certain"

"So how the hell did he manage to convince you that he was in the A&E department over the weekend?"

"By lying Nick, he told me he was, and whilst I didn't really believe him, I didn't disbelieve him either, I guess I am getting sloppy in my old age. That was all my fault, I asked the hospital, they said Lennard Post was in for observations over the weekend, that was good enough for me. Thing is, I didn't check with the hotel to see if he was still staying there, it just needed a quick telephone call. If I had done that it would have thrown his story into doubt, made me double check.

Who the hell was actually in the A&E department, goodness only knows. It was just someone using his name, it's easily organised. There are any number of people who he could pay, maybe some ex-convict from his time in jail, some down and out drug addict who was happy to get a smack on the head and spend 48 hours in hospital for a few hundred quid.

The local A&E department are way too busy to actually check who they are admitting, especially on a Friday night with all the pissed-up drinkers rolling in. If you tell them your name is Alfred Hitchcock, and your date of birth is the 40th of February 1900 they will simply record that and take it as fact. The point is, he is not where we thought he was, and he hasn't been since Friday night"

"Ok Lee, you weren't the only one who was misled. Debby sent DS Shacklady to the local hospital, she came back with the same info'. What we need to concentrate on now is Post and where the hell he is"

"Where did he live boss before he was convicted?"

"Good question Nick, but I am afraid that whole estate was demolished and redeveloped into a shopping centre ten years ago. He has no family, or at least in this country. There is an aunt in Australia and a couple of cousins in the middle east. To be honest he has no connection at all with anyone or anywhere in the UK, save the couple of jails he spent the last twenty-two years in.

We have to be more creative than that, we have to get into the head of Post, and that's not going to be easy, he is one fucked up individual. We have until Friday night to find him and get him into custody. If we don't, three innocent women will lose their lives, and that won't be the end of it, there will be many more, rest assured"

"Wait a minute Lee, didn't you talk to Post on the phone?"

"I did Nick, I have tried to ring him, but the number was unobtainable. It seems the phone he was using is no longer in existence, except at the bottom of the local canal. Post is a clever man, he has covered his tracks, so like Marcus said, we need to get creative"

"So, any ideas, because I am fresh out?"

"The only connection I can think of Marcus is Olivia"

"Who the hell is Olivia?"

"It's Post's ex-girlfriend Nick. I met her in the Prince of Wales pub in Steeple Claydon. She was shit scared but did speak to me about him and she tried to warn me off, saying he would kill me. He is nasty, very nasty Nick. The things she told me about Post would make your hair curl. From what she was describing I think Post has some kind of multiple personality disorder. Maybe that might explain why he thinks he is innocent of his wife's murder. I think he is able to control people with fear and intimidation. Often people like Post seem to acquire followers, acolytes, weak individuals who seemingly want to be controlled, be dominated.

Anyway, if we can track her down, perhaps we can persuade her to contact Post, see if he wants to meet up. She might know where he might be, perhaps some family or friends we don't know about. I don't have an address or even a second name for her, maybe you will have something in the original crime files"

"It's worth a try Lee, to be honest, we have nothing else. You go back to the Prince, see what you can find out, I will get the local uniforms out looking for her"

Before we could say our goodbyes, there was a knock on the door. It had that urgent and rapid cadence, perhaps a feeling of panic. Whomever was outside didn't wait to be called in. I turned to look just as the door burst open, a fresh-faced uniformed constable bowled into the office. He clearly had something he needed to communicate, but there was a nervous pause before he spoke.

"Sorry sir, but there's been another"

"Constable, take a breath, settle down and try to explain to me what 'another' actually means"

"Sorry sir, another young woman, she has been taken, or is missing, we don't know"

Marcus sat looking at the young man, it was immediately obvious what this half-garbled message actually meant. None of us wanted to ask the obvious question though, Marcus eventually did.

"Is there a body constable?"

"She is not, well, there isn't a dead woman, sorry sir, she is just missing"

"Can I assume you mean that a young woman is missing, but there has been no body found?"

"Yes sir, but my boss said she fits the profile of those taken"

Marcus looked at his Sergeant, then back at me. A cold and ominous silence descended on the meeting. It would seem that the threats were in fact real, the devil killer was collecting, and we had just three days to find him.

I drove away from the police HQ with a sinking heart. Marcus was right, we had nothing, Post could be anywhere, he might not even be close to here. Now there was another missing woman, it could have just been a coincidence of course. She did fit the profile of those two bodies found recently and of the three victims twenty-two years ago. Dam, that made five dead and one missing, and that's not counting Post's wife.

Post was certainly out to make a name for himself and that was a very dangerous situation. I had not been involved in any major serial killer case before, but I knew how difficult they could be to stop. A man bent on harm, hiding in plain sight, not drawing any attention to himself, not even from family and friends.

It was a common scenario, and I certainly didn't envy Marcus and his team. Soon the press would be all over it, his boss would want answers, the local community would want a resolution. Reporters would be blocking the entrance to the police HQ; Sky and the BBC would have cameras everywhere.

This of course was exactly what Post was after, he wanted to be known for his deeds, strike fear into everyone. He wins, so long as he remained in the shadows, away from those cameras and hidden from sight. He will laugh at those trying to catch him, treat all attempts to arrest him with distain.

It's perhaps at that point when he might just make a mistake, become overly confident. The trouble was, how many women would die before that happened. Marcus and his team must do whatever they could, if he did make a mistake and become detectible, they must be ready to strike.

In the meantime, I had to do whatever I could to help. The first thing was to go to the Prince of

Wales pub and see if any of the locals might know of his whereabouts. It might be that some of them are still in contact, or possibly know something about his background that might lead us to him.

By the time I pulled up outside the pub, the early crowd were arriving. It wasn't going to be busy at lunchtime but that might be helpful, at least when talking to the landlord. I opened the front door and walked confidently inside; it was at that point that I realised my mistake. It was mid-afternoon and the over whelming majority of the customers weren't local, just passers-by and the occasional workman. Nevertheless, I pushed on, walking straight over to Frank, the pub landlord. He looked up, he had that 'I don't remember your name, but I do recognise your face' look. He smiled and immediately came to the side of the bar where I was now standing.

"Good afternoon sir, I think I remember you from the other night, you were asking about that Lennard Post, weren't you?

"Afternoon Frank, I was and to be honest, I would like some more information if I can get it"

"Ok, first things first, what are you drinking?"

"Well since you ask, mine is a pint of bitter please"

He turned and took a glass from the shelf at the rear of the bar. Whistling confidently, he drew a pint of bitter from the pump, checked it for clarity and brought it back to me.

"So, Lennard Post, what's he been up to? He's out of jail isn't he, starting to kill folks again, or young girls to be more accurate"

That took me back somewhat, 'young girls, killing folks again', was it a lucky guess or just a throw away comment. I needed to settle down, this case was starting to make me edgy and that wasn't a good place to be.

"Killing people Frank, not sure what you mean"

"Well, he did his wife good and proper, tied her up and slashed her throat I heard. If you ask me, he's bound to do the same again, folks around here say he did something similar before he killed her"

"That's a bit of a shocker Frank, what were they saying?"

"They say he killed quite a few and touched up loads more before they arrested him. His wife was just the end of the line, his final killing before the cops got hold of him"

"Were you here when Post was about?"

"No, that was way before my time, but the conversation does come up occasionally, especially when you see another serial killer getting arrested on the news. It makes it worse when it's someone local, Post really stirred things up around here with his devil mask and all that"

"I hear he used to drink in here Frank, maybe he stayed in the village with someone?"

"Yeah, he used to sit at the other end of the bar, or so I am told. He didn't live in Steeple Claydon though, I think his place was in Buckingham. He did have a girl here though, you spoke to her the other night, what's her name.....Cranfield, that's it, Olivia Cranfield. She drives an old Land Rover Defender; I think it's an original 90. She loves that piece of junk, thinks the world of it. Her father gave it to her for a birthday present years ago. She wouldn't drive anything else; it's called Henry I think, I don't know how it's still running, should have blown up years ago"

Her dad owned the engineering works on the outskirts of Aylesbury, well off people, loads of cash. They passed away some time ago. I think she moved to her sisters in Aylesbury when she broke up with Post, but she lives in her parent's old place now. It's the posh Victorian house, near the paper shop, you can't miss it."

"Thanks Frank, I will give her a call. Do you think she ever started seeing Post again, or was it just the one relationship they had?"

"That's a good question, some say she moved to Aylesbury to be with Post, away from this place and the gossip. I can't really comment on that, but it seems to be the overwhelming feeling around here"

"But I thought she moved in with her sister?"

"Yeah, that's what she used to tell people, thing is, no one ever met her sister. Odd that, you would think someone in the village would have known her sister, wouldn't you? She would have been someone you went to school with, that girl who was your first date, all that kind of stuff, turns out no one ever did, no one ever met her"

That was somewhat of a shock, everyone knows your business in small communities like Steeple Claydon. You can't hide anything, especially people. Surely someone would have known Olivia Cranfield's sister, it would have been impossible not to.

"Does anyone come in here who used to be friends with Post, someone who might even still be in contact with him?"

"There might be, I doubt anyone would admit to that though, he has a shit reputation around here. If you are a friend of Post, I doubt people would have anything to do with you"

"Was his wife from around here, maybe there is someone I could talk to?"

"Can't help you there, no one around here ever knew her, I guess she was from out of town"

It seemed my only chance of finding something more out about Post, was to go and see his ex-girlfriend. I would doubt meeting anyone else would help, I think I understood the feelings people around here had for him, so they would never talk to me. The only person still here who really knew him was Olivia Cranfield, I needed to go and talk to her, try and find out anything more she knew.

By the time I finished my drink, and a rather nice round of chicken salad sandwiches, the day had brightened up considerably. Warm summer sunshine had broken through and the whole atmosphere around the village was brighter.

I remembered driving past the paper shop on the way to the pub. It was five minutes' walk away, so I decided to leave the car and appreciate the sunny afternoon. I enjoyed walking, when my knackered knee would allow, it gave me time to think, away from people, phones and emails. We don't dedicate enough time to being by ourselves, we don't get enough time to think, so I set off for her house in the afternoon sunshine.

I doubted if Olivia Cranfield would be able to shed any more light on Post, but I had to try. Perhaps she might know somewhere locally where he might be hiding out, but it was a long shot. It had occurred to me she might be a target of his, but I decided to reject that thought, she was much older than his victims and if he wanted to kill her, he would have done so many years ago. No, she was someone who might just have something to impart about Post, but sadly, I wasn't holding out any real hope.

It wasn't long before the paper shop came into view, and just as Frank had described, there was a large Victorian villa right next door. Now, given the time of day and it being the middle of the week, I wasn't holding out much expectation of Olivia Cranfield being at home, but I had to give it a go.

The heavy wrought iron gate swung effortlessly open, the path leading to the house opened up in front of me. The pathway was wide and meandered through extensive and well-kept gardens. To my left was the driveway, leading to the double garage next to the house. There was a new E200 AMG Mercedes Benz parked just in front of the garage doors. The bright red paintwork shone in the sunshine, it must have cost the best part of 60k, nice if you can afford it, I mused. Maybe that old Land Rover 90 her father had given her all those years ago had finally given up the ghost, nothing last forever, I guess.

In front of me was a four-story property, somewhat intimidating, substantial wooden bay windows with an imposing double door at it's centre. This was a very large villa, even by the standards of the time, and easily the biggest property for miles in any direction.

I lifted the heavy brass doorknob and knocked. At first there was no response at all, perhaps no one was at home, I started to leave. As I turned, I caught site of someone through the ornate stained-glass inserts to the front doors. The person slowly came into focus, coloured red, blue and green by the decorated glass. I hope that person would be Olivia, she might be the one person who could help.

The door slowly opened, eventually a familiar face appeared in the tiny gap. To my great relief, it was the face of Olivia Cranfield, perhaps the only person who could help find Lennard Post.

She screwed her face up, she was obviously shocked to see me, and probably quite annoyed.

"Hi Olivia, sorry to disturb you, I wonder if I might have a very quick word"

"Mister Hunter, I have already told you everything I know about Lennard. I don't want to get involved, he is a very dangerous man, and I am really scared of him, you should be too"

"Olivia, I have spent many years dealing with people like him, he doesn't scare me at all. To be honest, I don't think you should be scared either. He has nothing to prove by having anything to do with you. If he wanted to hurt you, he would have done so already, or even before he went into jail"

"I don't agree, as I said, he is an evil man, and best left alone. Forget about him mister Hunter, just go back to where you came from"

"Listen Olivia, I need a bit of information, it won't take a second. Post has gone missing, and I need to talk to him, I have some things I need to share. Do you know of anywhere he might be, I don't have an address for him, it's important"

There was an extended silence, she just stared past my right shoulder and into the distance. I didn't really detect any great fear in her persona, more of irritation at my arrival.

"I don't mister Hunter, the place where he used to live has been bulldozed, there is a shopping centre there now. I don't know of any other places where he used to live, we weren't going out together for that long"

The question of her sister was still conspicuous in my thoughts. According to Frank, no one had ever met her, or even knew her name. I didn't buy that at all, someone somewhere would know her, it was inconceivable that no one did. I was beginning to wonder if the rumours were right, and it was Post that she moved in with in Aylesbury and not her sister. This needed to be sorted out, no time like the present.

"I wonder if your sister might be able to help. She might have another location for him, what's her name?"

Her face turned bright red, she moved back slightly from the door, she was clearly agitated.

"What's my sister got to do with this?"

"You said that you moved in with her, to get away from Post"

"Well, yes, that's true. She won't know anything about him though, not at all"

"It might be worth a try Olivia, maybe you could give her a ring, see what she says"

"I am not bothering her now mister Hunter, she is very busy. Anyway, I have to go, so sorry but goodbye mister Hunter"

Without another word, she closed the door firmly in my face. I was left standing in the porchway like a naughty schoolboy at the headmaster's office. She certainly didn't like talking about her sister, if her sister did indeed exist, which I now doubted. As I turned to walk back to my car, I mulled over what if anything I had learned from the brief meeting.

She didn't have another address for Post, I could live with that. The relationship was many years ago, so why would she keep any details about him, she probably wouldn't. In any case, he might not have told her the whole truth about himself, so there was nothing to be gained there.

Then there was the question about her sister. Olivia became very agitated when I mentioned this, she clearly didn't want to talk about her. The locals in the pub might have a point though, thinking it was Post she moved in with, not her sister. Was this significant, perhaps not, again it was many years ago. She lied about it then, so she had to keep up the charade, even twenty-five years later.

So, it was most probably a waste of time, but at least I could put Olivia Cranfield out of my mind. I doubted if she knew anything of great interest about Post, even if she did, she was never going to tell me. I didn't believe the apprehension thing though, she never really displayed any real fear or emotions when talking about Post, not this time, that was obvious. So why say that she was frightened, maybe it was an easy way to get me to back off, perhaps it gave her an excuse to stop talking.

Was it really that important, she was probably a woman who wished she had never met the guy. Maybe she had been frightened in the past, when she was just a teenager, but I didn't really get that impression now. No, Olivia Cranfield was a dead end, I needed to move on.

So where to next? I had to speak to the lead detective in the original case, Peter Dexter. Also, I had to sort this thing out regarding Paul Willow, was he the man I met the other night, or some kind of deranged imposter? I remembered the ladies' pink knickers question though. If this guy contacted me again, that's the first thing I would ask him, odd question hey!

Wednesday evening.
Ready for the second object.

The sense of exhilaration was overwhelming in the devil's mind. His first object was secure in the cell, the fear in her eyes was delightful. She had begged for her life, to be released, but she was going nowhere. He had taunted her all day, slowly explaining what he had done to his other victims, and what he would be doing to her on Friday night.

She screamed until her voice became horse, but no one would hear her cries. Shivering, and curled up in the corner of a darkened cellar, she wanted to wake from this nightmare, but knew she never would.

He had gone out but before he did, he told her, "I will return my darling, and tonight you will have a companion, someone to share your terror with. Remember to tell her what I told you, the pain and the blood, and don't forget that I will be eating your flesh before you die, I can't wait.

There will be a third though, so plenty for you to talk about. You will all meet your end on Friday, so no need to worry about food. There are bottles of water in the corner, try to drink, you will need to be hydrated. When you are dehydrated, your blood loses volume and becomes thicker. I prefer to drink blood that is a little thinner, and it exudes from your slashed skin more easily, so keep drinking, there's a good girl"

He spun and left the room, the dimness returned, the smell of damp pervaded every part of her senses. She looked about her, through the gloom. There were three mattresses on the floor, a chemical toilet and several bottles of water, but nothing else. The floor was cold limestone slabs, and the walls cracked and degraded whitewash. There were no windows, just a heavy blue painted door at one end.

It was clear she was underground, perhaps in the cellar of a house. It reminded her of her grandmother's old home. She used to play in the basement, it felt just like this place did, cold and ghostly.

Pushing herself to her feet, she walked around, trying to see through the gloom. The single lightbulb was old and yellow. The light it shed was all but gone, perhaps like the last few days of her life.

She pulled and kicked at the blue door, but it held firm with a solidity borne from the quality of days gone by. The dirty brass handle would not move, it was fixed, resilient to anything other than the key to which the lock was married.

"You bastard, you won't kill me, not a fucking chance. One false move and you die, I will kill you with whatever comes to hand. Don't you ever threaten me, don't you ever, you slimy bastard. Just wait until I get that one chance, you won't even see me coming"

Enraged she turned and sat down on one of the mattresses. "So, there will be two more, well that puts the odds in our favour, that was a mistake wasn't it"

Marcus Cooke never felt relaxed in these kinds of places. Just next door was the mortuary with several dead bodies in the coolers. There was no odour of death in the main office, but he could smell it all the same. He could taste it as well, these places were the end of the line for so many people. It demonstrated that everyone was mortal, even if he didn't want to think about that outcome.

He had lost count of how many dead bodies he had seen during his career in the police. It never got any easier though, especially when it involved young people, such a terrible waste of a life.

He occasionally had nightmares, solemn dreams of death and murder. White bodies, drained of life moving ghostlike away into the night. It was mostly connected to specific cases, and the two recent murders had been no exception. Two young women, cut down in the first part of their lives, still to explore life and to be blessed with many adventures.

It had been made worse by the threats from the devil killer, three more victims, all to be murdered in a few days' time. These threats had now been reinforced by the disappearance of a young woman last night. Whilst it was true that people go missing from time to time, only to re appear a few days later, this latest incident was very serious indeed. The truth was, he was no closer to catching the devil killer than he was last week. He needed a break, something, anything that might point him towards a specific target.

Lennard Post was front and centre of the current suspects, but his whereabouts were unknown. For all Marcus knew, he might not even be in the country, let alone in Aylesbury. To make things worse, he was relying on a private detective to find Post. It felt wrong, with all the facilities and manpower at his disposal, he was depending on Lee Hunter to find his main suspect.

He wondered if things could get any worse, there was a strong fear that tonight they would, with the disappearance of another woman. Marcus had done everything he could, ensured every available uniformed officer was out on the streets. He had sent his detectives to the pubs and clubs around the town, watching, advising single females of the dangers. The local press and radio had publicised the disappearances and warned of the possibility of more.

In truth he understood whilst these measures might well be affective, they wouldn't last forever. The devil killer need only wait, postpone his plan for a few weeks. Eventually he would have to scale down the police presence and that's when the devil killer could strike. He was caught in nomans-land but at least he had done his best. In actuality, that was never going to be enough, and he knew it.

The door to the office opened and in walked Doctor Simone, a woman in her mid-sixties. Tall, elegant and extremely cultured. Originally from Paris she had that self-confidence, an inner grace and style of an educated and very sophisticated Parisian woman.

Marcus was drawn to her bravura, and an absolute knowledge and control of her subject. If Doctor Simone gave her opinion on something, she was always correct, being held in the highest regard by the police, the courts and the lawyers.

As she moved in behind her desk she smiled, a warm and friendly smile, enough to disarm the coldest of hearts. She drew her grey/blond hair behind her ears and began to speak. Her accent was soft and warm, a measured cadence and delivered with consummate ease.

"Good evening Marcus, sorry about the lateness of the hour but this week has been rather busy, as you might imagine"

"That's fine Doctor, I am afraid crime doesn't keep sociable hours, unfortunately"

They laughed; it had indeed been a busy period for them both. Times like this only added unwanted strain to their already busy departments.

"I only wish they would. Finishing work predictably from time to time might be rather pleasant, especially when I have tickets to the theatre. It would certainly help in saving one's marriage, not that I miss him, he was never a good husband in the first place, no style you know.

Now down to business Marcus, I have completed my reports on the two girls, and emailed them to you. However, in short, these are my findings.

The first girl found by the dog walker on Tuesday morning. Her name is Jessica Wright, twenty-three years of age, borne and a resident of Aylesbury.

In my opinion the cause of death was strangulation, and overwhelming blood loss, caused by nineteen stab wounds. These stab wounds were to the breasts, crotch, eyes and throat. The stab wounds were clean, there was no sign of ferocity, the perpetrator simply pushed the knife into the victim, rather like calving the Sunday roast. There was a red silk scarf around the neck, whilst not knotted, I presume this was used to strangle the victim.

Most disturbing of all Marcus, some of the woman's flesh is missing. Some strips from the stomach and buttocks. I can't confirm why this would be, but I might speculate that he is cannibalising them?

On to the second victim, found by a man on his way to work early this morning. Her name is Martha Folks. She is a Dutch citizen, living in Aylesbury and currently employed as an au pair in the town.

The wounds to her body are identical to those of Jessica Wright, identical in every detail. Disturbingly, this also includes the missing flesh. It would seem that we not only have a murderer Marcus, but one that is also a cannibal"

He sat back in the comfortable chair opposite Doctor Simone. His head was spinning at the news. Not only did they have a vicious murderer, but also a man willing to eat the flesh of his victims. Those poor girls, their end was unspeakable, the news to their parents would be unbearable. At least he would be spared that horrific task, his job was now to catch their killer and stop this from happening again.

"Can I ask about the red silk scarves Simone; did they have any labels?"

"They did Marcus, William Q of Paris. I must admit to not being familiar with that label, much to my shame"

Marcus chuckled to himself, she was a consummate professional, but she was always a fashion-conscious Parisian.

"I would be surprised if you did Simone, that company went out of business a long time ago. The thing is, those same scarves were used on four victims twenty plus years ago. Three young women and the wife of the suspect in these murders. What about DNA Simone, anything of note?"

"We are having tests run as we speak. There was almost no blood on the bodies, they had been very thoroughly cleaned Marcus. I could smell the sodium hypochlorite, whoever had done this didn't want to leave any evidence. Their hair had been washed, even under their fingernails had been scraped clean. They hadn't been raped, so no semen to analyse. It seems that your murderer was very thorough in covering his tracks. We will get the tests back shortly; I will keep you posted"

"Thanks Simone, let's hope he has left something, we need a break"

"Actually, there was something found under the first victim, Jessica Wright. It was a button, black with a brass-coloured outer edge. It's probably just a coincidence, some bit of rubbish thrown out of a car, or just fell from the coat of a passer-by.

There were no fingerprints on the button, but we have swabbed it and sent it to the lab. I will get it out of the evidence locker, you can sign for it and take it with you. It's a large button, probably from an overcoat, it had no markings or names"

"A button Simone, that's all we have, a bloody button. In all probability, just a piece of unwanted rubbish thrown out, discarded by someone. The body was deposited on top of it, and now it's in the evidence locker.

Strange isn't it, how a man can take three women from the middle of town, kill two of them, and throw their bodies out like a piece of trash. No one saw him take the victims, no one saw him getting rid of their remains. I can't find the probable perpetrator, and no one knows where he might be now. It's almost certain that he has another young woman, he plans to take two more and then kill all three on Friday.

You know what the saddest thing in all of this nightmare is? That's the extent of everything we know. It's a button Simone, a useless piece of black plastic with a brass-coloured outer edge, that's the lot, the sum total of this case, a piece of bloody rubbish"

She stared back at Inspector Marcus Cooke, his face was pale, tiredness written large on all of his features. This case seemed impossible, there was nothing, no clues to expand on. She had processed the bodies of the latest two victims, studied the reports on the first three, they precisely matched. There was no doubt that the same man was responsible, but who was that man and where was he now?

"Look Marcus, you aren't to blame for this situation, this man is well prepared, he covers his tracks and doesn't seem to take any risks. He has done this before, albeit twenty odd years ago. You are inevitably going to play catchup, but he will make a mistake and you will be there to take him. Stay with it, I will give you every possible piece of evidence I can. He will make a mistake, you will find a lead, you will catch this man, of that there is no doubt"

He slowly looked up at Simone, "thanks' for that, you are right, but the question is, how many women will die before that happens Simone? I haven't got any more time, he has one, he will take two more, three dead women on Friday, that's the sickening truth"

The room fell into silence, Marcus was right, he had run out of time and three more women would pay with their lives. Also, how long was this going to last, would Friday be the end, or was it just the beginning.

"What I don't understand Simone is, how the hell is he doing this in the middle of a very busy town? Kidnapping women and then throwing their remains back into the night and no one sees anything, I don't get it? It's impossible, someone must have seen something, I just don't understand. I don't buy the 'well prepared' bit or that he was 'just lucky', not a chance. The town is covered by CCTV cameras, there are a few blind spots, but not many"

"Maybe he knows the location of the cameras Marcus, perhaps he is aware of the blind spots. It's not impossible, and if he does, then he can plan his activities accordingly. How many people would know this information, who knows where they can operate safely?"

"I don't know Simone, perhaps some of the camera operators, maybe the engineers who installed them, in truth, does anyone really know. Most people just call for the tapes when they need them, the question of blind spots is not something that is often considered. In any case, money is short nowadays, even if someone points out a blind spot, in all probability, nothing would be done about it. it would just be forgotten about"

"So, who can operate in full site of everyone, with absolute impunity, and no one asks why? What gives a man a free pass to do what he wants. After all, if you can't hide something, emphasise it. It's called hiding in plain sight Marcus; you need to find out who that is. Who is operating where everyone can see him, and he doesn't really care, because nothing seems to be out of place"

Wednesday evening.
The Travel Lodge Buckingham.

I looked down at my Apple iPhone screen, 'number withheld'. I was bloody sick of these calls. Before I became a private detective, the anonymous calls were some scammers, or a man trying to sell me life insurance.

Now the calls were usually some lunatic, or a murderer, perhaps a gang land boss. Normally they would be threatening my life or telling me they had someone hostage who would be killed at midnight. Oh, for the old days and those anonymous swindlers from the far east.

I reluctantly sat up on the rather comfortable bed. To be honest today had been crap, and a waste of time. No one in the pub could help and Post's ex-girlfriend was not much use either. Olivia Cranfield almost certainly knew more than she was saying, but what was I supposed to do, beat it out of her? No, Post was out there, and, in all probability, no one knew where. If he was the serial killer, he could strike at anytime and anywhere, and no one would be able to stop him.

Right, do I answer the call, or do I grab a shower and go for something to eat? I had to say, the latter was by far and away the favourite. The trouble was, I would be wondering all night who the hell it was calling, and that would certainly spoil my evening meal. So reluctantly I pressed the green button and put the phone to my ear.

"Mister Hunter, this is Peter Dexter, I assume you remember me from our conversation the other day. If you recall, I was the lead detective when Post killed his wife. I trust you are keeping well"

Now there's a turn up, Peter bloody Dexter, the man in Spain, in his apartment, with his wife. The only thing was, he wasn't married, he hadn't got an apartment and he wasn't in Spain! Marcus had inadvertently blown that lie out of the water, the thing was, do I confront Dexter with it? There was also the conversation I had with his supposed ex mate and colleague Paul Willow.

Now there's a bunch of ammunition, where do I start, or should I leave it until later. I decided to sit on what I had, just play it straight and see if Dexter tries to correct the record. I would also leave Paul Willow out of the conversation, at least for the meantime. If Willow was genuine, it might be that Dexter doesn't know his suicide was a fake.

"Hi Peter, how's life treating you?"

"Great thanks Lee, I wonder if you fancy a meeting, discuss the case, see if I can be of any help"

"Oh, I am sure you will be Peter, what about the Indian restaurant in the middle of town, the Buckingham Fort"

"Love it there Lee, I will book a table, they know me personally, what about eight pm?"

"Sounds great Peter, I will see you inside"

"Sorted, see you at eight"

I started to wonder why he wanted to talk to me about the case. Well, Marcus had asked him to have a chat with me, I guess. I wasn't sure that would have persuaded him to pick up the phone though.

After all, he had been a senior detective, he had got his man, that man was guilty and served a lot of time for what he did. Talking to me wasn't going to change anything, and certainly wasn't going to earn him any extra pension.

Now, call me a suspicious old Hector, but he seemed to be going to a lot of trouble just to tell me how great he was, and how he solved the case. Perhaps he was one of those self-opinionated jerks who liked everyone to know just how brilliant he was. There were plenty of folks like that, and in all probability, he was one of them. He would spend all evening telling me how he had caught the most dangerous people in Britain, perhaps even Europe. He would then move on to his female conquests and end with his classic car collection.

I did wonder if this was about something more subtle than any of that though. Was this an attempt to cover things up, maybe see what I knew or was thinking? If, and it was a very big if, the man I met in Windsor was Paul Willow, then Dexter had some explaining to do. Perhaps he was feeling a little bit vulnerable, after all it had been a quarter of a century since the crimes had occurred. His life had been perfect since, but now Post was out of jail, the murders had started again, and I wanted to talk to him. That was bound to make him somewhat suspicious and more than a little jumpy, that's if he had anything to hide of course, and to be honest, I think he has.

Ok, let's grab a shower, get to the restaurant and see what he has to say, should be fun. I would play this without any obvious agenda, see what he had to say. I wouldn't tell him about the meeting with Willow, or my regular contact with Marcus Cooke. There would be no mention of Post's ex-girlfriend Olivia Cranfield, my meeting with Post in Southport or anything else of importance.

I would simply tell him that I wanted to get some information about the original crimes, from the man heading up the case. Marcus had told him that I wanted as much info' as possible on the Post case. He hadn't said why, or who I really was, so the field was open for me to put any slant on my request that might prove most beneficial.

The restaurant was very busy, especially for the middle of the week. I took this as a good sign, in my experience, if the food was great, a place is always in full swing. There was a counter, just to the right of the door, I decided to wait there until Dexter came to find me. It didn't take long, a tall, well-built man, maybe late sixties or early seventies came in my direction. He was well over six feet tall, somewhat overweight and almost completely bald. He was wearing a light grey suit, yellow shirt and cowboy boots, very stylish…not!

He confidently strode right up to me, with a broad and constructed white smile that must have cost him well over 10k. I couldn't help but notice the Omega Seamaster divers watch on his right wrist. It looked genuine, my bet is if it was, it was worth about the same as his dental implants. I had to wonder how an ex-cop on a police pension could begin to afford these things. Maybe an old aunt had left him some cash, or he had a win on the lottery, who knows.

With that smile reflecting the light, he extended his hand, a huge shovel of a thing, each finger replete with a gold ring.

"Good evening Lee, so glad you could join me. I have my favourite table, over here by the window, follow me"

He turned and strode confidently away towards the far end of the restaurant. I followed, trying to keep up with his long stride. Diners watched as he flashed past, he was indeed a very imposing figure, creating a draft as he walked by. Eventually we arrived, a small square table with a couple of chairs. He had already ordered himself a beer and had obviously been scrutinising tonight's menu.

"Grab a chair Lee, let's have a chat. Order anything you want from the menu; I have an account here so help yourself"

He winked at me as he finished the sentence, what a slimeball. We sat and exchanged pleasantries, the weather, the price of food etc. Eventually I decided to order Chicken tikka masala, with naan bread and a pint of Tiger larger. Goodness knows what Dexter ordered, it sounded exotic, let's see what it looks like.

"So, Lee old man, what the hell is this all about, been doing some detective work eh?"

He had that condescending tone to his voice. He gave a sly smirk, obviously he enjoyed belittling people. He clearly didn't know I was an ex-cop and had held the same rank as he. That would only play into my hands, so long as he thought I was some bungling amateur, then his guard might well be down! I needed to stay sharp, ask questions but not in the manner he might recognise as ex police.

"Well, you know Pete', just looking into a few things. I don't know where to start, I wondered if you might be able to help. My wife's mate is Deborah Smith, she is the partner of that policeman and friend of yours, Marcus Cooke.

I am looking to write a book on Lennard Post, I thought Marcus might be able to help but the case went back before his time. He recommended you; he said you were in charge at the time"

I could feel my face flushing bright red. I couldn't believe I had just come out with that crap. I am a writer, what the fuck was that all about, he was never going to believe it, surely! Also, If Marcus had said anything about me and my past as a cop, my cover story would be finished in an instant.

By the look on his face, Marcus hadn't said anything, other than I wanted to speak to him about Post. I must contact him and tell him to keep his mouth shut and leave the rest to me.

"A writer Pete', never met one of those before. Why the hell do you want to know about that monster? There must be more interesting people to write stories on, and ones that don't go around killing innocent young women. You know that twat is out and by all accounts, killing again. Now there's a thing, maybe that might be an interesting story line, I might write that book myself, if only I had the time left"

He rubbed his chin in an exaggerated manner, nodding at the same time in an approving fashion. I could have happily reached across the table and poured his beer all over his slimy persona. What a complete twat, shame Post hadn't come after him twenty-five years ago, he could have done us all a favour.

"Well, we all have a living to make, mine is writing. Not very exciting Pete' but it pays the bills. I bet you have a story or two to tell, arresting gangsters, murderers and terrorists. I don't think I would have the courage to do that, you must have nerves of stee'"

"Of course, you need to be a real man to do what I used to. It was tough at times, but the girls looked up to me, if you know what I mean"

He winked as he mentioned the girls. This was turning into a bloody nightmare, but at least he was talking, and the beer was flowing. That was a good combination and one that might reveal a little more than he wanted to do.

"So, Pete', what was the story with this Post guy, did you have a partner, or did you do all this by yourself?"

"I did have a partner, his name was Paul Willow. Bloody waste of time if you ask me, a wimp, work shy and not up to the job. He fucked up so many things in the case, Post got off with three other killings because of Willow. He couldn't stand the shame, drowned himself in the English Channel, good riddance to bad rubbish if you ask me"

"I read that Post wasn't guilty of the other three killings"

"Well, he wasn't prosecuted, but that was largely because of Paul Willow's bloody ineptitude, but take it from me Lee, he was guilty. He killed them and then his wife in exactly the same way. He stabbed them, then strangled them with a red silk scarf from Paris. What a mess Lee, blood everywhere, what a shit show"

I ordered some more beer, and then more again. It was obvious that Dexter was well used to drinking, but then so was I, after all, that's why I lost my job in the Met. One beer turned into two then three and four, I lost count after that. I had to concentrate on what I was saying and what Dexter was burbling on about. Most of what he said was rubbish or had nothing to do with the case, but at least he didn't suspect me, and he was nice and relaxed.

"What did your superiors think about all of this Pete', did they support you, or did you get the job done by yourself?"

"Bloody waste of time Lee, chief inspectors, superintendents and the like. That lot couldn't organise a piss up in a brewery, I sorted this out, not the bosses in their ivory towers. If it was left to them, we would still be looking for the killer, I needed to take control of the whole thing, get Post behind bars"

That was an odd statement, "I needed to take control of the whole thing, get Post behind bars", was this what Willow was talking about? Was Dexter alluding to stitching Post up, improving the prosecution numbers, making himself out to be some kind of wonder cop?

The truth was, either Post was some kind of deranged maniac, and Dexter by corruption, luck or judgment had got him off the streets. Or Dexter had thrown an innocent man in jail for most of his life, for no other reason than for statistics and personal glory.

In all probability, Post was the original killer, that's why the murders had started again, because he was out of jail, and couldn't help himself. But what if he wasn't the killer, what if Post was exactly how he betrayed himself, an innocent man, stitched up by a bent cop, one Chief Inspector Peter Dexter.

I was still convinced it was the former, Post was on the streets and the devil killings had started again. However, Post would know he was going to be the one and only suspect. He would certainly get caught, and end up locked up for ever, why the hell would he risk that?

As much as I was convinced of his guilt, there was a little light flashing in my brain. It was trying to tell me that Post being the devil killer was way, way too much of a coincidence. Was Post on the run, not because he was guilty, but because he was worried about the likes of Dexter? He might end up once again as an innocent man behind bars.

This theory would of course throw up one huge question, if Post was actually innocent, then who was the devil killer? Also, why was there so much of Post's DNA and fingerprints left at his wife's murder scene?

There was of course Paul Willow, and what he had told me. According to him, Dexter was corrupt and needed to be brought to justice, just like the devil killer. Dexter being a bent cop was of no real interest to me at this time though. However, if Willow was right and Dexter stitched Post up, then Post might not be the killer after all!

Obviously, Post was our first priority, and Dexter might have some information regarding him. Something not in the records, a contact, perhaps a piece of intelligence that might lead to his whereabouts.

I shook my head, I needed to concentrate on what was directly in front of me. Namely, the whereabouts of Lennard Post and had Dexter anything he could tell me about him, before more women lost their lives?

The question regarding corruption and Peter Dexter was nothing I could do anything about, other than report back to Marcus. It would be up to Thames Valley Police to follow that up.

I finished my main course and waited for Dexter to suggest what to order next. I could tell by the red look in his eyes that the alcohol had taken effect. This was the time to push the questions, his resistance would be low and his propensity to boast about himself would be at its strongest.

"So how did you get this case done Pete', how did you get Post locked up?"

"Well, there was a load of DNA evidence Lee. His wife's body was covered in his semen, and his bloody fingerprints were on the knife. It was easy to be honest. He said that it was all a plant, but why wouldn't he, I would say the same, I guess.

He banged on about not having had sex with his wife for years, so why would his semen be all over her? He even had witnesses saying that there hadn't been any sexual relations between himself and his wife for the longest time. If that was the case, if he hadn't been fucking her, why would his semen be all over the body?

He also said the knife was not one he had ever seen before, t must have been left by someone else. Good try Post, shame that your fingerprints were all over it eh!"

"Had his wife been having an affair, was this a crime of passion?"

"There were one or two reports stating his wife had been in a relationship with another man. I put this to Post, he said he knew about it. They had an open relationship, so there had been no problems in that respect. She had several relationships with other men, if he wanted to kill her over that, he would have done it years ago.

He was vaguer about affairs he had with other women. He said most of these had been with married ladies, and he wanted to protect their privacy. He seemed relaxed about the whole question of extra marital relationships, seemed very laissez-faire about the whole thing. No, I don't think this was a crime of passion, you know, catching his wife shagging his best mate. I never got that impression at all, it was a cold-blooded murder, he wanted his wife dead, so he killed her"

"So why has he never confessed. By not doing so he probably served several more years than he needed to. The Parole Board don't like to grant early release, unless you have both admitted, and come to terms with your crime"

"Arrogance Lee, the twat is arrogant. He just couldn't accept the fact that he lost it and killed her. Either that or he just wanted her gone, out of the way, so he slit her throat, end of problem. He just made it look like the devil killer, tried to make it seem number four in the serial killer's murders, blame someone else for what he had done.

You need to remember that psychopaths don't need a reason, they don't feel regret. They are by design, manipulative, unremorseful and exploitative. My personal opinion is that she was no further use to him, she got in the way, maybe stopped him from doing what he wanted. So, she had to go, he feels no regret, he doesn't see what he has done wrong. He is a narcissist; he can't distinguish between right and wrong"

"But surely if he was manipulative, he would have tried to pull the wool over the Parole Board's eyes. He would have done anything to get out of jail early. Confessed, done the anger management courses, signed off with the prison psychologist and got out"

"That's something you are going to have to ask Post, but remember what I said, he is calculating and cunning. He will say whatever he thinks needs to be said to get him where he wants to be, and he is good at it Lee, very good. To be honest I really don't think that he felt he had done anything wrong, killing his wife was just something he had to do, so he had nothing to confess"

"So, what about the other crimes, the assaults and then the three murders, why couldn't you prosecute him for those offences?"

"I tried Lee, but the lawyers wouldn't go for it. The crimes were almost identical, stab wounds, French silk scarves from Paris. It was uncanny, but Post always had a strong alibi, he always seemed to have an excuse"

The recent debacle regarding the head wound at the Red Rose Hotel, and the weekend he didn't spend in Southport hospital sprang very clearly to mind. Was Post an expert at covering his tracks, he certainly had me fooled. He probably paid someone he had met in jail to take a blow to the head and pass himself off as Lennard Post. Spend a weekend in the hospital, lots of lovely nurses to look after you, and get a pocket full of cash for your troubles. I guess it seemed like a good deal to some homeless drug addict with nothing to live for.

Dexter wasn't right though, not even close. The three murders of the young women were not the same as Post's wife. Yes, there were lots of stab wounds, some in similar places, but those murders were cold, calculating even pleasurable for the perpetrator. Whoever did them enjoyed the offence, it was something he had planned, looked forward to. He killed the women slowly, tortured them, let them bleed before strangling them with a silk scarf. Afterwards he cleared up, destroyed any evidence, made sure he left no clues, he was forensically very aware.

On the other hand, his wife's murder was frenzied. He left evidence, and lots of it. In any other circumstance, not a judge in the land, no lawyer or investigator would have connected them, but for one thing. The red scarves from William Q of Paris, that was more than a coincidence, it was a clear and unquestionable connection.

I had to find Post, I needed to question him about the scarves. Did he have a plausible excuse as to why the identical scarves had been found on the bodies of his wife, and the three young women. To be honest, I couldn't see any real reason other than Post being the murderer. The problem was, I couldn't put that question to him, because no one knew where the hell Post was.

"What if it wasn't Post who killed those women. Let's accept he killed his wife, but there were several sexual assaults, and then the three murders. Who's to say it wasn't someone else, the real devil killer"

"Lee, it was Post, no doubt at all. Let's remember what was found in the boot of his car, including the devils mask. You can dress this up any way you want, it was Post, no fucking doubt about it, it was Post"

"I am still a little troubled about the differences in the killings Pete'. His wife was frenzied, blood and gore everywhere, the other three were clinical, no evidence. Surely if his MO is that of a meticulous predator, it would have been the same outcome when he killed his wife?"

"Well, I guess you are right Lee, but perhaps there was something else in his mad brain when he killed his wife. We will never know because he will not confess. My guess is hatred. The three young women were pleasure, he enjoyed them, took great delight in watching them slowly die, suffer and scream as he tortured them. On the other hand, his wife was hate, plain and simple"

Dexter's last statement kind of squared things up in my mind. There were still questions I wanted to ask Post, things that didn't quite add up. I was sure he killed his wife and was almost certain he was responsible for the other crimes.

"Post seems to have gone missing Pete', have you any idea where he might be? His old neighbourhood is no more, so he must have somewhere else to hide. I have asked the locals, even an ex-girlfriend but no one seems to know.

Do you recollect anything from the original investigation that might be useful. He doesn't seem to have any family, or at least none in this country. Did he hang out with a group of people, a gang perhaps?"

Dexter sat back in his chair, looking off into the distance. I wasn't sure if he would actually tell me everything he knew, but I had no choice, I had to ask.

"He was a home boy Lee, so far as I remember he stayed around these parts. He was also a loner, no gang connections, I don't even think he had any friends. If he has disappeared, well your guess is as good as mine, he could be anywhere"

Well, that kind of killed the night, I was no wiser as to the whereabouts of Post. I was hoping Dexter might have some kind of an answer, but it turned out to be another dead end.

Post was a very clever operator, that was certain. He had given me the slip from the hotel, disappeared without a trace. He had also managed to kill two women and in all likelihood, would kill another three.

I wondered how many women would have died twenty odd years ago if he hadn't lost the plot and murdered his wife. His body count was currently six, in a couple of days it might rise to nine, and I feared that it wouldn't stop there.

Wednesday night.
A dark street.

The evening dew had started to form on the outside of the van. A thin veil of moister partly obscured his view through the windscreen. He reached out to activate the windscreen wipers but thought better of it. Any sudden noise or movement might give away his presence, stealth and patients were the key to a successful hunt.

He shivered, it rolled up and down his spine, he was vulnerable to the cold. He tapped the steering wheel, his black leather gloves giving a pleasing feel. He looked at them, smelled one, the rich aroma of leather made him smile.

"When will you come my love, it's late and I need to get back home. I have waited here for you for hours, I have been patient, but I know you will be here soon.

Tonight, you will join the first one, you will have much to talk about, a lot to look forward to. Perhaps you will become friends, who knows, but you will die together, that I am certain of"

The silence and emptiness continued, perhaps tonight would be a failure. There would be tomorrow of course, but he had promised Lee Hunter he would be ready for Friday. If he couldn't make the capture this evening, he would only have two victims for the big night.

The frustration caused him to bite his lip, the copper taste of blood filled his mouth. That familiar taste made him smile, it reminded him of the other women, and the tang of their blood. He could remember each and every one of them, where and when each had perished. That look on their faces as they realised they were going to die. That was the real pleasure, that look of absolute terror, there was no rush like it, he was totally addicted.

The devil killer looked about in frustration, he was certain he would find a victim here. A quiet street with meagre street lighting, a route into town, an easy means to access the pubs and clubs. He shook his head, tapped once again on the steering wheel, and exhaled.

"Right, perhaps I was wrong, maybe I need to move to a higher risk location. It's not too late, there will be plenty of prey about, all I need to do is find the right spot"

He reached forward and started the engine. It purred into life, revved slightly before settling down to a constant rhythmical beat. The climate control whirred into life, slowly drying the screen and bringing a welcome breath of warmth. After checking the mirrors, he selected first gear and pulled away into the night.

There were cameras everywhere in Aylesbury, but he knew their locations. All he had to do was be wary, don't take any unnecessary risks, just get the prey into the van. Driving around the outskirts of town he spotted several possibilities. Most weren't the kind of woman he was looking for, some were in the wrong location, others moved in pairs.

"Persistence is the key, just stay with it and take your time. You will be proud of me mother, look what I am doing and all for you"

He smiled as he turned right into a long street. He knew this area very well, the streetlights were inadequate and most of the properties were daytime businesses, so wouldn't be occupied at this time of night. This looked to be a promising location, it was a cut through towards the city centre, and there wasn't much traffic. He slowed, constantly looking about. There was a camera at the other end of the street, but it would be of little use if he stayed around here. The van juddered as it slowed, the devil killer selected a more appropriate gear and pulled over to the pavement.

Immediately a fine drizzle started to blow about in the increasing wind. He watched as the tiny rain drops danced in the van's headlights, caught in the breeze, illuminated and carefree. This vista only enhanced the feeling of cold, perhaps it was psychosomatic, perhaps it was real, but he shivered as he watched for prey.

It was getting late, maybe he had missed his chance, it seemed that two victims would have to suffice. There was a rising tide of anger, frustration borne from the lack of activity.

Maybe he would call it a night, come back tomorrow, perhaps take two victims, yes that might suffice. He would have to be extra careful, but it could be done, if he set off in time, there would be a chance.

He started the van's engine once more, tonight had been a failure, but it wasn't worth taking any unnecessary chances. Time was still on his side, there was still tomorrow, at a push, even Friday night before the main event.

The van started to move forward, as it did so he looked in the door mirror. He caught a glimpse of something, the mirror was wet, was it male, or female? He stopped the van, turned off the engine. He wanted to reach out and clean the mirror but that might alert whoever was coming his way. They were on the other side of the street but that might work in his favour. He could quietly get out of the van and approach from the rear.

He scanned the area once more, the lights were poor, the camera would see nothing this far away. The drizzle added an extra cloud of murk and confusion to anyone, or anything that might be watching.

"Slowly, take your time, don't rush. Yes, it is female, seems the right age, by the looks of her, she has had a few too many drinks. Good, a drunken victim, easier to capture, less fuss, less of a struggle. Now wait, let her get past, then slide out, quietly, don't make a noise.

Good, she is wearing heels, that means she won't run, or at least not at first. She is holding her jacket around her head and shoulders, protecting herself from the rain. That is perfect, she won't notice me approaching"

The woman came closer and closer, the rain persisted, she held the jacket closely about herself. She stumbled once or twice, the alcohol, high heels and slippery pavement making for a hazardous progression. Closer and closer, almost level with the devil killer's van, he wanted to pounce, the area was clear, but he held on. She was level now, he could see the blonde hair, long legs and petite figure, she was perfect for what he wanted.

"Soon you will be mine, I will play with you, enjoy the taste of your flesh. But first you can watch as I murder your companions, see their blood spill out onto the floor. Your mind will scream with panic, your heart will be close to exploding in your chest, but you will endure.

You will gaze with horror as I tear them apart, cut open their skin. You will wish this nightmare to end, but it is no dream. Then you will start to beg me, promise me anything I want, just so long as I let you go free. The thing is, I have heard all these pleadings before, all the assurances, every single word, but there will be no release, not whilst you live that is"

She was several feet in front of him now, completely oblivious to his presence, the menace lurking in the night. He gently pulled at the door release handle, it quietly clicked, freeing the door from its lock. Without any undue effort, he slowly opened the door, turning to his right and sliding his legs out and onto the road. The cold of the night went unnoticed as it swept over and through him. The fine drizzle caught his face, immediately wetting his skin.

His feet hit the wet tarmac, he pushed at the van door, but not to the point where it closed. Slowly and with great care he crossed the road, the syringe was in his coat pocket, loaded with the sedative that would render her helpless.

Closer and closer, his mind racing, heart pounding. He wanted to shout out, the exhilaration was almost too much to endure. This was what he had now become, what made his existence so real. There had been a break of so many years, but now he was back, now the killings would continue for years to come. The plan was for one hundred women, or maybe two hundred. Why would he stop, this was his gift to the world, to his mother. This wasn't wrong, it was meant to be, in future times people would study his work and marvel at his magnificence.

Closer now, he could smell her perfume, it was sweet, sophisticated, it carried through the night, beyond the filth and drizzle. She had no idea he was about to strike, the terror as the needle plunged into her would be overwhelming. The drug would overcome her, prevent struggle, she would soon be his.

He was within reach, she tottered in front of him, her heels slipping from time to time. She pulled her jacket even closer, the rain and the cold biting deep into her. He finally reached his prey, pulling the syringe from his pocket, carefully removing the plastic cover from the needle.

He stared at her buttocks, concentrated at the point where the needle would penetrate her clothing. He reached forward, wrapping his left arm around her throat, pushing forward with the needle, plunging it deep into her.

To his absolute disbelief, something went wrong. At the exact point where the needle was supposed to enter her body, it stopped. The syringe jarred in his hand, the needle point had hit something hard, perhaps her belt, or a buckle in the back of her jacket. He pushed it forward once more, but she had moved, turned askew and jerked to one side. The needle seemed to catch on something, it was pulled away and flung from his grip altogether.

Shock raged through him, then panic, what should he do, let her go, or drag her backwards towards the van? The split second of deliberation was all she needed, she turned and launch a well-aimed punch to the base of his nose. The familiar taste of blood assailed him, the pain striking like lightning through his nervous system.

"Fuck off bastard, you have picked on the wrong woman tonight"

There was another blow and then another, sending him stumbling backwards. Then an overwhelming pain in his groin as she landed a kick to his crotch. He lurched backwards once again, stumbling and slipping on the wet pavement. One final punch to the side of his head and the assault stopped.

He reached out with his senses, trying to orientate himself, pushing his arms forward to prevent any further harm. Stars whirled through his sight, pain overwhelming him, feelings of nausea rising in his throat. He felt detached from reality, halfway between the conscious world and somewhere darker and less familiar.

He opened his eyes, but she was nowhere to be seen. He panicked, he had to find her, stop her, she could identify him. He turned, the driving rain slapped him, he blinked, wiped away the cold wetness. He stared into the black night, but there was nothing to be seen. Turning right and left he peered into the whirling drizzle, the pain throbbing in every nerve ending.

Then, out of the corner of his eye he caught a movement. It was to the side of a small industrial unit, had she hidden close by, why hadn't she run? He looked about one more time, she hadn't run because there was nowhere to run to. If she had set off up or down the street she would still be in view, vulnerable. No, she had to be close by, hoping he would vacate the scene in panic. All she had to do was wait and in moments he would be gone.

"No, my dear, I will remain, you are close by, I will find you and this time I will not make the same mistake"

He turned back and gazed at the grey building, the industrial unit where he had seen the movement. It had a large steel roller door, a flat roof, dark bricks. There was no sign of further movement, but the square building had an entranceway to one side, maybe she was hiding there.

He made his way back to the van, opened the glove box and reached for his Maglite torch. He moved to the entrance of the unit and turned it on. To his left was the small alleyway, some large waste bins lay just inside. He shone the torch, its beam cutting through the night, shining left and right.

"Come out my dear, there is no escape from there, it's a dead end. If you come out now, I will let you go, we will say no more about what just happened. Come on, you won't get the drop on me a second time, if I come in there after you, it won't be pleasant"

There was a long silence, the only noise was a slight whisper on the breeze, maybe a rustling through some nearby trees. There was no response, perhaps he was mistaken, maybe she had run, escaped via another route. He closed in on the small opening, staying far enough away to prevent a sudden attack.

"Last chance, come out now and we can go our separate ways, you just need to promise you won't tell anyone"

It was then that another noise invaded the night. Faintly at first, then louder and louder. It was a second or two before it fully registered in his brain. The noise, it was a siren, a far-off siren, and it was getting closer.

"Shit, a mobile phone, she has a mobile phone, why didn't I think of that. She has called the cops; they are on their way. Right, get away from here, get back to the van, I can be away before they are anywhere near the place. Should I go in there, kill her, do I have time, will they be here before I finish?

No, leave, get away, there will be another time, she knows nothing. It is dark, she can't identify me, I need to go"

With some reluctance, he turned and started to run back to his van. Rising panic began to surge through him, the siren getting closer with every second that passed. He jumped into the vehicle, started the engine and drove away with all the speed he could muster.

At the end of the street, he had a choice to make. If he turned left, he would pass under the camera but be traveling away from the city centre and most certainly the cops. He pulled hard on the wheel and turned right; at lease it would be away from the camera. The windscreen wipers worked hard to disperse the increasing rain, swishing from right to left.

He raced through the gears, accelerating as hard as he could, if anyone pulled out in front of him now, there would be little he could do. On he sprinted, into the night, waves of panic but also anger. If only he had been more careful, if only he had acted more professionally, his mother would be so angry.

He strained to see if he could hear the police siren, but it was too noisy in the cab. She would certainly have given them a make on his vehicle, they would be looking for his white van.

"Dam, shit and dam. How the hell was I so careless, this will set my plans back. What if they find me, she might be able to describe me. Shit, what will mother think, she will hate me again. I have tried to be a good boy, but now look, I hope she doesn't send me back to that place, that special school"

The night lightened and darkened depending on the streetlights. Houses, people and bus stops flashed by, left and right. Vehicles came and went, cars, lorries and the occasional bus, but there were no police vehicles. As time went by, he became more confident that he had managed to slip away.

The darkness had cloaked him, the city hidden his escape in the noise and clamour of the evening. He slowed the vehicle, calmed his nerves, he wanted to move with everyone else, not stand out like a man running for his life. His pulse began to return to normal, his breathing becoming regular.

His thoughts turned to the woman, would she be able to recognise him, give any particular details. Had she taken photos of his vehicle, noted down registration marks. He had tried to cover his tracks, he had the devil mask on, the number plates on the van were false, he should be in the clear.

"This time you win, but I will be back, and there will be no mistakes. I will find my newest victim tomorrow, she will pay for tonight, her suffering and torment will be unmatched. Soon you will accept my life's work, understand why I do these things. Beyond that, you will praise me, bow down to me and call me the devil.

This agony has only just begun, it will not end for a thousand years. I will persist beyond each and every one of you mortal fools. The screams of my victims will radiate out and be felt by all humanity. Their blood will make slick the ground over the whole world, their sacrificed lives will be legion.

The devil killer will soon be at his work again, and you will tremble, you will cry in absolute fear and terror"

Midnight Wednesday.
The office of Inspector Marcus Cooke. Thames
Valley Police HQ, Bicester.

The night had turned drier, the smothering drizzle had finally dispersed. Marcus had answered his work mobile just before getting into bed, his tiredness swept away by the news. Jumping into his car he drove straight to the Police HQ, buoyed by the call. He hadn't expected any good news regarding the devil killer, so this was a welcome break.

A young woman had called the police saying she had been assailed by a man wearing a devil mask. By her own reactions and skill, she had fought him off and made her escape. This was a remarkable turn for the better, investigations like the devil killer case often rolled along very slowly, often with very little in the way of useful information.

He had ordered that she be treated in accordance with protocol and with the utmost compassion. A trained female officer was already with her, this could just be the break they needed.

He sped through the Oxfordshire countryside, his siren and blue flashing lights turned on, illuminating the streets as he passed. He just hoped she was in one piece mentally, prayed that she had something to identify the killer.

By the time he reached the HQ, it was close to one a.m. on Thursday morning. Marcus parked his car, slammed the door and ran across the carpark and into the building. He was greeted by his deputy, Detective Sergeant Nick Walker.

"Boss, glad to see you, this was one hell of a stroke of luck"

"Not sure the woman will agree Nick, but I know what you mean. What's her name and what kind of state is she in?"

They walked quickly down the main corridor and towards the family room. Marcus pulled down his sweater, straightened his hair and took a deep breath. He needed to appear calm, so the victim would relax, as much as possible.

"She's ok boss, seems to have come through the ordeal very well, all things considered. She is a self-defence teacher, spent several years in the army, she obviously knows how to take care of herself. She gives classes to the local universities, schools and women's groups. That devil killer really picked on the wrong person this time"

The two men chuckled as they walked briskly down the corridor. The thought of that pathetic man coming up against a trained soldier made both of them laugh.

"I would love to have seen the look on his face when it all went wrong boss, I bet it was a picture.

He might even think twice next time, might put him off for a while, give us a chance to get to him"

"You might be right Nick, the trouble is, it might just make things worse. Stir him up, make him angry, a bit like a wasp's nest after you twat it with a stick"

Marcus reached for the door handle, turned it and walked into the room. Sitting to his right on a long sofa was a woman, possibly thirty with short blond hair. She was dressed smartly and had a controlled air about her. On the opposite side of the room, on an identical sofa was a WPC, smiling widely but looking very tired indeed.

"Good evening, my name is Inspector Marcus cook, this is Detective Sergeant Nick Walker, I hope you have everything you need?

She looked up and smiled, "I do thank you, everybody has been very kind"

"That's good news, my Sergeant tells me that your name is Sarah Donaldson"

"It is, pleased to meet you"

She stood, they shook hands, Marcus and his Sergeant sat down opposite with the WPC.

"So, Sarah, thank you for staying so late. I just need some information off you whilst it's fresh in your mind, it won't take long"

"Inspector, you can stand down the sympathy and softly spoken words routine. I really appreciate what you are doing and understand you have been trained to undertake such interviews.

However, I am an ex-soldier with twelve years in the army. I have been in combat four times, been injured by a roadside bomb. I spent weeks stranded in the arctic and survived. I qualified as a physical training instructor, an unarmed combat specialist, and a diver, so I am more than capable of dealing with what happened tonight.

Thank you all the same though, it's nice to know you are there, even though your coffee is crap"

"Sarah, thanks for that, so we can cut through the BS and get on with things then. Oh, sorry about the coffee, you are right, it's shit"

She smiled, "right on Marcus, let's get on with things, I am tired"

"Right Sarah, you have given a formal statement to my WPC, I will go through that later. I just want to recap some points with you. At least I don't need to skirt around the distressing bits, that's really going to help. Please recap for me the events of the evening"

"Ok, I was on my way home from a wedding reception. To be honest I had too much to drink, but I was not completely pissed. I became aware of someone behind me, but it was too late. Before I knew it, he had his arm around my throat and tried to stab me in the back.

My training just kicked in, I just reacted. I turned to one side, stepped back and attacked the prick. Smacked him on the nose, kicked him in the bollocks, punched him a couple of times. He staggered backwards, dropped something on the ground, I thought it was a knife, turned out to be a syringe.

Anyway, I thought about killing the little fuck, but he might have had other weapons. It was dark, raining and I had a gut full of Champaign, so I thought it best to make a retreat and observe. There was no way he was going to harm me, so long as I stayed away from any knives or even guns he might be carrying.

He came looking for me, but he was nowhere near, I was on the other side of the street behind a builders skip, what a useless twat he was. Anyway, I took the opportunity to call you lot, as soon as he heard the sirens, he jumped into his van and left.

I ran out and tried to get the number plate, but it was too dark, sorry Inspector. It was a white transit, looked in good condition, fairly new. I guess there aren't more than ten million like it eh?"

Marcus laughed, she was right, there was little point in trying to trace that vehicle. But at least it was something, an addition to the information already available, evidence that might prove useful at a later time.

"Was his face covered Sarah?"

"I couldn't really see, it was dark, and I was fighting for my life, he might have been wearing a mask, maybe just a balaclava, but I really can't' be sure. I guess he's the guy you have been looking for. If I had been a little more on it, I could have put him down and waited for your guys to carry him away, sorry Inspector, but I couldn't take the chance he would pull a gun and blow my head off"

"That's ok Sarah, the most important thing is that you are safe and sound"

"There was one thing though, something I think is very important. He was dressed as a cop, full uniform, stab vest, radio, blue sweater, no helmet or anything. Seemed a little strange given that he was creeping up on me. Because he looked like a cop, I would probably have believed him, if he had just approached me in a normal manner. He would have had a better chance of overcoming me"

The room went quiet, Marcus looked across at DS Nick Walker, "Dressed as a cop, that's the first we have heard about this"

"Boss, it might explain why people have not reported anything previously. There is nothing suspicious or out of place. He is a cop, sitting in a white transit van, nothing strange about that, in fact you released a statement saying there would be extra police and patrols after dark. If you asked anyone, they would have said he was one of the extra patrols, out to catch the devil killer, observing, looking after young women on their way home.

This might just have been the perfect cover. We need to look back at the CCTV footage. Are there any images of a male police officer, near a transit van. I know that's going to be an almost impossible task, but I think we might just find our man if we did that"

"Nick, have you any idea of how many male police are now in the area, looking like this guy. Talk about a needle in a bloody haystack, that's just about impossible"

"So, we better get started boss, it's going to take an awful long time, time which we don't have"

Marcus closed the door to the family room behind him. Tonight had been a good one, the devil killer had not managed to take his prey, in fact she had got him. He knew this would not be the end of things though, far from it. He was masquerading as the local police, given the amount of officer's now in the area, that meant he could be anywhere, ready to strike once again.

He would check to see if there had been any more missing persons reports in the last twenty-four hours. With a bit of luck, none of them would be due to the devil killer, but luck was not going to solve the case, or keep his hostage safe after Friday night.

He would phone Lee Hunter in the morning, maybe he had some further information regarding Post and his potential whereabout, maybe!

Dawn Thursday morning.
Driving to the park and ride again in Windsor.

I was not a fan of getting up in the morning, truth was, I was not a great fan of getting up at any time. My bed was warm and comfortable, and the booze from the meeting last night was still causing my stomach to turn over. Peter Dexter seemed to be immune to the effects of alcohol, and it was some time before he began to loosen up. Not that he told me anything I didn't already know, but at least I was certain that he didn't have any important leads hidden away.

He did seem convince that Paul Willow screwed up so many things in the case, that Post got off with three other killings. He was certain that he committed suicide because he couldn't stand the shame and drowned himself in the English Channel.

Well, that's Dexter's story and since I had no other, I was willing to believe it to be the truth, at least for now. Given that account and that of Marcus Cooke, a picture was beginning to emerge. Post was the killer and Paul Willow made such a mess of things that Post literally got away with murder. After being humiliated by his bosses and in the knowledge that three women had died at the hands of Post, he killed himself.

That didn't excuse Dexter and the fact that he was as bent as the day was long. He obviously manipulated people and events, but that didn't change the fact that Post was the killer and Willow was a complete bloody idiot.

So, why the hell am I off to Windsor just after dawn to see a certain Paul Willow? He had phoned me at some bloody awful time this morning saying he wanted to see me. Beats me why he picked dawn, why not after lunch, and why had he phoned me at all? Anyway, I am up now and on my way, all I can say is this better be important, very important!

I guess it never does any harm to listen to another side of the story, see what someone has to say. After all, there are always three side to any story, yours, mine and then the truth! Maybe Willow might have a lead on Post, perhaps he was trying to make up for past mistakes? In any case, I had to listen to what he had to say, even if he wanted to drone on some more about Dexter, I had to give it a go.

One bonus traveling at this time in the morning, there was no rush hour. Anyone with any amount of sense would still be fast asleep, unlike me, and Willow of course. This meeting still didn't seem to make any sense though. If this was really Willow, and I doubted it, why contact me? He had nothing to gain from trashing Dexter's reputation, I doubted if anyone would listen twenty years after the event.

So, what was I going to hear? A load of moaning about Dexter and his corruption or Willow protesting about his innocence. I had already asked him about his alleged suicide, he just put that down to Dexter playing games. I did have the 'ladies pink knickers' card up my sleeve. According to Marcus, Paul Willow would know Dexter wore them on his wedding night.

I pulled over to a small café, I needed a strong black coffee, one sugar. The light of the dawn was now well established, it brought with it the first warmth of the day. There was a slightly damp but clear feel, a typical English summers morning.

So, I was bound for a meeting with Paul Willow, an ex-detective and suicide victim, how the hell is that supposed to make sense? I closed the car door behind me and pressed the lock button on the key fob. There was a satisfying clunk from the car as I walked away.

The café was warm and smelt of toast, bacon and coffee. The woman standing behind the counter looked up and smiled.

"You're early darlin', what can I get for you? Coffee, toast, or a full breakfast"

The thought of eating a fry-up breakfast at this time in the morning made me wretch. Well, maybe the alcohol still lying in my system did that, but I wasn't about to eat anything that's for sure.

"No, just a black coffee, one sugar thanks"

"Take a seat my sweet, I will bring it over"

I liked sitting in cafes, for some unknown reason they helped me think. Sitting with a bland coffee and staring into the distance focused my mind. Perhaps being away from anyone who might interrupt me was beneficial for my very simple mind.

The overly friendly woman came over, she was way too effervescent for this time in the morning, much too happy to be real. She placed my coffee on the table in front of me and smiled.

"If you need anything else darlin', just give me a shout, here to help and fulfil your order"

I smiled and thanked her, she walked away and served a lorry driver who had just entered.

So, what did I want from the meeting? I didn't want to listen to him trying to vindicate himself. I didn't want to hear him blame Dexter for everything that was wrong in the world.

I wanted to know anything he might have concerning the possible whereabouts of Post. I needed to know his thoughts on why these murders had started again, and why had Post risked being thrown back into jail until the end of time? It just seemed all too convenient, it just didn't sit right somehow.

Having said that, why wouldn't they start again, if Post was the killer, he was now out and up to his old tricks. There wasn't a judge in the land who wouldn't throw him straight back into jail. Murderers are released on what's called a life licence, in other words, they are always prone to being recalled to jail, even for unrelated crimes.

However, from my conversation with Post, he didn't strike me as an idiot, far from it. He would know that every cop in the land would now be searching for him, and what would happen when they caught him, which they certainly would. So why start killing again, because he is a psychopath, the police and courts would say. He can't help himself, but because there are no vulnerable women in jail, his killing instincts became dormant.

That was perfectly right of course, he can't kill what he can't get at, but now he is out, he has plenty of targets to go at. I tapped my fingers on the table and gazed at the dark brown coffee in the white mug on the table. I didn't have to make my mind up right now. I am not the police, it isn't my number one duty to get Post. What I wanted was the truth, if Post was going back to prison for the rest of his life, I wanted to know that was the right thing, not what seemed to be correct.

I finished my pick-me-up and said goodbye to the woman behind the counter. The morning outside was glorious, warm, dry and very summer like. It brought a smile to my face, maybe today was going to be a good one, maybe!

The remainder of the drive to the park and ride was somewhat uneventful. I listened to some pointless drivel on the radio, someone complaining about the parking prices in the city. I eventually arrived, parked at the back of the carpark and waited for Willow to arrive.

It didn't take long before a somewhat dishevelled man came into view. He was wearing the same clothes as last time, a grimy grey overcoat with shiny black buttons that had a golden edge, one of which was still missing. He had on those grubby dark trousers and muddied black leather shoes. He looked all around before approaching the car, stopping to check several times before eventually arriving at my passenger door. He stooped down and gently knocked on the window, his fingers were grubby, fingernails encrusted in grime.

He certainly wasn't living the high life on a police pension, more like existing at the local doss house. If this was Paul Willow, and he wanted to stay anonymous, it was certainly working. There was no way anyone was going to recognise him, even if he ventured out into the public domain.

"It's open Paul"

He gently opened the door, taking one last look around before he took a seat. It wasn't long before the 'Eau de Ken' began permeating the car, it wasn't nice but there wasn't much I could do about it.

"You keep looking around Paul, is someone chasing you?"

"I have to be careful mister Hunter; one false move and I am a dead man"

That seemed a rather strong comment. A dead man, he was an ex-cop, not some ex-KGB spy. Who the hell would want a broken old tramp dead, it didn't seem to make any sense.

"Why are you so fearful of your life Paul, who the hell is going to kill you. Call me Lee by the way, it sounds a lot less formal"

There was a long and drawn-out silence, he just stared out of the windscreen, hardly moving at all.

"There are people Lee, powerful people you don't know about. They control things, including the lives of people who won't conform to their rules. I don't conform, I never did, and I never will. Therefore, my life is in continuous peril, and I must take every precaution"

Now this was beginning to sound like some half-baked conspiracy channel on YouTube. 'They' control the world, 'they' control our lives, 'they' control our money, 'they' listen to us on our mobile phones. Thing is, no one ever says who 'they' are, but 'they' are certainly watching us via the TV screens, or something like that.

"Who the hell are 'they' Paul, what rules haven't you conformed to?"

He shot a glance straight at me, as if I should have known the answer, to whatever the hell he was babbling on about. Ok, be polite, listen to what he has to say, get him out of the car and get on with my case. It won't take long I am sure and if it does, I will open the door and push him out. I was in no mood for some half-baked conspiracy freak pretending to be a dead cop.

"Look Paul, I am really busy, and I need to find Lennard Post as soon as I can. If I don't, another woman will lose her life. All I want to know is where Post currently is and where he might be hiding the girls. I would really appreciate your help, but if you don't know anything of any use, I do need to move on"

There was another long pause, this time it didn't provoke any obvious kind of reaction from Willow.

"Lee, I know you think I am a has-been cop with an axe to grind against Dexter, but that's not the case. In fact, nothing could be further from the truth. Yes, Peter Dexter is a disgrace and a shameful example of what can become of a corrupt police officer. I have however stated my opinion on the man and informed you, and others, of his practices and why people escaped justice, or were wrongfully convicted for crimes they didn't commit.

The point I was trying to make to you is that Dexter is corrupt and would stop at nothing to gain credit with is superiors or get the job done, no matter how it was concluded. Last time we talked about precisely that, and his willingness to use whatever means necessary"

Again, there was a long pause, this was just going over old ground, he was not telling me anything new. This meeting was turning out to be a complete waste of time. I was just about to throw the old tramp out of the car when he piped up once again.

"Look Lee, I tried to warn you off the case, that was the purpose of my last meeting with you. I know you are an ex-police detective, so there would have been little point in trying to scare you. I had to try and be a little more subtle than that. I thought if I told you about my fights with Dexter, and how he delt with people who got in his way, it might encourage you to leave this case alone. I hoped perhaps you would continue trying to secure Lennard Post's innocence, and forget all about Dexter, seems I was very wrong. It appears that Lennard Post, Peter Dexter and I are permanently linked together, and nothing will ever change that"

I sat back for a while, what the hell did that mean, of course they were all linked together. You two arrested and then investigated the crime which led to Post's imprisonment. As it turned out, even with Dexter's corruption, it got Post off the streets for a while. However, he was now out again, and murdering once more.

One thought was burrowing its way into my mind though. Was Willow trying to tell me something, but being a little too subtle about it? I hated stupid games like this, just come out and bloody tell me. Why be elusive, what the hell would he have to gain.

"I get the feeling you aren't telling me something Paul. Is there something going on here apart from Dexter's corruption. To be honest I am not worried about that, the police can sort that one out all on their own.

All I want to know is where the hell is Post. I am not even that bothered about his previous crimes. Did he murder his wife or didn't he, I couldn't give a toss to be honest. Did he sexually assault those young women, did all that turn into three murders, who the hell knows"

The more I get to know of this tangled web of lies, corruption and deceit, the less I want to do with it. To be honest, I was seriously thinking about giving Post his money back and going to see my daughters. The trouble was, I couldn't give him anything back because I hadn't got a fucking clue as to his whereabouts!

"Look Paul, I don't like playing games, I spent too many years in the met pratting around like this. If you know where Post is, tell me, if you don't, I have things to do and I will bid you good day"

He turned his head to look at me once again. He had a look on his face, anger, I think. I wasn't playing his games and he didn't like it, or I wasn't getting some subliminal message he was trying to send. Either way, he wasn't very happy, but who cares because neither was I.

"I don't know where Post is mister Hunter, he used to live in Aylesbury, but I think that area is now some shopping centre. So far as I remember, he didn't have any family, friends or acquaintances. Lennard Post was an absolute loner in every way. To be honest, I don't ever remember a man so detached from everything and everyone.

It was only later on in his life, after meeting the woman who became his wife that things started to change for Post. He seemed to grow up all of a sudden, he changed from and absolute loner to a man with a wife and a job"

Odd that, with all the stories I had been fed about Post, I forgot the fact he had actually been married, had a job and a place of his own. Ok, people grow up, when I was a teenager, I was no more use than a chocolate fire guard. In fact, my parents threatened to throw me out. I turned out ok in the end I guess, my wife might not agree with that statement, but I think I did.

If I grew up, turned out ok, then so might Post, people usually do. The trouble was his wife was now dead. To make things worse, his DNA and fingerprints were all over the murder weapon and his wife, so I guess Post was one hell of an exception!

I had been employed by Post to clear his name, give him a new start. That investigation hadn't got very far before the murders started again, so I guess that kind of blows that job out of the water.

"What was it that Post did for a living Paul. I hadn't got that far with all that's been going on?"

"He used to work for the local farmers. Drive the tractors, work in the yards, help during harvest. By all accounts he was a hard worker and good with the animals. I guess he found his place in life and developed from there. He met his future wife in Aylesbury, bought a house, and you know the rest"

"You mean he killed her, and the rest of those women?"

"Well, there you go Lee Hunter, that's the story Dexter set up. Have you ever asked yourself why Post wants to clear his name? Have you ever thought he might have a case?"

I opened my mouth to speak but something stopped me. What was it Willow just said, 'thought he might have a case'. What the hell did that mean, surely Willow must have known Post killed his wife, even if Dexter had tried to fit him up with the other cases. Was this what he was trying to illude to, surely not.

"Are you trying to tell me that Dexter fitted Post up with the murder of his wife?"

"I am not telling you anything Lee, all I can apprise you of are the facts, you need to work the rest out for yourself. Dexter was a bent cop, he fitted people up for crimes they didn't commit. Post wants to clear his name, he has never admitted to killing his wife. That alone cost him several more years in prison. The parole board don't like letting people out who haven't 'come to terms' with their crimes.

It takes iron determination to do something like that, spend more jail time just because you want to appear innocent. Makes you wonder if Post really was the killer, what do you think mister Hunter?"

He had a point of course, but that didn't explain why the murders had started again, soon after Post had been released. It was as clear as the day is long, Post killed his wife and those other women. There was DNA evidence, red silk scarves, the devil mask in the boot of Post's car, what more do you need? The trouble was, all the other noise whirling around this case. In truth it was a bloody sandstorm, and you simply didn't know what was coming next.

"Post has made some very serious allegations regarding Dexter and you. Post had said that you were on the take from local businesses, and you were well known for it. You tried to extort money from his dads engineering firm. When Dexter and you came around one afternoon, threatening him, he assaulted the two of you for your trouble.

You tell me Dexter is bent and Post might not have committed the crimes. Post tells me you are as bent as Dexter and were on the take. So, who do I believe, what is the real truth to all of this?"

"Mister Hunter, all I can do is tell you the facts, make of that what you will. You need to join the dots and build the picture.

It wouldn't have surprised me at all if Dexter was on the take. To be honest, I would be shocked if he wasn't. So far as my involvement in any of that, I can honestly say that I had no participation in any such crimes.

In my opinion, Post was not responsible for the three murders or the assaults on the young women. As to who might have been guilty, I will leave that up to you to work out. Did Post kill his wife? I have my doubts Lee, but the evidence is very compelling and can't be easily explained away.

So, before I go, I have to say again, you must leave this case alone. If Post is the killer, he will eventually track you down and kill you too. Dexter is a very dangerous man Lee, if he thinks you are getting too close to his corruption, he will also kill you, don't doubt that for a minute.

You are in a place beyond your wildest nightmares Lee, leave it alone and forget all about Post, Dexter and this case"

"Before you do Paul, I need to ask you one question. It might seem a little strange, but it will confirm your identity. Who was the best man at Dexter's first wedding?"

"That was me Lee"

"Did Dexter wear something on his wedding night, just for a bet?"

There was a short silence, Willow smiled and then turned back.

"Yes, the knickers, I think they were pink. He wore them to the ceremony and on the wedding night itself. Goodness knows what his wife thought, she must have been bloody shocked when he got undressed"

That was it, only the real Paul Willow could have known that. It certainly confirmed his identity.

"One last question Paul. Why a fake suicide, why not just move to Spain?"

"No one bothers looking for a dead man Lee, it was as simple as that. Moving somewhere would not have helped, well not in the long term anyway. No, I had to die, fake my own suicide, then there would be no need for Dexter to ever come looking for me. Now, if you have no more questions, I must be on my way. I have spent too much time already out in the open"

 Without another word he opened the door and left. I didn't see where he disappeared to, I just sat there in a state of shock. What the hell had just happened? Had I been warned off, or given some sound advice, or what? I wasn't sure, I tried to piece together what Willow had just said. It seemed on one side I had the serial killer Post, and on the other Dexter, the bent cop. At least I did have one certain fact though, Paul Willow was actually the man I had just been talking to, the pink knickers story had confirmed that.

 The drive back was somewhat uneventful. Having spoken to Dexter and now Willow I had made no discernible progress. The only thing left was to go back to Steeple Claydon and talk to the people there. Someone must know something about Post, an old hang out, a friend or an ex-girlfriend, something!

Dusk, Thursday.
The outskirts of London.

The daytime had just about faded away, leaving that strange half-light, not day, but by no means the dark of the night. The streets and roads were crowded, rush hour was well underway. People left and right, cars queueing to leave the city, the M40 and the M25 junctions were manic as usual, a ribbon of humanity stretching far into the distance.

He had arrived here in plenty of time though. He knew these roads, how busy and clogged with traffic they would become. This mayhem was exactly what he wanted though, busy people rushing to be somewhere else. The level of noise was high as was the palpable stress emanating from the commuters.

All he had to do was to act calmly, be part of the mass, not stand out. If he came here at night, the myriad cameras would pick him up immediately, there would be no hiding at all. He had cleaned his white Ford Transit van, now resplendent with orange stripes and a reflective POLICE sign on each side. To all intents and purposes, this was a police vehicle, and no one in the city would even give it a second glance.

This wasn't a hunting mission though, this time his target was known, her address already locked into his sat nav. He had resigned himself to only having two women to play with tomorrow evening. That was a disappointment to him, but he would do his best. He was certain the young women would enjoy their time as terror and agony enveloped every atom of their minds and bodies.

He had set up the camera, the whole thing would be videoed and broadcast on the internet for everyone to see. The devil killer would become a worldwide phenomenon, and everyone would want to meet him. This was the highpoint of his career, the first major step to fame and fortune. There would be regular broadcasts, featuring other victims, perhaps a weekly show.

So, he drew a deep breath, he had arrived at the address in the sat nav. Inside the apartment on the second floor was his victim and he couldn't wait to meet her. She was young and very pretty. They would love her on the show on Friday night, he had a special treat in mind for her, it would be magnificent.

He exited the vehicle, staying controlled and focused. He straightened his uniform, checked the number of the apartment and moved off towards the entrance. To the right of the main door was a large list of occupants with their corresponding bell push.

"Right, where the hell are you, it should be second floor, apartment four, in other words 204, I hope"

He scanned up and then down the list, and there it was.

APARTMENT 204 – V. HUNTER.

"Good, it's so thoughtful of you to tell me exactly where you are. Now press the bell and wait for an answer, I hope you are in darling, I don't want to be disappointed a second time"

There was a long pause, he pressed the bell for a second time. He looked around, his disguise was perfect, but being here in full sight was not a good thing. He shuffled his feet, maybe he should go back and sit in the van, the less………

"Hello can I help?"

"Ah good evening, I am police sergeant Dobson, Thames Valley Police. I need to speak to a miss Victoria Hunter as a matter of urgency, is she in?"

There was another short pause. This was a critical moment, the whole plan could fall right here, right now. He had to stay calm, be matter of fact, there was no rush.

"Sorry, what is this about?"

"I need to speak to miss Hunter. There is some concern reference her safety, nothing to worry about, but I need to speak to her"

"Safety, what the hell's happened?"

"Police intelligence officers have raised some concerns about the safety of a miss Victoria Hunter, in connection with a current case. All I need to do is make sure that miss Hunter is ok and confirm that all reasonable security precautions are in place. This won't take more than a few minutes, afterwards you are advised to ring a family member and tell them that everything is ok"

"What kind of precautions, what the hell has happened?"

"I need to make sure the windows are locked, and the security cameras are working. This information we have is of a minimal level of concern, so I don't actually think there is anything to worry about"

"Ok, well can you put yourself in front of the security camera and show your ID etc"

He stood in front of the security camera to the left of the bell panel and showed his police ID card.

"Ok sergeant, come up, it's apartment 204, please make sure the front door is closed behind you"

The electronic lock clicked and then buzzed. He slid inside, took one last look about and made for the lift. He selected '2' on the control panel and waited for the lift car to arrive. Eventually the silver doors opened, and he stepped inside, the doors closing behind him with an almost silent swish. It wasn't more than a few seconds before he arrived at the second floor. Again, the doors opened, this time revealing a long-carpeted corridor. A friendly woman's voice announced, "second floor, please mind the door when exiting"

Turning right he quickly arrived at a door marked, APARTMENT 204. There was a small nameplate to one side, V. HUNTER. He pressed the doorbell and waited, smiling as he did so.

"So, miss Hunter, on the other side of this door you wait for the devil killer. I will take you and everyone will see you die. Your father, the glorious detective Lee Hunter will feel your pain and his own as you scream and beg for mercy. He has meddled in this case once too often and for no reason other than making money. The others too will hear you cry, see your blood spill on the ground. It will be glorious; I will be famous over the whole world"

She opened the door, he smiled, seemed very friendly and certainly looked the part in his police sergeant's uniform.

"Ah, miss Hunter, can I come in. Nothing to worry about but I need to check a few things"

"Certainly, no problem"

He reached and clicked the transmit button on his fake radio. "Sergeant Dobson to control, I am entering the apartment of Victoria Hunter to complete security checks"

He walked past her, the room was well lit, a large panoramic window gave extended views of this part of London. There was the underlying smell of cooking, perhaps breakfast this morning.

"Hey, great views miss Hunter, I wish I could afford something like this"

"It's my mum, she has her own real estate business, this apartment came onto her books. We got a great deal on it, lots of work needed but its great and it's all mine"

"Oh, I wish I had a mum like that. Listen, can you show me around, I need to check the security of the place. Your dad has asked us to keep an eye on things. He has had some threats, something to do with the case he is working on. He doesn't think they are serious, but we need to take every precaution, you understand?"

"Yeah, no probs' it's not the first time. Follow me, we will start with the bedroom"

She turned around and led the way. He pulled the syringe from his waist pocket and flicked off the plastic cover from the needle. He closed the gap between them. He could smell her perfume, her hair looked so clean. He was right behind her now, they entered the bedroom, he reached forward.

The needle entered her buttock, it penetrated her jeans so easily. He pushed the plunger, she spun around but it was too late. There was a look of shock on her face, followed by that familiar vacant expression as the drug started to take effect.

"You are mine my darling, try to relax, when you wake you will have a friend, you can chat, talk about what is to come. In the meantime, I will inform your father of your fate, and tell him to watch the channel tomorrow night. The show will be wonderful, he will enjoy watching you die"

Thursday mid-morning.
Prince of Wales pub, Steeple Claydon.

I pulled up outside the pub, it wasn't open yet, but I needed to plan what I was going to do next. There were no options left, I had to find Post and it had to be today. If his threats were real, and it seemed as if they were, two more women would be dead by tomorrow night.

I was wracking my brain trying to come up with a plan when a car flashed by. It wouldn't normally have caught my attention, but the speed and the make did. It was a E200 AMG Mercedes Benz with bright red paintwork. Where the hell had I seen that car before, it was around here somewhere, but where?

You don't see many about, best part of 50k, who the hell can afford one of those? Well Tony Bianchi I guess, but he was way up north, and red wasn't his colour anyway, far too flash. No, it was local and recently, it stuck in my mind because of the model and the colour. It was parked somewhere; I remember it shining in the sunlight.

Then it came to me, it was in the drive of Olivia Cranfield's place, Post's ex-girlfriend, over at the Victorian villa. Why would she drive a car like that? I remembered the pub landlord telling me she had an old Land Rover Defender 90, something her dad gave her. Seemed too much of a contrast if you ask me, fifty-year-old piece of junk and a brand new 50k Merc'. It set my curiosity off, was that her car, or someone else's? I started my car, put it into gear a drove down the road to the home of Olivia Cranfield.

In all probability it was a boyfriend, some flash twat after her money. But it wouldn't take more than a minute to find out, so I set off to see what I could see. I was at the corner of Addison Road within seconds, but the Merc' had disappeared. Maybe it wasn't the vehicle I had seen previously, maybe someone passing through.

Then I caught a glance of the shiny red paint, it was there, right up the drive, in front of the garage. I had to take things easy, I didn't want to be noticed, just stay calm and stay out of the way. I let the car roll down the slight hill and left at the junction, it gently came to a stop, staying tight to the left had curb. There were a few trees near to the edge of the road, the dark shade that they cast might provide a little cover.

I turned the engine off and strained to look over to the Cranfield house. The red Merc' sat motionless in front of the garage, there was someone inside it, but I couldn't make out who. Ok, wait here Lee and just stay calm, whoever was in that car wouldn't stay inside it for long, be patient.

It occurred to me that I was sitting watching a red car, outside someone's house, for no apparent reason at all! Why had I reacted, was this case really getting to me, perhaps it had.

It was at that precise moment the door of the car opened; the driver was someone who seemed familiar to me, but I couldn't place who it was, not at this distance anyway. He eased himself out and stood erect on the driveway. The sun caught his face, illuminating him from behind, causing me to squint, shade my eyes from the bright light. He checked the car was locked and walked slowly to the front door of the house.

I wondered if it looked like Peter Dexter, the ex-lead detective in the original case. Possibly, but no, don't think so, this person seemed a little taller, but it was almost impossible to judge. I was convinced that it was someone else, it felt like someone I had already met. So, what was that person doing here, whoever it was? Maybe it was Dexter, I tried to think of a connection between someone like Dexter and Olivia Cranfield, but none came to mind. Maybe they were just friends, perhaps they had formed a relationship all those years ago. Why didn't he tell me though, surely if they were an item, he would have told me, but maybe he wanted to keep that quiet. Anyway, it was something for me to ponder over tonight, back in the Travel Lodge.

I reached forward to press the 'start' button, just before I did so, something sprang to mind. It was something Paul Willow had said during his bloody hidden meaning parlour game, in the park and ride carpark.

He said, "Lennard Post was not responsible for the three murders or the assaults on the young women". He would leave up to me to work out whoever was responsible. He also expressed doubts about who killed Post's wife, even though the evidence is very compelling and can't be easily explained away. He also emphasised on several occasions that Dexter is a very dangerous man, and if he thinks "you are getting too close to his corruption, he will kill you".

Was I putting two and two together here and coming up with six? Was Paul Willow trying to tell me something, was he trying to say Dexter was responsible, but responsible for what? He obviously thought Dexter was capable of just about anything, he really did think he might kill me if I got too close. He was certain that Post wasn't the killer of the women and had serious doubts about him killing his wife. So, if he was trying to tell me that Post wasn't the killer, who was......Peter Dexter?

Of course, this set off a huge firework display in my mind, surely not, that can't be true. Dexter was a bent cop, he was on the take, he manufactured evidence, but a mass murderer, I don't think so. I have known people like Dexter before, bent, underhand, can't be trusted, but never much more than that. This would put him on a different level altogether, and why had the killing stopped when Lennard Post had been locked up?

No, I think Willow was way off the mark, perhaps his fake suicide was an indication of the trauma and stress he undoubtedly suffered during his career as a detective. Attending murder scenes, long hours away from his family, the pressure to get the conviction, and Peter Dexter to deal with.

I can see why someone would want to fake his death and disappear. I might have joined him in those circumstances, perhaps I did. My suicide was not a swim in the channel, it was a bottle of scotch, every night down the pub and boozy lunchtime meetings. Alcohol had the same effect though, it completely screwed my life and career and caused me to disappear, this time to a north-western seaside town.

I sat back in the car seat. It was absolutely preposterous, there was no way Dexter was the killer. I have known many killers and Dexter was not one of them, he didn't have the right temperament. But what if Willow was right and I was wrong, I am not infallible.........no chance. Dexter was a slime ball, a no-good ex-cop, nothing more than that.

I couldn't scrub that thought from my mind though, what if Dexter was my man, as ludicrous as that might seem, I had to act and find out. It wouldn't take long, and to be honest, I didn't have long. The murders would be tomorrow night, that left just a few hours to find the killer, whoever that might be.

Right, I would call Marcus and get his guys on the case. They could have a look around this Victorian villa. These places had large cellars, plenty of room to hide his victims. The girl might be down there right now, a five-minute call and all this could be sorted, or more likely Dexter would be struck of my list of possible suspects.

"You want me to do what Lee, not a bloody chance. I will need a warrant to go poking around in the cellars of that place, and on what grounds? I need evidence, and the ramblings of some old tramp, pretending to be someone who committed suicide twenty years ago isn't going to cut it. The magistrate will laugh me out of court that's for certain. In any case, why do you believe this vagrant, he is just after a few quid, a bit of sympathy, he needs locking up for wasting your time. Surely you don't believe he is who he says he is, that's impossible, he's supposed to be dead for fucks sake, feeding the little fishes at the bottom of the English Channel"

"I do Marcus and it was you who gave me the info'. Remember the pink knickers on Dexter's wedding night. Well, I asked this guy who was the best man at Dexter's first wedding and if he was wearing anything unusual. He was spot on Marcus, he said he was the best man, and Dexter was wearing pink knickers, just like you said! Now that might have been one hell of a lucky guess, but I don't bloody think so, do you?"

There was a long silence, "Lee listen, I really appreciate you giving me a call and the fact that you have spoken to, whoever it is you have been speaking to. But there is no chance that I will get a warrant for that search, pink knickers or not. I will however send a uniform down there to ask if they can have a look. You know full well Lee, if the occupier says no, then it's game over"

I wanted to tell him to go and get that warrant but he was right of course. Magistrates don't hand these things out like parking tickets, and he had no evidence other than what I had told him.

"Also Lee, Dexter has a reputation around these parts of being a good cop. Someone who got the job done and kept everyone safe at night. If you try and screw around with that kind of standing, then you better be absolutely certain you are right. The word of some pisshead pretending to be a dead police detective isn't going to help. You need proof, photographs, statements, concrete evidence Lee, otherwise no one will listen to you, Dexter's name carries authority around here.

Also, don't forget that Dexter is terminally ill, people will try and respect that"

"Dexter is ill Marcus, what do you mean?"

"He has terminal Pancreatic cancer Lee, that story about being in Spain at his villa, it's a cover story for when he has his chemo' sessions. He doesn't want anyone to know about the cancer. He calls his cancer nurse his wife, goodness knows why, I guess the treatment and the booze have screwed up his mind, can't blame him there. Being in Spain with his wife is his way of saying he was undergoing some more chemotherapy, with his cancer nurse"

It was a shock hearing about Dexter's illness, I kind of understood about his cover story though. Maybe I should respect that a little more, I know other people certainly would. It definitely ironed out a few creases in his story, but it didn't help with my task.

He was also right about evidence, the fact that Marcus himself wasn't listening to me told me a story, so I had no chance with anyone else! I had to get closer, try and get something Marcus would take notice of, but what?

Right, let's see if the uniformed police are allowed to look around, if they are not, I will. Where the hell was smelly Ken when you needed him. He would be in and out of that place in a flash. Trouble was, he was two hundred miles away and probably smacked out of his head on some substance that would normally kill anyone else who dared take it.

So, I drove back to the pub and parked outside. Time was running out and I needed a break in this case, a bloody big one, and my phone was just about to deliver

Midday Thursday.
The office of Inspector Marcus Cooke. Thames
Valley Police HQ, Bicester.

Sergeant Nick Walker had stormed into his boss's office and delivered the news. His heart was pounding and mouth bone dry.

"You are fucking joking Nick, she's gone missing, who the hell told you that?"

"Her sister boss, Emma Hunter. She says Victoria should have been home when she called. Her place is a complete wreck and the next-door neighbour said she was escorted out by a policeman"

"So, her flat is a complete wreck, so are most people's places at that age. Anyway, if she was escorted away by some cop, then she will be at the local nick, right?"

"They have checked boss. There was no arrest, no official call to the premises, nothing at all. Given what Sarah Donaldson told us, after she had fought off the devil killer, and him being dressed as a cop, the alarm bells started to ring. If the local constabulary had arrested anyone, they would have known about it. This could be the devil killer boss; we need to find her and bloody quick"

Marcus Cooke and Detective Sergeant Nick Walker stood motionless in the office. If he was right, the devil killer had Lee Hunters daughter and there was nothing they could do about it.

"Listen Nick, get the call out, we need to find out what the hells happened to her. Uniformed police don't just turn up and take people into custody. There are procedures, arrest warrants, records, orders are given. Someone must know something"

"Boss, the call has been made. I talked to my ex-manager in that area, there were no arrests of that kind. No one called at her address and took her in, no one. This is the same bastard that tried to take that ex-soldier, Sarah Donaldson, this time he succeeded"

"Right Nick, we need to tell Hunter, but we need to be careful. I know him, he will go undercover and try to find this sick twat himself. Once he finds him, a short time later someone will spot a body gently drifting down the Thames, and it will be wearing a devil's mask!"

"He didn't strike me as that kind of guy boss"

"Listen, Hunter is a no-nonsense kind of operator. When it comes to family, nothing's off limits. Also, he has contacts, big contacts in the underworld. If he calls them in, the devil killer will be toast, don't doubt it for a second"

"Is that a bad thing Marcus, after all, the devil killer has killed I don't know how many women.

This might be a chance to put a stop to him, permanently!"

"The thought had crossed my mind Nick, but we are above all that kind of stuff. We need to tell Hunter, keep him under wraps and go and find the devil killer. I am going to call him, get him into the station. That's when we tell Hunter and not before. In the meantime, you get everybody who is, has been, or is going to be a cop, and get them looking for the devil killer, understood"

"Crystal boss, I am on it"

Marcus Cooke sat back in his office chair with a pronounced frown on his face. There was another woman gone, disappeared. Would she be added to the list, three or perhaps four twenty plus years ago and two already this week. He had two more someplace, goodness knows where. He had promised to kill them tomorrow night, and he had no doubt that he would live up to his promise.

Added to his problems was Lee Hunter. He was an ex-police detective, so he knew how things worked. He also had contacts who could put an end to someone's life without a second's thought. That combination was not one Marcus wanted on his patch.

The problem Marcus had, once he told Hunter, there was absolutely nothing he could do to stop him walking out of the station. Once that happened, there was no telling where it would finish. The first thing he had to work out was how to get Hunter into the office without him suspecting anything. That wasn't going to be easy, but he would have to try.

"Right, find Hunter's number and give him a call. I need to come up with some kind of bollocks, I just hope he falls for it"

Inspector Marcus Cooke pulled his mobile out of his pocket, found Lee Hunter in his directory and pressed call. The phone started to ring but almost immediately went to voice mail.

"Hi, Lee Hunter, sorry I can't take your call, just leave a message after the tone and I will get back to you as soon as I can"

The line clicked, Marcus grimaced, drew a breath and spoke.

"Lee, it's Marcus here. Listen mate, I need you to pop into the station, soonest please. I have some recent photos of Lennard Post. Seems he might have changed his appearance since being released from jail. Since you were the last person to talk to him, perhaps you might be able to confirm that they are him, or what he might have changed. Just give me a call and we can arrange a time, it is urgent Lee, so as soon as you can. Ta"

He pressed end call and stood up, slipping his phone back into his pocket.

"Well, if that doesn't work, I don't know what will. Let's hope he falls for it and calls me back, very soon"

Thursday afternoon.
Sitting in my car outside the Prince of Wales Pub.

My phone started to ring, I glanced down at the caller ID, I don't know if I felt relief or disbelief.

"Well Lennard Post, I have been looking for you, where the hell are you hiding?"

"Good afternoon, mister Hunter. If you don't mind, I will keep that to myself for the meantime. You see mister Hunter, there are people who would gladly see me dead, and I have no intention of complying with their requirements.

I read in the papers that two women have been found murdered in the Aylesbury area. I would suspect those murders have been blamed on myself, am I right mister Hunter? Anyway, I have no desire to be locked up for another twenty years, so I am staying, how do you say, incognito.

I need to prove that I have absolutely nothing to do with these recent events. That's very hard to do when I have been arrested. The only way you can accomplish that mister Hunter is being out in the free world, poking around, asking questions, not banged up in some stinking hole in the ground.

Therefore, the reason for my call is simply to find out what progress you have made in my case. Last time I was convicted of a crime which I did not commit, the murder of my wife. I was very lucky not to be tried for the other three murders at the time, the so called, devil killings.

Since it would appear the methods in these recent killings are reminiscent of the devil killer, then my name is certainly going to be in the frame"

I had to take a few seconds to think about a reply. A few moments ago, I was trying to track Post down so I could hand him in to the police. Now he is asking me if I have managed to clear his name for the murder of his wife.

This was a difficult juncture in the case. I needed to get my hands on Post before he killed anyone else. Telling him that I thought he was a mass murderer would not help me do this, in fact, if anyone ever met him again it would be a bloody miracle. So, what to do, pander to his delusions, or call him out for what he was? I decided to go for the former, it felt so much safer.

"Sorry Lennard but no progress at all. I can't seem to find anyone in the area who knew you, except your former girlfriend, Olivia Cranfield"

Saying that name reminded me of the confusion regarding that woman. She was Post's ex-girlfriend, but had she moved to Aylesbury to be with her sister to get away from Post, or had they moved in together. This might be a good opportunity to test that out, see who was telling the truth! Since seeing someone, possibly Peter

Dexter hanging about her house, I needed to get to the bottom of Olivia, so to speak.

"Oh yes, young Olivia, what a little cracker she turned out to be mister Hunter. I have never known such a rampant nymphomaniac, she tired me out. She wanted to go to swingers' parties, have friends film us making love, all sorts of things. At first it was fun, but it got quite nasty at times, it wasn't what I wanted to be honest"

This was exactly the opposite to what she had told me of course. I wasn't in the least surprised though, after all, that kind of relationship is not exactly what you might want to admit to. However, it did confirm what kind of thing they had together, whoever was to blame, it didn't really matter. There was something else I wanted to know.

"Did you two move in together, somewhere in Aylesbury?"

"We did mister Hunter; it didn't last long. I had work to do, and she kept me up most of the night with her sexual demands"

"I heard say that she moved in with her sister at some point, can you confirm that Lennard"

"Sister, she didn't have a sister, I am absolutely certain of that. Who told you that mister Hunter?"

"She did Lennard, she said she had to get away from you and moved in with her sister"

I could hear Post laughing at the other end of the phone. It was clear that Olivia had spun me a line, but why? Surely, she had nothing to gain by lying to me, did she? I sat there trying to figure out why Olivia Cranfield had lied. So far as I could make out, she had nothing to gain from doing that. Post was out of the way, he was no threat to her, and I think she knew it.

So, what was in it for her, was it something to do with her reputation locally? No, I didn't see that, Post was the villain, everyone I spoke to confirmed that. She was seen as the innocent victim, nothing more.

Was she on some sort of sympathy trip, or attempting to throw me off a particular trail, that could be the case. Had I stumbled upon something that I didn't know existed? Perhaps so, that's often the way of things, but I just hadn't figured it out yet. What the hell could that be, she wasn't involved with the devil killer, or was she? Was she just another person trying to blame it all on Post, she wasn't alone on that score.

If the locals had their way, he was responsible for the assault's, the three original murders, the murder of his wife and most likely the two latest killings. In fact, I could also include the local police in that. When you stood back and looked at the whole picture, everyone seemed to have it in for Lennard Post, including me!

"Well, so far as I know, there was no sister mister Hunter, I am certain of that, just the one and only

Olivia Cranfield. I have to admit to only knowing her for a few months, but she never spoke of a sister. Perhaps they didn't communicate, maybe they had fallen out, had become estranged, it does happen"

"Perhaps so Lennard but it seems strange that she told me she had moved in with her sister in order to get away from you"

"Well, if you ask the locals, I bet they won't know of any sister, I will put money on that mister Hunter"

He was right of course. I had spoken to the landlord of the pub I was sat outside. He knew nothing of a sister, so perhaps Post was telling the truth.

"If you want mister Hunter, I can take you to the place we stayed. It's still there in the centre of Aylesbury. I can assure you we moved in together and no sister was ever mentioned"

I wondered if it was time I discussed with Post my doubts regarding him and his case. Everyone and his dog knew Post was responsible for the original and the latest killings. In fact, Post himself admitted going into hiding because everyone would suspect him.

"Lennard, we need to discuss the elephant in the room here. You admit yourself that everyone thinks you are responsible for all these killings. I have to confess that I also regard you as a prime suspect. All the DNA evidence, the mask in the car and most of all, the killings have restarted since your release.

All this cannot simply be dismissed as 'made-up' or an attempt by the police to 'stich you up'. For example, your semen on your wife's body, that's a fact, you simply can't explain that one away"

"Let me tell you something mister Hunter, and I am more than happy to back this one up with hard evidence.

When I was eighteen, I had a serious car accident, in fact the doctors were just about to turn off my life support machine. It was only the pleadings of my grandparents that saved my life.

Of course, I knew nothing of this, I was in a coma having undergone some very extensive surgery, including several pelvic operations. The feeling amongst the doctors was, even if I regained consciousness, I would never walk again.

Anyway, to cut a very long story short, the damage to my pelvic region had led to the nerves between my spinal cord and my penis being damaged. This left me with a condition called Anejaculation. In short mister Hunter, I was unable to ejaculate and to this day, I am still incapable of that.

Now, given this condition, you have to ask yourself, how I was able to leave my semen all over the corpse of my wife. Any doctor would confirm this mister Hunter, it is an absolute and complete medical impossibility. I am more than happy to send you my doctors report, the report from the prison medics, or in fact undergo any medical examination to prove this. So, you have to ask yourself, how the hell did my semen get all over the body of my dead wife?"

I sat there reflecting on what Post had just said. Of course, he could be lying, why not, it certainly sounded feasible and who was I to question it. Would he be able to prove it, he said he could, or was he just trying to call my bluff, knowing I wouldn't check.

"Lennard, I have to admit, it does sound feasible but for one thing. It was your semen, so how did your DNA find itself at the murder scene? You can't just use anyone's, they check these things Lennard, it wouldn't work"

"Good Point mister Hunter, so how did that happen? When you go into court and try to tell them, and they won't listen, what can I do. I tried to tell the judge about the Anejaculation, but they just laughed at me and refused to listen to any evidence I had.

My useless barrister wouldn't believe me either. He wouldn't argue with the court, seemed he didn't want to cross the judge for fear of damaging his reputation. I was truly screwed mister Hunter, and I spent the next twenty years in jail for it.

So, you explain it to me. I get that the court wouldn't listen to me, that my barrister was fucking useless, but how did my semen get onto my wife's body? It would take an operation called TESE, or testicular sperm extraction to do this, and I certainly didn't have it. It's not a major operation but without it, no semen, no sperm and no DNA mister Hunter"

Ok, so let's presume Post was telling the truth, he must know I would check. He couldn't have left his semen, so where the hell did that come from?

There was more of course, his fingerprints on the murder weapon, how was he going to explain this? I needed to find out what he had to say.

"Mister Hunter, that one is even easier to explain. Yes, they were my fingerprints and yes, the knife was found at the murder scene. Yes, the knife was one from our kitchen and yes, I had used it to butcher several rabbits I had caught that morning"

"So, what's that got to do with the murder weapon?"

"Don't you see mister Hunter; the blood was not my wife's. Something else I had to try and explain but no one was willing to listen. Ok, when I got to my appeal, that was my chance to prove the blood was from the rabbits and not from my wife, job done"

"So why didn't you, that was surely a way to blow a hole in the case"

"Because mister Hunter, the knife had gone missing. Strange that, a pivotal piece of evidence, and a way to prove my innocence had simply vanished. The court ordered the police to find it but with no success. They also managed to find some doctor who assured the court I could ejaculate; the whole thing was more of a stich up than the original trial.

The police had it in for me mister Hunter, they wanted me behind bars for as long as possible. They couldn't get me for the devil murders, in truth they couldn't really pin my own wife's murder on me. They corrupted the evidence for that, can you imagine finding out your wife is dead, and they think you did it? I was a convenient target for them, a local ne'er-do-well who no one liked. I had no family, no one to stick up for me.

Moreover, I had taken on two corrupt local police, namely, Detective Chief Inspector Peter Dexter and his best mate, Detective Inspector Paul Willow. I had put a stop to their vial extorsion racket, and they didn't like it. So, they stitched me up mister Hunter, got me out of the way, for a bloody long time. By the time I got out, they would be retired and living it up somewhere in Spain.

That's the brutal truth of the thing, twenty years of my life because I stopped them preying on local people. The same people who laughed at me when I asked for their help. I guess there were others in their pay mister Hunter, perhaps the judge in the case, maybe that's why I got nowhere with my evidence. I also suspected my own barrister, maybe Dexter and Willow had something on him as well.

The problem I had then and still have to this day, is I have no evidence to prove any of this. I just need someone to believe me whilst I find some, that's why I called you mister Hunter. I just knew you would believe me after a previous case of yours involving corruption in the police"

"This all sounds a little far-fetched Lennard. Ok, perhaps it's slightly believable regarding your wife's murder, but what about the rest of the murders and the recent killings?"

"The truth is, someone is responsible for the assaults and the killings, there is a real devil killer out there. I was just a convenient target to blame this all on, an easy conviction, something to make the baying top brass and public go away. Now it's all started again since my release, odd that don't you think mister Hunter!"

"So, if you aren't the devil killer, who is?"

"That's up to you to figure out mister Hunter, all I can do is stay out of the way until you do. I was always convinced it was someone involved in the original case though"

"Why do you say that?"

"It fits, someone was enjoying himself assaulting and killing all those women twenty plus years ago. Maybe they wanted to stop the slaughter, perhaps their conscience got a grip of them, maybe they were sickened by what they were doing, who knows?

One thing was certain though, they needed someone to blame it on, a patsy. So, providing they could stop themselves murdering any more women, they could blame it all on me, even if they never managed to prove anything.

Very convenient don't you think, and a full proof way to get away with murder, and label someone else as a serial killer. They also disposed of the one person who stood up to their extorsion and criminal activities, namely me. Two successful outcomes in one swoop. It's a great plan mister Hunter don't you think. However, now I am out of prison, they are free to indulge their sick perversions once again, all at my expense!"

"So how the hell did they distort or completely change the evidence in the case against you?"

"Good question, I am certain we will never find any proof of that, these people are far too clever to leave a trace. My guess is Dexter and Willow had in their pay a couple of senior judges, maybe some lawyers as well. It wouldn't be out of the question that the police coroner was with them also. Given that scenario, they could fabricate or change any evidence they wanted.

Listen mister Hunter, this was a very lucrative endeavour they had going. Extorsion of local business, protection racquets, even importing booze, cigarettes and porn. Once my father had been beaten for not paying up, I made it my business to find out everything I could about Dexter and Willow. It didn't take long; in fact, it wasn't that difficult at all. They had got lazy, very lazy, after all, who the hell would think two very senior detectives could be doing such things. All they had to do was get me out of the way and it didn't matter to them how they did it, then they could get back to making money, big money"

"Right Lennard, let's say you are correct, telling the truth and that I believe you. There are a few problems with the whole set-up though.

One, they meddled with the evidence or made it up altogether. I have to say that wouldn't be the first time I had come across that scenario.

Two, let's assume you were convicted, wrongly, for the murder of your wife and suspected of the original devil killer murders, just to get you out of the way. I can go for that, a meddling member of the public wrecking the lucrative activities of two bent cops. That person needs to be got rid of, yes, I have seen that before.

Three, let's also assume the real devil killer was able to stop his psychopathic murder spree, just to wait until you came out of jail so he could start again. Not sure that could happen Lennard, serial murderers don't operate like that, but let's assume this one can. Maybe he can pick and choose, perhaps he is not some deranged lunatic but someone who enjoys killing and can stop whenever he wants. Maybe he was sickened all those years ago, just as you stated. He wanted to stop, so blame it on poor old Lennard Post and get away with murder.

All of these things are credible, individually Lennard, but all three together, it's a huge leap of faith and one I find difficult to accept. Also, whilst we can attribute points one and two to Dexter and Willow, who the hell is the real devil killer? Is he someone who was part of the original case as you suggested. Or is he just someone who took advantage of the situation and got away with his crimes by allowing it to be blamed on you? To be honest, I can't see it being Dexter or Willow, they don't strike me as complete psychos, so if it's not them, who the hell is it?

I have to say Lennard that this is always going to be your problem. You have served time for your wife's murder, we can dismiss that for now. But the killings have started again and as you said, once they catch you, you will take the blame and they will throw away the key. We need to find the devil killer, once that happens, you are in the clear. Then we can start the job of proving your innocence for your wife's murder"

Did I just say that to him? Five minutes ago, I wanted to catch him and throw him to the wolves. See him banged up for ever, do I believe him now, has he succeeded in lying to me or is he telling the truth? His story seemed very convincing, especially as I had come across such cases before. Money corrupts, especially in large quantities, it can get people to do the most extreme things.

This didn't explain the devil killings though, that was nothing to do with money, corruption or bent cops. It was cold blooded carnage, killing for pleasure, gaining enjoyment from the screams of your victims. People like that don't just stop and then start up at will, especially twenty years later. Whoever this person was, if it wasn't Post, was a real piece of work. Able to pick up where he left off, enjoying murder and misery like someone picking up an old hobby, enjoyed many years ago.

I think it was time I nailed my colours to a particular mast. Either Lennard Post was telling the truth, if that was the case, I would work with him. Or, he was lying, and taking me for a ride. I decided on the former, take Post at his word, and try to find the real devil killer. The trouble was, where the hell do I start?

I was just about to inform him of my decision when my phone vibrated. I looked down at the screen, there was a text, it read.

'A message from - Marcus Cooke.

Lee, for fucks sake put the phone down. I need to speak to you, NOW!!!! Phone   me back immediately'

A dark place.

The cold of the basement permeated into the two women, the damp had a sickly odour, redolent of corruption and death. They sat on a pile of dusty old rags, staring into the half-light, pondering their fate. The silence was deafening, any minute now he could come and take them, rip their life away like some unwanted toy. There was no escape, this was the end, and they knew it.

"No one knows where we are, there won't be any rescue. Have you seen the masks he wears, he is the devil killer"

Victoria didn't reply, she found it impossible to re direct her thoughts away from her impending doom. The man had entered the dark cellar two or three times, occasionally he would wear the mask of the devil, sometimes not. She tried to figure out how to get away from this, but there was no way out, no window and only one door. She had tried the lock, but it held fast, the door was solid, there would be no escape.

"He said he would slit our throats, eat our flesh and it would be on tv. He said terrible things Victoria. Tomorrow, we are going to be murdered, our blood spilled, and everyone will see"

Again, Victoria Hunter stared into the gloom, she wanted to think that her father would come and rescue her, but it seemed impossible. There was no indication of where they were, a basement in a house but nothing more than that. Even if she had her mobile phone, she would not be able to summon help.

Victoria turned to the young woman sitting next to her. She was dishevelled, dirty, her clothes were covered in a dusty grime. Her eyes conveyed panic and fear, she wanted answers, but Victoria had none to give.

"Listen, whatever your name is, I can't give you any comfort. We are trapped here, and he intends to kill us, that's for certain. He is the devil killer, so we know what's going to happen to us, if we don't do something about it. The trouble is, I can't think of anything we can do.

The only two advantages we have are numbers and surprise. We are two, he is one and he may not be expecting an attack. That's our only hope, we need to plan an assault, the next time he walks through that door. There will be no holding back, no stopping. If we die in the attempt, then at least we go out knowing we tried our best"

"My name is Amelia by the way, I kicked at that door, spat hate at that monster but I am still here. This place has drained my will to live, he has said so many terrible things to me, I don't know how to fight back"

"Hello Amelia, my name is Victoria, and we will overcome this bastard, don't doubt that. The first thing we need to do is plan how we attack him and get through that door. There is no way we are going through it unless he opens it first. So, how do we put him down, how do we disable and overcome him?"

Amelia looked around the gloom of the cellar. There was nothing in the room apart from the dirty rags they sat on, and a small chemical toilet in the corner. There was nothing sharp, hard or anything that might damage him.

"I don't see what we can do Victoria, he has even taken our shoes and belts. We could throw the contents of the camping loo all over him, but that's not going to stop him. I don't see what we can do, we are stuck here, he will kill us and there is nothing we can do about it"

"There is always something you can do Amelia; all we need to figure out is what. My dad was fond of saying, 'whatever you do do, don't do nothing'. I have no intention of doing nothing, so let's make a plan"

"Ok, well we have ourselves. He is quite a big guy, but if surprised we could physically overcome him, I guess. The chemical toilet is heavy, hitting him with that will certainly put a few stars in his eyes"

"There you go Amelia, you are planning already"

"But how do we pick it up and hit him with it, he would see us coming and simply leave the room, locking the door behind him"

"Right, good point, so we have to get him over to the toilet. What about me sitting on it as he enters. He is a sick twat that's for sure, the sight of me with my knickers around my ankles will certainly get him aroused. If I say the right things to him, he might come over and try something. That's when you attack the bastard, hit him with everything you have. I will stand up, pick up the loo and smash it down onto his sick fucking head"

"That's too simple Victoria, that's never going to work"

"Yes, you are probably right, but if you have a better plan, I would love to hear it"

For the first time the look of terror on Amelia's face disappeared, there was even a slight smile on her lips.

"Ok, that's the plan, I hope you can get him over to that loo, otherwise we are screwed"

"I will, don't worry about that. This twat may me some screwed up psycho, but he likes young women. One sat on the toilet, pants down will be a treat he won't be able to resist"

Thursday evening.
The office of Inspector Marcus Cooke. Thames
Valley Police HQ, Bicester.

I sat there absolutely motionless; I couldn't believe what I had just been told. I felt angry, crushed but most of all, helpless. I hadn't ever felt like this before, it was like a nightmare, an utter horrendous black dream. I tried to regulate my breathing, control my heart as it pounded in my chest. Neither action had much effect, I felt myself losing control, not just of my mind but my body also. The world around me seemed to be tail spinning like an out-of-control aircraft, heading towards the earth, within moments of certain death.

Marcus hadn't held back, perhaps it was the modern way of doing things, get the bad news out quickly and see what happens next! He sat me down in the office, told me what had happened and the probable identity of the man in the police uniform, the devil killer. They then stood back and assessed my reaction. Detective Sergeant Nick Walker brought in a very hot coffee and sat quietly next to me. He had that 'false sympathy' look on his face, it was almost convincing. I knew deep down just how difficult it must have been for both of them, but my only real concern was for my daughter.

I knew the drill, they had to see my reaction, note what I might say or perhaps what I might do next. They were of course worried that I might go and look for this bastard, they were right on that count. However, as much as they might want to see the end of the devil killer, they had a duty to stop that from happening.

Also, they must have known about my connection to Tony Bianchi and his ability to get things done, and not always legally. I had already thought about that, I wondered if Tony had any connections in this part of the world. He might know someone who could help find my daughter, and then tear the devil killer limb from limb.

"Lee, I know that look. You are going to try to find this guy and when you do, well I hate to think. You know what's going to happen if you do any harm to him. We will have to arrest you and put you at the mercy of the courts. The judge will sentence you regardless of what has happened to your daughter.

Please, please leave this to us, we are best placed to do this, and you know it. We will find her and bring her back to you, we have everyone out there looking, it's only a matter of time"

I wanted to scream at the top of my voice, jump up and leave right now. Every fibre in my body wanted to find the psycho and kill him, hateful revenge was the only thought in my mind. Marcus was right though, I would only make things worse, dragging him out into the street and kicking him to death was not the thing to do. Sitting back though, that seemed impossible, he had my daughter, and he was going to pay for that.

"Marcus, please tell me you have a lead on where she might be"

"Listen Lee, I will only ever be honest with you in relation to this situation. I don't know where your daughter is, but we will find her, have no doubt in that Lee. We are calling in favours, bending arms up backs, we are doing everything we can.

If you go out there like some latter-day Charles Bronson vigilante, then it's just going to make things worse. You are going to get in the way, blow operations and give that sick fuck the heads up. If he runs, we might never find him or your daughter, and don't forget the other girl he has, her life will be at risk also. You have to stay out of the way Lee, that's a bloody order"

I wanted to argue with him, but he was right. The thing was, I couldn't simply sit back, I had to do something, I had to find my daughter. If I was being honest, that wouldn't be limited to the legal, if I got my hands on him, he would certainly be dead.

"Lee, we have a team at your wife's house. They are specially trained officers, they are a great help, highly skilled, they do more than just sit there and drink tea. They talk to people, make phone calls, liaise with HQ, organise social media. Your other daughter is there too, why don't you go and sit with them?"

I couldn't bring myself to look at Marcus or Nick Walker, if I did, they would read my thoughts and surely lock me away. They were right about the special team currently with my wife and other daughter, but they didn't need me prowling around grinding my teeth. I needed to be out there and finding the devil killer, and I needed to start right now.

I agreed to stay out of the way, that was a lie of course, I knew it and I assumed Marcus did as well. They would do everything they could, I was certain of that, but it wouldn't be enough. This needed another approach, it wasn't going to be legal, it wasn't going to be nice, but it might well be successful. So, the first phone call I was going to make was to Fat Tony Bianchi. He would relish this kind of job and stood as much of a chance as anyone else in finding the devil killer.

The late afternoon sun stung my eyes as I left the police HQ. On any other day or occasion, it would have been a glorious evening, one to sit with friends and enjoy a beer or two. This one was not though, I was fully aware of what the devil killer had in mind for tomorrow night, and now it included my daughter, Victoria.

I looked down at my phone, pulled up Tony's number and hesitated. If I pressed call, then a whole set of events would be set into motion. There would be no going back, the likes of Tony Bianchi wouldn't stop coming for you once he started. This would certainly end up in bloodshed, beaten bodies or even worse. Did I really want to drop another lunatic into this situation, was I really making things worse? Of course I was but at least I stood a chance of getting my daughter back.

"Hi Lee, what's up mate, did you find that Post fella?"

I wanted to end the call, I had done the wrong thing, I knew that now. I was an ex senior police officer, what the hell was I doing asking for help from the likes of Tony. I would just make small talk and end the call"

There was a long silence, I guess Tony sensed something was up.

"Hey Lee, you done something bad mate? Someone screwed you over, tell me who they are, they will regret messing with you, and that's a promise"

I did smile, he was a very bad man, that was for sure, but his heart was kind of in the right place, well only if you hadn't pissed him off. To be honest, I wouldn't have solved the last case without him, and I needed all the help I could get, right now!

"Listen Tony, something has happened. I need your help, but before I tell you why, promise me you won't come down here and start World War three"

"Anything for you Lee, just say the word"

"Tony, you need to promise me that you won't start beating people to death"

"This sounds serious Lee. Ok, I won't, not unless you tell me to"

"The devil killer has kidnapped my daughter. He has another girl as well and he is intending to murder both of them tomorrow night. No one has any idea where they are, and I don't see any hope of anyone finding them before he does so"

"Right, it's that fucker Lennard Post isn't it. I am on my way Lee, I will kill the bastard, and not quickly either. I have a fucking great machine, it electrocutes people, they soon start talking when I plug them in"

"You see Tony, I knew you would say that. You promised not to, we have to be more careful"

"Well ok, I guess you're the boss and it's your daughter Lee. So, what's the plan, what do you have in mind?"

"I need a couple of contacts down this neck of the woods. A couple of heavies, two guys who will apply pressure to selected people, find out things the police can't. I need them to be able to stop short of actually disembowelling anyone though. They have to be a higher class of thug, ones that will stop when I tell them to"

"Right Lee, give me an hour, I need to make a couple of calls. Go and grab a coffee somewhere, Tony Bianchi is on the case, and I won't let you down, and that's a promise"

The line clicked and went dead. That last statement worried me somewhat, "Tony Bianchi is on the case". One thing you could be certain about when dealing with Tony, he was very good at pain, death and violence, and he thoroughly enjoyed it.

I sat there and wondered if I had done the right thing. I should have left this to Marcus and his team, but that's not the kind of person I am. My daughter had been taken by some psychopath on a killing spree, and I was determined it wasn't going to end like that. My daughter wasn't going to be doing the dying here, it was going to be the devil killer.

A dark place.

The plan was set, and the two girls were primed and ready. This was going to be their one and only chance to live, if this didn't work, death would surely be their one and only fete. They sat in the gloom of the basement, each in their own world, contemplating what had brought them to this situation.

Victoria Hunter, the daughter of an ex senior police officer and now private detective knew she should have known better. She had been duped by a bogus police officer. He seemed credible enough though. He had the right uniform, an ID card, why wouldn't she believe him. Now she was here, and no one knew where here was. The worst part of this situation was the thought of dying alone, with no one to hold her hand. Her lifeless body would be dumped somewhere, perhaps never to be found.

They had both decided that dying whilst trying to escape was better than letting the bastard cut their throats. They were ready, as soon as they heard the door being unlocked, their plan would snap into place. Victoria would entice the devil killer further into the room whilst Amelia would attack him from behind. Both girls understood that this first attack would only knock him off balance, but it would be enough, it had to be enough.

It would give Victoria just enough time to pick up the portable toilet and bring it down on his head. With luck it would knock him down, stun him for a few precious seconds. It was in those moments that they would make their escape. They would lock the door and run for their lives, hoping that a passing motorist would come to their aid.

It wasn't long before they heard signs of someone coming towards the cellar where they were being held. They both looked at each other, fear gripping every nerve, self-doubt washing over them.

This was their moment, there was no going back. A gentle silence descended over the dark and grimy cellar; a small spider skittered across the floor, going about its business, oblivious to the events about to unfold. It felt like the stillness before the storm, a peaceful moment prior to a tempest erupting. Did their fear settle slightly, perhaps a quiet confidence descended.

Victoria swiftly moved over to the portable toilet, pulled down her pants and sat in wait, whilst Amelia dragged the rags they were sitting on closer to the door. She would be able to spring at the man and close the distance much more quickly from here.

They both shook uncontrollably, waves of nausea pulsating in their stomachs. Victoria struggled to catch her breath, the fear of what was to come almost overwhelming her. Amelia was shaking so violently she could hardly focus her eyes across the room.

The steps came closer and closer, the girls wanted to abandon their plan, self-doubt stalking them, it wasn't going to work, and they knew it. There was the familiar crunching sound as his feet moved across the stone floor towards the door. They could hear his breathing now, he was so close, then the sound of the key as it entered the lock.

That peaked their levels of fear and panic, this was it, there was no going back. The lock creaked a little as it turned over, the tumblers falling into place. He stopped for a second, put something on the floor, kicked violently at the swollen wood, two, three and then four times. Then there was silence as he picked up whatever he had placed on the dirty stone floor outside in the corridor. The door groaned a little, complaining at being woken from its sleepy task of imprisonment.

The heavy wooden door swung inwards, displacing dust and some cobwebs from the ceiling above. The particles spun wildly in the half-light, it brought a simple silence to the area. Their nerves now settled, the plan was in action, this was their chance at freedom.

It seemed to take an age for the door to slowly open, the tension building all the time. Amelia wanted to scream out, "stop, it won't work" but her mouth was dry, and no sound was possible. The door opened just a little more, jamming for an instance on a piece of errant concrete. He pushed it back and forth, crushing to dust the material caught beneath its path.

Eventually he entered, wearing his devil mask. It was bizarrely impressive with black and red features, a sickly grin with white fangs. Portents of evil, murder and bloodshed radiated from this plastic face, the air in the cellar turned icy cold. For just one moment time stopped, the whole world calmed itself, awaiting the outcome of their exploits.

He entered, looked about the dim room and stopped. The sack he held in his left hand dropped to the floor as he spied Victoria.

"Oh, my darling. What a delicious image you are, sitting with your pants down. I must admit to being somewhat aroused by what I see. I wonder, should I approach, perhaps I might enjoy a view of your womanly parts. Or should I wait until tomorrow. You will be completely naked by then, tied to my operating table, with terror blazing like a hot sun in your eyes"

Victoria hesitated for a moment, she knew what to say, but the words would not come forth.

"Why don't you tell me Victoria, what would you have me do, what pleasures do you want me to bless you with. After all, I am a man, I could bring exquisite gratifications to a woman like yourself"

This was it, she either spoke now or the plan would fail. Their lives depended on what she said next, and she knew it.

"Come Victoria, tell me what's on your mind. Don't be shy, I am hard now just seeing you sat there, you would really enjoy me making love to you"

"I am not sure you could satisfy me devil man. I am a woman with huge needs, sometimes it takes two or even three men to quench my desires"

"But I am a man with great potency, let me show you"

"You will be wasting my time devil man, I will destroy you before you even start"

That seemed to provoke him into action. Unzipping his trousers, he started towards Victoria. She could hear him breathing, rapidly, almost out of control.

"We will see about that my darling, I will………."

His world suddenly turned upside down. He felt a huge force hit him from behind, thrusting him forwards. For an instant he couldn't comprehend what had just happened, but it didn't take more than a second to realise that he had made a mistake. He had let his lust and ardour get the better of him, he had walked straight into a trap.

As he stumbled under the weight of the impact, he instinctively put his hands out in front of him. Two or maybe three steps again but this time there was no standing upright. The palms of his hands hit the rough concrete, grinding shards of stone and dirt into his skin. The sharp pain made him yelp, like a dog being punished by his cruel master. Next his knees impacted, dull stabs of agony shot up his legs and into his pelvis. He wanted to roll over, see who was assailing him but he was unable. The mask a slipped, temporarily blocking his vision.

He rolled over and tried to sit upright, holding his hands up in an attempt to fend of his assailants. He felt a terrible blow to his ribs, a kick, his liver screamed in agony. There was uncontrolled anger boiling up within him. He needed to grab someone, take control, but there was no one out there.

He tried to reach upwards but there followed a devastating blow to his head. Red, white and blue flashes ran through his mind, spinning wildly in his vision. There was another impact and another, then his world went quiet and dark.

"So, look at you now big man, devil killer, now just a piece of shit lying there on the dirty floor. That will teach you to mess with Amelia and I, looking at me with lust in your eyes, I fucking think not, you dirty bastard. Don't you ever speak to me again, don't you ever threaten my life, don't you ever treat me like a victim.

The next time you see me will be in court, just before the judge locks you up for the rest of time. You will rot in some dirty fucking cell, just like we had to. You will cry every night as someone rapes you, just like you were going to do to us"

The absolute fury and rage boiling inside her was overwhelming, she could have happily killed him right here, right now. She kicked him in the ribs four, five or even six times. She kicked him so hard that her ankle exploded in red hot pain, but still she continued, unable to quench her vengeance.

"Victoria, stop, we need to get away, there might be someone else here. This is our one and only chance to escape, we have to go"

Those trembling words penetrated into her conscious mind like a warm zephyr, slowing her adrenaline, calming her fury. She could feel her breathing slowing, the red mist dispersing. She landed once again into the real world, finding herself gazing down at the body in front of her.

"Sorry Amelia, you are right, let's get the hell out of here"

She turned and made her way to the door. The corridor outside was wide and dimly lit, the floor was paved with old flagstones, polished by generations of feet. The walls were clean and whitewashed, the whole place smelt of damp.

"Come on, there is no point in waiting, if there is anyone out there, then too bad. We overcame that bastard, let's do the same to them"

Amelia smiled, taking some comfort from her words. Victoria however knew all too well the consequences of meeting someone else. They had taken the devil killer by surprise; they wouldn't be that lucky next time.

Out an in the corridor, they looked right and left. To the right the corridor ended in a stone wall, to the left another door.

"Right, follow me, that door might lead to the outside world, if it does, we run for our lives and don't look back, do you understand me, Amelia?"

She nodded, that was all the confirmation Victoria needed. They moved quickly across the stone floor, breathing deeply, adrenalin keeping them far from exhaustion. It felt like the whole world had slipped into slow motion, the door seemed to hover in front of them like something in a dream. Any moment now it would open, and someone would come through it and stop them in their tracks. There was a rising tide of panic in their hearts, what if the door opened into another room, what if someone was waiting.

Eventually they reached the red wooden door. It was strong and robust, like the door to their cell.

It had a brass handle, splattered over time with whitewash and covered in a blue green verdigris.

Victoria turned, tried to control her breathing, and spoke to Amelia. The young woman looked terrified, fear blazing in her eyes, almost on the edge of panic. Victoria had to get her to control herself, clear thinking is what was needed now.

"Listen Amelia, this is it, we go free once we open that door. Take a deep breath, you need to concentrate and not panic, there is no need for that. We have done the tough stuff, so let's get out there and run for freedom"

This seemed to calm her just a little, bringing that nervous smile back to her lips.

"Ok, turn that handle and let's get out of here, I will be right behind you Vicky, let's go"

"Right, standby"

Victoria turned and reached for the handle, grasping it firmly in her right hand. She took a deep breath and swallowed hard. Should she open it quickly, or take her time? She decided to open the door swiftly, if there was anyone on the other side, perhaps it would take them by surprise, and give the women a split second's advantage.

She turned the handle to the right, but the motion quickly locked. She then reversed the action, turning it to the left but again it stopped.

"Come on Vicky, what's the problem?"

"It's locked, the dam thing is locked"

The two girls looked at each other, neither knowing what to do next.

"Ok, wait, the door is locked so the only person with the key must be that twat lying in the cell, he must have it on him. We need to go back, search him, get the key"

"I can't do that Vicky, what happens if he wakes up, he might be on his way right now"

"You wait here Amelia, he won't be waking up any time soon, I promise you that. I will be back in a few seconds, then we get out of here"

"No, please don't leave me, someone might come through that door"

"Amelia, get a grip, no one else is coming through the door, it's locked! The only key is in that man's back pocket, and I am going back to get it. You wait here and take a chill pill, sit down and try to breath"

Amelia reached out and grabbed her arm, "don't Vicky, I can't stay here by myself"

Victoria wrenched her hand away, and without saying another word sprinted off into the half-light, towards the devil killer. She could hear her heart pounding like hammering drums in her ears, the taste the fear was pungent and overpowering.

Amelia was right, he might now be conscious, clearing the numbness and disorientation from his brain and readying himself to gain a swift revenge. What would she do if he was standing in the cell, should she fight him, would she be able to overcome him for a second time? Of course, there was no choice, she would have to attack him, their lives would depend on it, at least she would try, that's all she could do.

The dash back to the cellar was almost complete, her lungs were bursting, her mind screaming for her to turn back, but she carried on. Eventually she came to the solid blue door, this was it, she slowed slightly and made the turn.

Her eyes immediately alighted on the area of the stone floor where the devil killer had been laid out, but he was not there! She screamed in panic, stopping, turning, a black cloud of horror and fear swept over her. Her mind spun, whirled, where was he, without that body she had lost control.

"Looking for me my dear, I am behind you, by the door"

She turned, the blue door swung closed, hiding behind its solid mass was the devil killer. He quickly moved in front of it to prevent any attempt to escape. Blood trickled from a cut somewhere on the top of his head. He appeared unsteady but generally in control.

"I can't believe you came up with such a clever plan. It certainly worked I have to admit, well for a short time. Now, how am I to punish you two, and yes, your friend won't be going out of that door any time soon, the key is in my back pocket"

He laughed out loud, swaying as he did so, coughing and wiping the blood from above his right eye. Victoria Hunter stood in the middle of the room, rooted to the spot, unable to think or plan any kind of reaction.

"So, have you got any suggestions darling, perhaps I can whip the flesh from your backs, no, maybe burn your faces with my welding torch. I must admit I am tempted but I really don't want to spoil the entertainment. The viewers would be so disappointed seeing two mutilated victims undergoing the ceremony.

No, back into the cell I think, I can wait, it's only a short while now, I can indulge myself then. So, please step to the back of the room, this time I will be emptying the room and putting the two of you in handcuffs. Come on back………"

He didn't get time to finish his sentence as the door opened behind him. It hit with considerable might, taking him completely by surprise and forcing him forward and to his knees. Into the room came Amelia, red faced and full of rage, there were no signs of fear now, just overwhelming anger.

"Whip the flesh from my back, I don't think so, slimy bastard"

Screaming like an ungodly banshee she jumped onto his back, grabbing his head and thrusting it forward. Her whole weight and momentum carried them both prostrate onto the floor. She smashed his head into the stone two or three times, screaming as she did so. It made a sickening crunch as it impacted, spraying droplets of blood in all directions.

Victoria lurched forward and grabbed her around the shoulders.

"Stop Amelia, that's enough, you are going to kill him"

The words fell on deaf ears. She thrust her fingers around his throat and started to squeeze.

"Amelia for goodness sakes, stop. He has the key, let's get it and go, he isn't going to hurt us now"

Slowly the anger and hate ebbed and the violence ceased. She sat there on his motionless back, breathing heavily, tears in her eyes, splatters of blood covering her face.

"This bastard isn't going to hurt us any more Vicky, I won't let him"

"Then get the key out of his back pocket and let's get out of here"

Amelia reached into his pocket and retrieved a large rusting key. It was attached to a dirty leather fob with 'good luck' stamped onto it.

"Right, let's go, we don't know if anyone else is involved, we need to get out of here and as far away as possible"

The two women ran as fast as they could down the corridor and towards the end door. This time there was no hesitation, Victoria thrust the key into the lock and turned the handle, they were free.

They burst out from the door like two corks from a Champaign bottle and into the daylight. It temporally blinded them, causing both women to squint, and turn away from the dazzling light. It took just a few seconds for their eyes to begin to adjust.

They found themselves standing at the rear of a large imposing property. In front were three stone steps leading up to a garden with large lawns, ornamental flower beds and fruit trees. Somewhere in the distance was the sound of running water and the smell of roses and honeysuckle wafted about them on the breeze.

Climbing the steps they looked about, it seemed oddly normal, free from horror, pain and fear. The contrast from their prison in the cellar could not have been starker. They stared at each other, waiting for the next move.

"Vicky, let's go, anywhere seems good, just as long as we get far away from this place"

"Right, there are fields at the end of this garden, let's go in that direction. We don't want to go around the front of here, we need to get away, we don't want to meet any partners of that bastard"

There was nothing more to say, they set off towards the fence at the end of the garden. Soon they would be free and away from the hell of the devil killer and back in the world they knew.

Late Thursday night.
The back room of the Tiger Inn, Aylesbury.

Tony Bianchi had made phone calls, called in favours and organised for a meeting with two local men. Assistants, as he had put it, a couple of guys who are willing to help. I dreaded to think what that help might consist of, but any port in a storm. Also, and more importantly, they might well know things or people connected to the present situation that the police would never know. It was worth a try I guess, not sure about the kind of help these guys would be willing to give, but hey, what's the worst that could happen.

Anyway, I had driven over to Aylesbury and following the address in the sat nav for the Tiger Inn, I arrived at the appointed time and location. The place, a very small pub, was located on a back street, off a back street, deep in the older parts of the city. It felt remote and well away from the forces of good. The street itself was a narrow one-way alley, a classic from a spy novel, dimly lit, no signs of life, not the place to go alone on a dark night.

I parked the car a few yards from the pub, drew a deep breath and readied myself for what was to come. When I got out, I could feel eyes upon me, this was not somewhere for a fun night out, or anyplace to bring a date. This was a deal making place, somewhere where people met to hammer out agreements, carve up earnings, and not of the legal kind. In essence, the Tiger Inn was a den of iniquity, a centre for crime and the local gang bosses. As soon as you entered you would be swimming in a sewer of wrongdoing and criminality, it was somewhere to be avoided at any cost.

I stood on the narrow pavement looking at the façade. It was double fronted, yellow painted bay windows sat either side of an ornate porch and double fronted wooden doors. There was a level above that mirrored somewhat the ground floor. Above all of this was a large, illuminated pub sign, 'The Tiger Inn'.

In front of the entrance stood two guys, both towered well over six feet tall. They were clearly body builders and had that, 'mess with me and die' look on their faces. It was clear that no one was gaining entry without first attaining the approval of these two gorillas. I steadied myself, tried not to look scared and marched confidently up to them. I looked up, they were intimidating but I had to approach, I only hoped they had got the message about my meeting, if they hadn't, I guess I wouldn't need to worry about tomorrow!

"Evening guys, my name is………"

"Yeah mister, we know who you are, and why you are here. Richard and Stephen are waiting upstairs for you. Go straight in and to the top of the stairs. Turn right, first room on the right. Don't go anywhere else, don't make me come and look for you, understood?"

"No problems, I will go straight there"

I felt like a naughty schoolboy on my way to the headmaster's office. Don't get me wrong, I was used to people like this, I had dealt with them for years during my time in the Met. The thing is though, I was alone here, and no one would come to help if things went wrong. I wasn't anticipating anything screwing up, I was sure Tony Bianchi would have seen to that. However, here I am, all alone in the centre of Dodge City and Wyatt Earp and Doc Holliday were not around to rescue me.

Without saying another word, or even looking up I walked through the front door. To my surprise the interior was warm and full of music. There was lots of wooden panelling, bright colours and lighting. It almost seemed friendly, a large bar to one side, men and women laughing, drinking and seemingly very relaxed and having a good evening. I blinked a few times, it was so at odds with the exterior and the threatening guards at the front doors.

The barman looked over, he smiled a mouthed something, perhaps asking if I wanted a drink. I smiled back, shook my head and quickly made for the stairs, as instructed by King Cong at the front door. I remembered what the guy had said, "don't make me come looking for you, understood?"

The upper floor was small but beautifully decorated and maintained. It didn't take long to find the room, I nervously knocked. There was a muffled voice from inside, I wasn't able to make out what had been said, so I decided to enter anyway and see what happened next. The room had the same feel as the bar, wooden floor, bright white walls and lights. There were heavy curtains drawn across the windows, I guessed privacy was very important when meetings took place in here. The only furniture inside was a long oak table. It had six heavy looking chairs either side and one at each end. There were several small watercolour paintings on the walls, each depicting scenes of Aylesbury in days gone by.

Facing me and sat on the edge of the table at one end was a man, maybe early thirties, tall and very well dressed in chinos, a very expensive looking light brown sweater and white trainers. Sat on a chair at the other end was another man, slightly older, perhaps not quite as tall. Again, he was dressed in expensive looking casual clothes, dark trousers, a white shirt and dark red v neck and black leather shoes. It was the older man who spoke first, he had a clear and well-paced cadence to his voice.

"Good evening, mister Hunter, and welcome to the Tiger Inn. My name is Richard, and my friend here is Stephen. Please forgive the security at the front door, we value our privacy here, it's nothing personal you understand"

He gently pointed at the other man sitting on the edge of the table. That man smiled and nodded. There was no real friendship in the gesture, it was more automatic than well meant. He tracked my movements as I entered the room and closed the door, without ever taking his eyes of me.

"We understand that an associate of yours has asked for our help, one Tony Bianchi. We are more than happy to oblige, he is known to our organisation and comes with the highest recommendations. Stephen and I have instructions to render whatever assistance you ask for without question mister Hunter"

That last statement made me smile inside. Tony had come up trumps again, I wondered how far they would actually go when he said, "whatever assistance you ask for without question". I had no intention of testing that, I could guess what they would do and probably enjoy every minute of it! Anyway, it was time to start the conversation and see what they knew and how they might be able to help. I needed to find my daughter and time was slipping away, these two guys were possibly my very last chance.

"Please sit mister Hunter, Stephen will fetch us something to eat and some drinks, what would be your preference?"

I sat down at the table, I smiled politely and said I would be happy with whatever turned up. Eventually Stephen returned with drinks, followed by several trays full of food, it all seemed very civilized and very surreal. Here I was, an ex-cop, sitting in an upstairs room of a gangland pub, talking to, well goodness knows who!

Richard and Stephen eventually sat down on one side of the long table, and I sat on the other, this was my chance, I had to make it count.

I tried to talk slowly, ensuring I covered all the details of the case I was involved in. Explaining everything was going to take some time, but I had to get it right and leave nothing out. Any little detail might prove useful to them, perhaps triggering information known only to their organisation.

I told them that I was a private detective, assisting and ex offender who is trying to clear his name. The man, Lennard Post, had been in jail for the murder of his wife, and connected but never charged with the devil killings. Those killings had started up again. At first, I didn't believe he was the killer, either in the past or in the present day, but things had now changed.

Now my daughter had been taken by this psycho and tomorrow night she would be murdered along with another woman he had. No one seemed to know who the devil killer is, or where he might be hiding the two women. I even covered, in some detail, the meetings with the detectives in the original case, Peter Dexter and Paul Willow.

I sat back, took a long drink from my pint of beer and waited for one of them to say something. I assumed it would be a shrug of the shoulders and "sorry can't help". They both seemed very relaxed, almost nonchalant, as if they hadn't been listening to a word I said. Eventually, Richard turned to Stephen and asked if he needed any more information, he shook his head and reached for another ham sandwich.

"Right mister Hunter, that was some story I must admit. Very good of you to give us all the details, very honest, thank you. I appreciate honesty, we don't come across that too often in our line of work, respect to you for that.

One thing I am a little unsure about though, sorry if I missed it in your statement but I need to clarify one point. It would seem from what you have said that you are not familiar with the name, Albert Walker?"

I looked across the table at the two men, they had a look on their faces of bemusement and why didn't he know this name. I must admit to feeling a little disconcerted at this reaction and what it might mean.

"Sorry Richard, Albert Walker, no I have never heard of him"

Richard reached for a handful of salted nuts and then took another drink from his glass. He looked across at Stephen and then back at me. After finishing his drink and his snack, he began to speak in his steady tempo.

"I am surprised mister Hunter that you don't know that name, Albert Walker was a very well know man in these parts. Perhaps because you are based in the north of England might account for your lack of knowledge on this matter.

Albert walker was of course around before I became involved in the firm, but everyone knows what happened. I guess you might now call it local folk law, but I am certain that the truth is much more than that. Albert Walker died in a car accident, must have been twenty odd years ago now. He was never missed, the snivelling little shite. By all accounts he was a nasty, nasty man, no one trusted him an any matter or with anything. To be honest, the human race was well rid of him, he served no purpose whatsoever. I sometimes wonder how he didn't find himself with a bullet in his head years before. I guess he just managed to survive without really pissing off anyone of real importance.

Anyway, one winters night he hit the back of a broken-down lorry in a thick fog on the A34. Died at the scene, the fire brigade took three hours to dig his body out of the mangled wreckage of his car. They cremated what was left of him and scattered his ashes in the garden of remembrance at the local crematorium. From what I am told, no one attended the ceremony, what a shame"

"So, what's this got to do with my case Richard?"

"It's got a lot to do with it mister Hunter. You see, everyone in these parts, well perhaps not including the local police, knew exactly what Albert was up to in his spare time"

"And that was what exactly"

"Mister Hunter, everyone knew that the devil killer was in fact that little twat, the one and only Albert Walker. The man you seek has been dead for a very long time, his ashes have blown away, he is no more"

I sat there staring at the two men, what had he just said, Albert Walker, dead for twenty years was the real devil killer? I had to try and digest this revelation, was it just local gossip or did the underworld really know the truth? It seemed credible, in my experience, the local mob quite often knew the truth about things like this. They didn't have to worry about proof, court cases or taping interviews after reading someone their rights. So, what did that mean for the case, well it would confirm that Post was not the devil killer.

"So why didn't the police know about this Richard, surely they must have at least suspected this man, even if they didn't charge him"

"Oh, mister Hunter, the police certainly did know about Albert. You need to ask them why they didn't do anything about it, but I have my own theory regarding that.

When your friend mister Bianchi contacted our organisation, he mentioned you were looking for this devil killer, so I made some enquires before your arrival. It seems everyone around here, and I mean everyone was certain of Albert Walker's guilt. That of course was borne out by the murders ending when he died. A dead man can't kill mister Hunter, not even a snivelling little bastard like Albert Walker.

Your client, Lennard Post was only associated with the murders because he was meddling with some very powerful bent cops. He was never going down for the killings perpetrated by Albert Walker, they would have never been able to make that stick, not even to senior detectives. He was just stiched up as they say, the devil killings were just a very convenient scenario. The real killer was dead anyway, so I guess the detectives weren't that worried about chasing Albert Walker, nothing to be gained there. I think the killings just became a very opportune way to get rid of Post by simply associating him with the killings. After all, it's not what you are actually guilty of, but more likely what everyone thinks you are!

Anyway, they never managed to pin the killings on your client, that was never going to work, not sure what the hell they were thinking to be honest. He had alibis mister Hunter, he could account for his whereabouts at every turn, even spent the night in the drunk cells in Buckingham police station on the night of one of the murders"

"Ok, but he actually went to prison for the murder of his wife, how do you explain that?"

"The feeling around here is the bent detectives murdered his wife, or at least paid someone to do it, and made it look like another of the devil killings. This was their big chance, get rid of the meddling Lennard Post for ever and clear up the devil killer case, all in one go, a thousand brownie points all round.

I guess they saw their opportunity, a golden one at that. So, they planted a load of evidence, paid off the judge, the local Coroner and his defence lawyers. Good plan, but as I said, he would never have gone down for the devil killings, there was never any supporting evidence. However, just the association with the killings made sure that he spent a very long time in jail for the murder of his wife, which I don't think he actually did!

Simple really, Post messed with the wrong people. His wife ended up paying the ultimate price and he spent twenty years in jail. The real devil killer was forgotten about, and things moved on"

These revelations whirled around me like a force ten storm. I had no reason not to believe what Richard was telling me, why would I? He or his organisation were not involved in any of this, so why not tell me the truth. It made sense, in fact Post had been telling me as much since the first day we met.

"So, who actually killed his wife?"

"I don't know mister Hunter; my assumption would be the people who he messed about with in the first place. I would suggest the bent cops, that's where you need to look mister Hunter, no doubt about that. As for the murders starting up again, I really don't know. It seems clear to me they want Post back in jail, and the murders put him front and centre, it seems somewhat obvious to me"

"I am not sure about that Richard, why do they want Post back in jail, he poses no real threat. Throwing accusations around at bent cops twenty years after the fact is never going to accomplish anything"

"Perhaps not mister Hunter, but it prevents him from achieving anything regarding his accusations concerning the now retired police detectives. Don't forget, if I am right about the murder of his wife, they might end up spending the rest of their lives in jail. They have a lot to lose mister Hunter, especially if Lennard Post gets people to believe him, I am sure they don't want to take that chance. So, they just blame Post and get him back behind bars, after all, who is going to believe a man in jail suspected of resuming his killing spree"

"So that begs the question Richard, who the hell is doing the killing now?"

"I don't know mister Hunter, and that's the truth, but I don't mind betting it's one of those ex-detectives, I am not sure who else could possibly be in the frame. There is no word on the streets mister Hunter, my organisation has no information whatsoever regarding the possible killer. It seems obvious that the present-day killer is also holding your daughter, so we best get looking before the deadline tomorrow night. Have you got any ideas of where we need to start?"

"I certainly do, and it begins with Peter Dexter"

Thursday night.
Somewhere in the darkness.

The night was warm and dry, the stars twinkled brightly, painting a chaotic but mesmeric picture. A silver moon cast its shiny light over the ground, throwing blurred shadows about the countryside. An owl tooted somewhere off in the inky blackness, the blanket of the late evening camouflaging its position.

Amelia and Victoria ran through the night with complete abandonment, giving no thought to their own safety. They stopped from time to time, forcing air into their lungs in an attempt to stave of complete exhaustion. There were no signs of life nearby, just distant jewels of illumination in the darkness, indicating towns and humanity far away in the night.

Eventually, perhaps inevitably, as they crossed a small stream their lack of care cost them dearly. Amelia slipped and fell forward, but slipped again, twisted and fell back into the cold water. There was a scream and then a sicking crack as the muscles and ligaments in her ankle tore and split.

Victoria reached out into the half-light but was unable to prevent the fall. She stopped, turned, there lying in the streams muddy bottom was Amelia. She yelled again, writhing in pain, holding tightly onto her damaged ankle.

"I slipped Vicky, twisted as I fell back. My right ankle is a weak spot I am afraid, the result of a bloody skateboard accident many years ago. That's me Victoria, I know this pain, it's cursed me for many a long year, and when it gets like this, I am finished. I can't go any further, no chance of walking anywhere, let alone running"

Victoria gingerly slipped down the steep bank and into the stream. Its icy fingers wrapped themselves about her feet, ankles and calves. She gasped as the cold swept through her, immediately quenching the fever of their exertions.

"Shit Amelia, I can't leave you here, it's not safe. There is a road not far away, I am sure I heard a car go by. You have to make the effort, I will support you, we need to get to safety and staying here isn't going to help"

Amelia looked up at the shadow of Victoria, outlined by the dim light of the moon. She was right of course, for all they knew the devil killer could be a hundred yards behind them. They had to keep going, find a passing motorist, get a lift to the nearest place of safety.

"Ok, but it's going to be slow work Vicky, this is going to hurt like a bitch"

"It will hurt even more if that sick bastard finds us. We have no choice, let's get to that road and away from here"

Slowly and carefully the two women clawed their way out of the ditch and onto the field. They cautiously began to limp towards where Victoria thought she had heard a car just moments before. It seemed to take hours to go any distance at all, moving forward with no sense of accomplishment, but for the occasional barbed wire fence marking the edge of another field.

"Vicky, we are going round in circles, I am sure that is the ditch I fell into. We have to stop, wait until it gets light and then move on"

"Listen Amelia, we have to keep going, there is a road out here and we are going to find it. I know it hurts but we will be safe soon, I promise you"

The two kept moving, trying their best to ignore the pain. It wasn't long before Victoria's faith in what she had previously heard bore fruit. Off in the distance, far to their right a light immerged, sweeping left to right as it moved.

"There Amelia, there in the distance, it's a car. We will be at the road in a few minutes, hang on"

They trudged on, across muddy fields and over another fence. Closer and closer to the road as another car passed by in the darkness. It seemed to take an age before they finally reached the side of the road. It was a minor affair, just wide enough for two vehicles to pass. Each verge was overgrown, late summer flowers proliferated, soft undulations rolled away into the darkness.

They waited in the shadows of the night but to no avail. There were no cars in either direction, the road was now dead. Amelia crumpled to the grass verge, her resistance to pain had overwhelmed her, she could do no more.

"No one is coming Vicky, it's too late, everyone is in bed. My ankle is shot, I can't go any further, you are going to have to leave me here"

"I am not leaving you anywhere, we are staying here together. A car will come don't worry; all we have to do is wait"

The night stilled once again as the two women sat waiting at the side of the road. They both knew that eventually a vehicle would pass by, even if they had to wait until morning. Their only fear was, the driver of the vehicle would not help, plunging them into danger and terror once again.

It was well past three in the morning before they caught sight of the next vehicle to pass by. Off in the distance the lights began to grow brighter as they worked their way towards them.

"Listen Amelia, we can't afford for this car to pass us by. You wait here, I am going to stand in the road, they will have to stop"

Amelia didn't reply, she was exhausted and on the verge of collapse as the pain and exertions of her journey overwhelmed her. She sat on the damp grass and stared into the night, she needed rescue, medical care and a warm bed.

Victoria stood, straightened her muddy clothes and ventured out into the road. It was still dark, the possibility of the vehicle not seeing her in the blackness was very real. She might be knocked down as it passed, broken and thrown into the verge, but she had to take that chance. Amelia was done, finished, she needed help and this driver was the only hope she had of getting it.

The car drew closer and closer, soon it would be upon them. Perhaps it would be an official vehicle, police or a local businessperson on their way to work. It was only moments away now, Victoria moved to the middle of the road and waited. Eventually it arrived, turning around the gentle right-hand bend no more than fifty yards away.

The lights were slightly yellow and the noise of an old diesel engine throbbed and occasionally coughed as it approached. This was certainly not a new car, perhaps an old farm vehicle or a poachers four by four on its way home after a night shooting rabbits.

She started to jump up and down, shout and wave her hands as vigorously as possible. The vehicle, perhaps an old Land Rover started to slow. Much to her relief she could hear the engine idle and the driver changing down gears. There was a gentle squeal as the brakes were applied, it was stopping, they were safe.

The old Land Rover eventually came to a stop just feet in front of her, the engine coughed and came to a stop. The driver drew the handbrake, it's clicking clearly audible from where Victoria was standing. The door opened, creaking as it did so, and someone got out. Their face and form were hidden by the glare of the vehicle's lights, but eventually they approached and became fully visible.

It was a woman, she stopped for a second or two before continuing the few remaining steps to where Victoria was standing. The woman looked to her left at Amelia lying on the grass verge then back at Victoria.

"Hi, my name is Olivia Cranfield, sorry but what the heck are you two doing out here at this time in the morning?"

"Oh, am I glad to see you, my name is Victoria, and this is my friend Amelia. It's a hell of a story but we were kidnapped by some fucked up psycho calling himself the devil killer. We managed to escape and just ran as far as we could. My friend has hurt her ankle, we need to get her to hospital and phone the police. Have you got a mobile, I need to phone people and tell them that I am safe"

"Well Victoria, seems I wasn't dreaming, you were actually standing in the middle of this old road at four in the mourning. Erm, sorry about the phone, I dropped it in the sheep dip yesterday, it's knackered I am afraid. Look, I am no more than fifteen minutes from home, you can use the house phone, we can call an ambulance and the police and your dad Lee Hunter from there. I have some pain killers and bandages at home, we can make your friend comfortable until they arrive"

"Oh, thank you Olivia, my friend is finished, she can't go another step, you are a life saver. Let's get her in the Land Rover and get to your place as soon as we can"

"Ok, you two girls get into the back, she can lay across the seats, she will be more comfortable that way"

The two women gently pulled Amelia to her feet and slowly made their way to the waiting vehicle. It smelt musty inside, full of strange odours, but they didn't care, they were safe, and their ordeal was over.

The engine throbbed into life, Olivia crunched the gears and they slowly started to move away. There was a slightly disconcerting whine from the old four by four, but it felt warm and safe. Soon they would be at her house and making those all so important phone calls. They bumped along, Olivia steering a steady course around the worst of the crumbling road surface. She didn't speak more than a few words for the whole journey, seemingly preoccupied with driving home safely.

Victoria stroked the head of the now sleeping Amelia, she lay motionless across the back seat. Victoria smiled, soon she would be making those calls and rescue would arrive shortly after.

There was something troubling her though, something Olivia had said. She replayed the conversations over in her mind, but nothing stood out. Why did she feel like this, they had been picked up by a passing stranger who was now taking them back home to phone the authorities. Olivia seemed normal enough, there was nothing threatening about her, nothing to worry about. That feeling persisted though, what was it, something she had said, something that didn't make sense.

Then something else caught her eye. A gently glowing light in the box in front of the gear stick. It had that recognisable tone, a colour and illumination often seen in the dark. Victoria stared intently, it could have been anything electrical, a sat nav, pager even a power pack. She tried to dismiss her suspicions, but it was unavoidable, that faint glow was clearly caused by a mobile phone on standby!

Olivia had definitely said her mobile phone was dead, dropped into a sheep dipping tank yesterday. So why was it here in the Land Rover, perhaps it was someone else's, yes, maybe her partners phone. People leave their phones all over the place and spend the next couple of days looking for them. So, nothing to worry about, it was someone else's and she didn't have the code to open it.

She would wait until they got to Olivia's house then phone her dad, the one and only Lee Hunter. She hoped he wouldn't go on at her for falling for the fake cop thing. No, he would be sympathetic, she couldn't wait to feel his strong arms embrace her, then she would certainly be safe.

It was then, at that precise moment that the thing which had been troubling her hit. It smashed into her mind like and out of control truck. It was that statement by Olivia shortly after she had stopped. She had said, "we can call an ambulance and the police and your dad Lee Hunter from there". Victoria had not said anything about her second name, all she had said was her name was Victoria. How the hell did this woman know her dad was Lee Hunter?

Things started to whirl around in her mind, panic began to rise, the mobile phone in the front of the vehicle, and Olivia knowing her dad's name. Who the hell was she, had they escaped the devil killer only to fall back into is blood-stained grip once again?

Thursday night to Friday morning.
Keeping watch.

Richard, Stephen and I had decided to start with Peter Dexter, it was a long shot, but we needed to start somewhere. They wanted to pull him in, beat the truth out of him and dump him in the canal if he didn't talk. It took me ages to convince them it was the wrong thing to do, even if it might make them happy. It almost certainly wasn't Dexter, I was reasonably sure of that, so all I needed to know was, where Dexter was and what he was doing.

Eventually they agreed to my demands and set out to monitor Dexter over the next few hours. My thinking was, if he was out in the open and doing whatever he normally does, we could eliminate him from the list of possible killers. The devil killer had two women, he would be busy preparing for whatever he had in mind for Friday night, he wouldn't have time to be doing anything else.

I told them to start with his normal haunts, including the Indian restaurant in Buckingham where we had first met. This did the trick, they found him eating and drinking his way through a prodigious meal, several bottles of beer and an ice-cream Sunday to finish. They followed him to his home, and stayed there until 4am, there was no further activity, we decided that Dexter was not our man.

So, who did that leave, and where might that man be hiding? I had by now accepted the idea of Albert Walker being the original killer, and the idea of either Peter Dexter or Paul Willow arranging the murder of Lennard Post's wife. It also seemed possible, even probable that one of them might have started the killings again, in order to implicate Post and get him sent back to jail, but which one.

Well, it wasn't Dexter, he was probably sleeping of a hangover of biblical proportions, killing two innocent women tonight was the furthest thing from his mind, and most likely impossible. So that left Paul Willow, the broken and suicidal lesser partner in the original case. The thing was, why would he want Post back in jail? After all, he was supposed to be dead at the bottom of the English Channel, Post couldn't do him any harm there. Perhaps he just liked killing women, maybe he had got a taste for it after murdering Post's wife. Post being free gave him the opportunity to indulge himself again and blame it all on him, who knows.

The problem I had was his location. Willow had always contacted me and told me where to meet him. I had no idea of where he was hiding and, in all likelihood, I would never find out. I was just about to give up on the idea of ever finding him when the very obvious answer to the problem came to me in one of those blinding flashes.

We had met on both occasions in the park and ride carpark, Winsor. That place must be bristling with CCTV cameras, I had the time and the date when we met, all I had to do was get to those recordings. We could trace Willow's movements, find out where he came from and where he went. It was the only chance I had, it was 5am and Marcus Cooke was about to get an early morning call.

"Lee, what the hell do you want, it's still bloody dark"

"Listen Marcus, I think I have an idea of who the killer is. I need to access the CCTV footage for......"

"Wow, wait a minute Lee, what the hell are you talking about, and as for accessing the CCTV stuff, not a chance there. Just take a breath and slowdown, who is the killer and why the CCTV footage? Just remember that this guy has managed to evade all the cameras in Aylesbury, we have checked and doubled checked, not a thing. Why wouldn't he be as careful in Winsor? You will be wasting your time and the camera operators"

"Marcus, I think the killer is Paul Willow, well at least this time. Originally the killer was Albert Walker, long story but he is no more. It is my assumption that Willow murdered Post's wife and together with Peter Dexter stitched Post up for the killing all those years ago. They also tried to convict him for the devil killings just for good measure. That failed but they are out to get him again, or at least Paul Willow is, and this time he might just succeed. Post knew things about the two of them, criminal activities, including protection rackets. He confronted both of them, so they hatched a plan to lock him up until he dies, that very nearly succeeded"

"Lee, what the hell have you been drinking, or snorting, you are off your head. Peter Dexter is a rampant alcoholic, he has terminal cancer and will in all probability be dead within the next six months, so he won't give a fuck about anything. Even if you are right, I would guess getting rid of Lennard Post for a second time will be the furthest thing from his mind. As for Paul Willow, he is dead, you are burbling on about nothing Lee, it doesn't make any sense"

"I know what it sounds like Marcus but please trust me. My daughter is going to die tonight, I am right about this, I need your help"

There was a long silence before Marcus replied. "Listen Lee, I can't begin to understand how you feel, but we are looking, and we will find her. Going stamping around on some absurd mission isn't going to help. Please go to your wife's place, stay with your family, they need you"

"Listen Marcus, it's not going to take more than a few minutes to check the CCTV footage. I have the precise times, dates and the place where we met. All it needs is a phone call from you and they can review what they have. It's not much to ask, it has to be worth a try"

There was another long silence. "Ok Lee, but when this idea of yours turns out to be nothing at all, will you promise me to go and see your family"

"I will Marcus, I promise and thank you for your help"

I gave him the times and dates of our meetings. I knew it wouldn't take long for the review to take place and the answer to come back. So, I went to the all-night café in Buckingham, ordered a very strong black coffee and waited for Marcus to call. It seemed to take hours, time that I simply didn't have but eventually my phone rang.

"Hi Marcus, what do you have for me?"

"Ok, they reviewed the camera footage and came back to me with the following information. Your car was indeed spotted in the carpark at both times and dates. The vehicle was approached by a man wearing a grey overcoat but otherwise looking scruffy. It seems that he entered your car and was seen talking to you about things they could not identify.

He was seen leaving your car and walking from the carpark, down the side street toward the old town cinema. It wasn't clear where he went from there but a man matching his description was seen getting into an old Land Rover Defender. There was an unidentified woman driving the vehicle, they drove from the town centre and away from the CCTV coverage. It wasn't possible to get the number plate of the vehicle, so we can't identify to whom and where it is registered. I don't suppose that is of much help Lee, but it's the best we can do"

The deluge of information washed over me. A Land Rover Defender, a woman driving, it seemed to evoke some memory, but I couldn't pin down what exactly it meant. There was something in my memory, I had seen that vehicle somewhere, but where?

"Listen Marcus, all this seems to ring a bell. I know this vehicle and a woman driving, I have seen it somewhere locally. Is there any chance you could run a search for this type of vehicle?"

"Lee, with all due respect, this is a very rural area, not central London. There are hundreds of old Land Rovers around here, maybe even thousands, most of the people living in these parts will have owned such a thing at one point in their lives. In any case, what would that prove, some old tramp got out of your car and got into a Land

Rover, so what, it's hardly a crime. I would suggest you have a think, maybe drive around and see what you find. If it helps you can ring me, and we can discuss any further moves.

Lee, you have to listen to me. If you think you have found something, don't go storming into somewhere just because you think it's where your daughter is. You're just as likely to end up arrested, that's not going to help anyone, let alone your wife and daughter at home.

Even if you think you know where Victoria is, goodness knows what will happen to her and you if you confront this psycho. Just take a breath, a very deep breath and pick up the phone, ring 999 and wait, do you understand me?"

I assured Marcus that I wouldn't do anything rash. The trouble was, I wasn't sure what I would do if I thought my daughter was close by. I needed to go for a drive, get out of the café and the people coming and going. He was right, maybe I would come across the vehicle, things would come back to me. All I needed to do was call him and the cavalry would turn up.

There was a problem with that though, that was the slow rusty wheels of the law. If I rang Marcus, and said I think my daughter is in a house, because a Land Rover Defender is parked outside, can you imagine what he would do. He might send a uniformed officer over, who might or might not be allowed into the house. Even if my daughter was there, they might be holding her somewhere nearby. Without some sort of surveillance operation, there would be no guarantee of ever finding out, no assurance of ever finding her in time.

I felt suffocated, time was slipping by, and I couldn't seem to get any further. I felt crushed, pains in my chest, pounding drums in my ears. My daughter was going to be murdered and very soon, I couldn't think of what to do next, I had run out of ideas.

Friday mid-morning.
A dark place.

The man held the shotgun right at her stomach, if she moved in the wrong direction or tried to run, he was sure to pull the trigger. There was no noise at all, apart from her feet on the gravel driveway, it seemed as if the whole world was holding its breath, waiting to see what happened next.

He was limping somewhat, and had a bloodstained bandage wrapped around the top of his forehead. His right eye was partly closed, and his breathing seemed laboured. She on the other hand seemed bright and cheerful, happy at her success at capturing the two women, she was almost overwhelmed with excitement.

"Remember your promise, you said I could watch as you tortured these two tonight, you promised"

"I did Olivia and don't worry, I am a man of my word. You can do all the filming; I want to record every moment of their pain and terror. They have caused us a great deal of trouble so they will pay for that, and you will have a seat on the front row"

She laughed, bouncing down what remained of the driveway like a young girl on her birthday. She ran the last few yards and opened the door to the cellar; she led the way into the corridor and back to their prison cell.

"Come on you two, the devil killer wants you under lock and key. There will be no escape this time, only death"

She laughed as first Victoria and the slow-moving Amelia moved inside. The damp and darkness enveloped them once again, that familiar tang of dank and fear. The woman was right, their hands were cable tied behind their backs, there would be no second chance, this was the end for both of them.

"I will be back later, you will be tortured to death, I will drink your blood and eat your flesh as you watch. My lover Olivia will film everything, and we will broadcast it to the world. Your end will be celebrated, your fear plane to see, what a show we will put on together. Just try to relax and meet your end with dignity. Yes, it will take hours to die, yes, the pain will be unbearable, but it will be glorious"

The door slammed shut, leaving the two women alone with their fears. Rescue seemed impossible, freedom a distant dream. Amelia began to cry uncontrollably, collapsing to the ground as she did so. Victoria tried to stay strong and calm, but it seemed useless, they had tried their best and failed. The darkness eventually swallowed them up, the crying stopped, and the two women faded away.

"I am glad you managed to find those two Olivia; my plans would have meant nothing without them. You are very special to me, please promise that you will never leave me. Ever since those days when we last obeyed our true master's commands, I have grown ever fonder of you. Together we will spread fear over the whole world, they will grow to know us and our master, bow down to us. You will become my goddess, the rock from where we will draw our power. We are awakened once more; our twenty-year sleep is over.

Our glorious lord has commanded that we start his life's work once more. This time it will be without the assistance of Albert Walker, Killed on the A34 all those years ago. Albert Walker was a loyal and great servant to our master. He abducted many victims for our master so he could carry out his work. Some of those victims were never known by the police, but Albert's time is now passed, it is up to us to obey our master's commands. Our master has commanded me to carry on his good work, start again, begin the killings once more. I have obeyed Olivia and so did you, filling the place of Albert, and doing so with great courage. We will bring forth terror and pain, drink the blood and eat the flesh. Just before our victims die, we will wrap their throats in the red silk scarf so beloved by our lord and master.

He commanded us to pause, disappear from view and wait his release from the bonds imposed upon him. It was difficult, but we had to be patient Olivia. Now he is free, discharged from prison and about to continue his work.

He murdered his wife, so much blood, inconceivable agony, it was wonderful to watch, absolute rage, I have never seen anything like it Olivia. He extinguished her life, but it was clumsy, and he paid a heavy price, even though I tried to cover it up, but that meddling Peter Dexter just wouldn't leave it alone. He tried to stop me Olivia, tried to diminish the work of our master.

That is all behind us now, and tonight our master will join us here and the real killer will live again, bathed in blood, expert in his work. It won't be me doing the killing Olivia, but Lennard Post, or as some heathens have come to know him, the Devil Killer"

Olivia screeched with excitement, "I gave myself to Lennard so many years ago Paul, we were teenagers then and I was ready to follow his every word. We tried many times to conceive a child, a strong son to carry on the good work of the devil killer. It wasn't meant to be, no child was made. We went our separate ways, but I never lost my love for him or my willingness to do whatever he commanded. We now have Lennard back after so many years, and we can start again"

"After he split with you Olivia, he married another woman, and tried to conceive a son by her, but again nothing was made. It was decided that Lennard's wife would become his victim. A trial of her faith and courage. I was there when he took her life, unlike me, she was totally unaware of the real Lennard, unknowing of her only task in life, to breed another devil killer. She died screaming, it was glorious, Lennard was exalted, he became delirious with the exhilaration of his work. He made mistakes, left evidence and was caught by that bumbling alcoholic detective Peter Dexter"

"He is free now Paul and we will continue; this night will be glorious. We have killed two already, they were just practice, to ensure our skills are honed to perfection. Tonight, Lennard Post, Paul Willow and Olivia Cranfield will kill, and the world will know fear once again"

"Indeed Olivia, if only I had succeeded in persuading Dexter that Lennard was not the killer of his wife, we wouldn't have needed to wait for so many years. Dexter was determined though, he wanted Lennard in jail. Lennard had intervened in a dispute over protection money, accusing Dexter of extorting money from his father.

An argument broke out between myself and Dexter, he couldn't understand why I was sticking up for Lennard. He of course was unaware of my connections to Albert Walker and Lennard, and the murders I had assisted them with.

We never mended that rift and soon I found myself out of the police force, thanks to the lies of Peter Dexter. I faked my suicide and obeyed the command of my master to disappear and wait for his release. Now our time has come Olivia, the long wait is over.

Soon Lennard will join us, the stories of his innocence that he proliferated have confounded so many people that they now believe every word he utters. They think he is innocent and wrongly imprisoned, what fools they are. He is certainly his father's son, cunning, cruel and ruthless"

"I can't wait to meet him once again Paul, it's been so many years since he last held me in his arms. Perhaps this time I can assist in the pain and bloodshed of all his sacrifices"

"I am sure he will call upon you Olivia, have patients my love"

Friday afternoon.
A blinding flash.

It's strange how things arrive in your consciousness like a flare. Sometimes it's the realisation of something, other times it's a memory. That's why I go for a drive if I am trying to recall things, the act of trying to stay alive on the roads of Britain allows my mind to relax, in an odd sort of way. It's normally then that the bit of information I am trying to recall comes back to me.

Anyway, I was driving back from Aylesbury to the Travel lodge on the outskirts of Buckingham when that flash went off in my mind. To be honest I nearly crashed as the recollection came back to me. It was that Land Rover Defender and where I had seen it before. It was in Steeple Claydon at the home of Olivia Cranfield, it was her old pride and joy, her personal project, a present from her father.

Now, Marcus Cooke was right of course, those old things are two a penny in these parts, but this was more than just a coincidence. I glanced over at the clock in my car, it was almost five pm, time was running out, as was the life of my daughter. I had to do something, and I had to do it now, but what? I could call Marcus, that was the right thing to do, he could send someone out to Olivia's place. That might take an hour or even longer, it's

Friday evening and the police would already be busy.

The trouble was, the right thing to do is not always the best thing to do. My only priority was to get to Victoria and bring her to safety. Of course, that might have nothing to do with Olivia Cranfield, in fact it almost certainly didn't. Thing was, it was all I had and those hackles on the back of my neck were itching, that usually meant I was on the right track.

Right, but I had a problem. Olivia Cranfield was not the devil killer, that was for certain. So, if she wasn't, he must be in there with her, I would have to get past at least two people at the same time, never a good idea. Ok, I had to get help and get it quick, but from where and who?

I decided to call my new friends, the two brothers, Richard and Stephen. At least they wouldn't be weighed down by the need for search warrants, permits and court orders. The trouble was, they wouldn't be weighed down by any rules at all, legal or moral. I had dealt with people like this before, and indeed Tony Bianchi was one such person. Controlling people like that was difficult, death, violence and criminality were their stocking trade and their pleasure.

I would ask them to wait outside, they would be my minders. I would call for their services if required, and only if! So, make the call, get them over here as soon as possible and go and knock on Olivia Cranfield's door. Good plan Lee, let's get it under way.

I reached for my phone a scrolled down to the number given to me for the two brothers. It wasn't long before someone answered. I kind of dreaded the reply, if they said they were on their way, then fire and brimstone could break out. On the other hand, if they didn't come, I had no one else to turn to.

"Hi mister Hunter, how can I help"

"Hi Richard, I need you two over in Steeple Claydon and quick. I think I know where my daughter is, and I need some help. Time is short and we need to get to her, I can't do this by myself"

"Ok mister Hunter, we will be with you within the hour, give me the address and sit tight"

The phone clicked, had I just done something I would later come to regret? There was every possibility should these two guys start World War three, then Marcus would not hesitate in prosecuting me.

I took a deep breath and drove over to the old Victorian home of Olivia Cranfield. I parked the car under an old oak tree some distance from the property and waited. All seemed quiet for a Friday evening, it was exactly six pm and all I had to do was wait. The sun had started its slow descent towards the western horizon, insects and birds were making their last search for food before dark.

I sat there, perhaps in a few minutes I would be re united with Victoria, holding her, reassuring her that this was all over. I felt a primary anger towards this psycho, taking women's lives for no other reason than to fuel his own sick fantasies. How many lives had he destroyed, how many mothers and fathers and perhaps even children were now grief-stricken because of him.

I had an overwhelming need to feel his throat between my hands, watch his face turn blue, his eyes bulge and redden. I could hear his rasping words, begging me to let go, giving him back his life. Perhaps it wasn't going to be the two brothers that started the violence and vengeance, maybe it would be me.

I wash shaken from my thoughts as a car passed by, it was the bright red E200 AMG Mercedes Benz. Now I do remember where I had seen this very expensive motor before, it was outside Olivia Cranfield's house. I was unable to identify the driver as the sun blinded me as he exited the vehicle, but this time the sun was behind me, and identifying him would not be an issue. I started my car, engaged first gear and slowly moved forward. I stopped just close enough to see the house, but not near enough to spark any suspicions from the occupants.

I hunkered down as low as I could. The Mercedes Benz slowly pulled up in front of the garage to the side of the Cranfield home. The perfect red paintwork shone in the late afternoon sun, whoever owned this motor certainly had a significantly large bank account.

"Come on, get out of the bloody car, let's see your face. Whoever you are will certainly answer a lot of questions. Are you Peter Dexter, not likely, or perhaps Paul Willow, I doubt it. Maybe you are someone I have never met, a stranger from the darkness, an unknown name"

Eventually the car door opened, this was it, this person was entering the place where I was certain my daughter was being held. This man was, in all likelihood the devil killer or at least and accomplice. I blinked my eyes clear, I reached for my phone and quickly selected 'camera'. If I needed any proof, my trusty Apple iPhone would help me to provide it.

The door swung open, and a man got out. Annoyingly he was facing the wrong way, but he would have to turn at some point in order to walk towards the front door. I turned the camera on and pointed it in his direction, selecting maximum zoom as I did so.

Eventually he turned and his identity became clear, it was unmistakeable, and he was someone I had certainly met before. The man now walking towards the house was the one and only Lennard Post. I shook my head, this couldn't be right, I had discounted him, the devil killer was not Post. How the hell had he managed to deceive me, even Paul Willow had said he was not responsible for the murders. Peter Dexter had been in no doubt, maybe he was the only man who had correctly worked all this out.

I didn't notice dropping my phone, the shock of this was too much for me to comprehend. I had been a very experienced and senior cop, and now a private detective, seemingly I knew nothing at all. Lennard Post had consumed me for breakfast, deceived me every step of the way, and apparently others as well.

It was then that other possibilities began to whirl around in my traumatised mind. Had I been taken for a bloody fool by not just Post but others as well. Was it possible that I had been blinded by a much larger picture and more than one person laying smoke screens. Sometimes it's easy to get lost in a case, chasing one subject when in truth there are several. It's not uncommon, especially if the subject you have in your sites seems to be the wrongdoer. Maybe this deception went further than just little old me. Perhaps Lennard Post had taken in the police and goodness knows who else. There had to be others, but who?

Well, Olivia Cranfield for one, it was her house, she was the ex-girlfriend of Post, conceivably their relationship had been more persistent than she had let on. Perhaps she had been covering for him, possibly offering him a home upon release. I had to open my mind, discount no one, anyone could be involved in this. Why had Paul Willow met me, he had been so insistent that Dexter was the main man. I was certain that Dexter was no more than a pisshead ex-cop now months from death. He had nothing more sinister to do with the case, other than being the lead detective twenty years ago. Paul Willow had also been seen getting into Olivia Cranfield's old land Rover, or at least a vehicle matching its description.

It all seemed to come together in some sort of logical story. Lennard Post was the real devil killer, Olivia Cranfield had been more than his ex-girlfriend. She had been his accomplice all those years ago and was now assisting him again.

What of Paul Willow, was he part of all this, or had he just been a mentally ill man casting so many aspersions that no one knew the real truth, including himself? There was no doubt he had been psychologically broken by Dexter, maybe he was just a damaged person searching for some sort of revenge.

It wouldn't have been difficult to add to the already confused picture. Post always protested his innocence, Dexter had been implicated in the murders, Willow had committed suicide and then re appeared. It was like trying to put a jigsaw together when missing the picture from the top of the box and half the pieces.

I had to go with what I saw, otherwise I would become as confused as Willow. I had to assume Lennard Post was the real devil killer, originally assisted by Albert Walker. Now Olivia Cranfield was his assistant, ready to help in his murderous spree. What the hell Paul Willow had to do with all of this, who knows. In that house was my daughter, another woman, Lennard Post and Olivia Cranfield.

Richard and Stephen were on their way and as soon as they arrived, we were going in, no matter what anyone had to say. This was it, if I was wrong, I would get arrested, if I was right, I would get my daughter back.

Olivia opened the front door, she checked left and right to see no one was watching. She smiled as Lennard Post leant forward and gently kissed her.

"Well tonight is the night darling, I can't wait, let's begin the preparations, is Paul here, he is very important to our work"

"He is Lennard, come in I will make us all a drink, I am so excited"

He entered, she closed the door behind them and followed Post into the kitchen. Sitting at the oak table was Paul Willow, he looked up and smiled.

"Paul, what the hell has happened to you?"

"Those two bitches jumped me and tried to escape. We got them back though, I mean to make their lives hell tonight, if you will permit me Lennard"

"Paul, you can indulge yourself as much as you like, so long as you don't kill them, I want to do that, tighten the red scarfs around their necks. How about using the hot irons on their skin, we can heat them with the gas torch, you will enjoy that"

"Thank you Lennard, I will go downstairs and get the irons, that will be great fun"

He quickly disappeared, heading down towards the cellar with a huge grin on his face.

"What time are you planning to start Lennard?"

"Immediately, have you got the cameras sorted?"

"Yes, it's all set up in the room next to where we are holding the two women. The table with the chains to hold them are there, I have the cameras and lights hooked up and all your torture equipment ready. We can make a start whenever you like"

"Right, well I am bloody starving so let's eat first. There is no point in starting something when you are hungry, you lack endurance. We need to make this last as long as we can. People will be watching; we need to look professional and put on a good show"

They both laughed, their lives had been building up to this and they were intent on enjoying every moment.

The Raid.

Seconds felt like hours as I waited for the two brothers to arrive. Every time I checked my watch it seemed to have stopped, it hadn't of course, I was just desperate to see them arrive.

The evening had turned into a sunny spectacular, faultless blue sky and a balmy breeze. It seems crazy that only yards away from this summer perfection were two killers and two victims, one of which was my daughter. I had to keep a grip on the steering wheel of the car in order to prevent me from tearing across the road and kicking in the front door of the house. The realism was, if I tried that they would either overpower me or simply run for the hills. They were cornered, they just didn't know it yet. I knew where they were, and once Richard and Stephen rocked up, their fate would be sealed.

I didn't notice the arrival of the brothers, it seemed they had parked their car around the corner. Simple thing to do I guess, but parking up behind me would have only drawn unnecessary attention to our gathering. Stephen gently opened the rear door of the car and the two men slid quietly inside.

Richard leant forward slightly and whispered in a very calm and controlled manner.

"Mister Hunter, what's occurring, I guess you think your daughter is somewhere nearby"

"She is Richard, that Victorian villa across the road. It is my assumption that she and another female are being held inside. I am also confident that a female, namely Olivia Cranfield is also inside, she is one of the kidnappers. Her former and possible current partner, Lennard Post has turned up. They are planning to kill the two prisoners tonight and broadcast their crimes on the internet"

Stephen was the next to speak, "How certain are you mister Hunter, for instance, that there are only two perpetrators in there and not ten?"

"I have been watching for some time now, there are only two in there, no need to worry about anymore. Also, that red E200 AMG Mercedes Benz parked in front of the garage. That belongs to Post, he arrived not more than forty minutes ago, no one else has arrived"

"So, what's the plan mister Hunter?"

"Well Richard, let's keep it as simple as possible. Stephen goes around the back, you and I go to the front door and basically kick the thing in. Once you hear that Stephen, you do the same at the rear and we storm in as well. We disable anyone we come up against and go and find the two girls"

"I like simple mister Hunter, but in my experience, simple is never quite as easy as it first seems. For example, what if we can't kick the front door in, what happens if they see us coming and arm themselves?"

"Yep, I get that Richard, but I don't see any other way. The police won't come to help, not until there is something of note happening. If we can't get that door open, it will at least make Post and Cranfield sit up, and keep them away from their victims. It won't matter if they arm themselves if we can't get in, but it will keep them occupied. One of us can then phone the cops, they will have to turn up and we can take it from there. I doubt if Post and Cranfield will want to fight us and Thames Valley Police's finest all at the same time"

"Ok, let's do it, no use in waiting, Steve, you get the back door, we will go to the front. When we get inside find these two and let the fuckers have it, no mercy, clear?"

"Yep Rich, let's go"

It felt somewhat surreal, like something out of Butch Cassidy and the Sun Dance Kid, just before they made that fatal dash into the open. I had taken part in numerous dawn raids before, but they were with loads of armed cops, and most importantly of all, a bloody search warrant!

Anyway, the details didn't really matter to me. My daughter was in there and I didn't care about anything else, other than getting her out. We were moments away from pulling her from the grip of a psychopathic nut job, who should never have been released from jail.

It was one of those slow-motion moments, we exited the car and began to run across the road. Stephen disappeared somewhere to my left and I followed Richard up the main path to the front door. He didn't slow at all, once in range he jumped into the air and levelled a huge kick at the front door. The whole frame and door shook with the impact, it shuddered, the noise was immense. Splintered wood, dust and bits of cement flew in all directions, but the door held fast.

I just kept going, passing Richard as he rebounded backwards down the path. I followed his example and threw everything I had into a shoulder charge. I knew it was going to hurt, but I had no choice. I hit the solid door with everything I had, but again with little or no apparent effect. As I spun to one side, with burning agony raging in my right shoulder, something, or someone flashed past. It was Richard mounting a second charge at the seemingly impenetrable old door.

This time there was success. The central panel exploded into a million shards of coloured glass, spinning in all directions. More wood splinters, two of which hit me square in the face. Next came a wave of grey dust, it temporarily blinded me, but soon cleared. I flicked the dust and wood splinters from my face and looked down at the wreckage of the door.

"Right mister Hunter, let's go, Steve will be doing the same to the back door, we need to get busy"

I didn't ask any questions, I simply folded in behind and charged into the house. I could hear banging from the rear. It was Stephen no doubt, and then there was another almighty crash as the back door gave way. There was a staircase to my right, leading up to the next floor. For a split second I considered running up it, but logic told me that in all probability, my daughter would be either on the ground floor or more likely, in a cellar.

Richard disappeared into a side room, I took the next one, but no one was here. Everything seemed strangely normal, here we were entering someone's home, but the room was like any other place, neat, tidy and seemingly oblivious to the invasion. As I left and made my way back into the hall, I caught site of Stephen coming from the kitchen at the rear of the property.

"Nothing at the back mister Hunter, how about the front?"

"Nothing, they must be below us, there must be a door somewhere leading down to the cellar, we need to find it"

"It's here guys, to the side of the stairs"

I looked behind me, Richard was opening a painted white panelled door leading underneath the staircase.

"Come on, they must be down here"

He didn't wait for a reply, he disappeared, I turned and ran to the open door, I could here Stephen running behind me. On the other side of the door was another staircase leading down into a well-lit but damp smelling cellar. At the bottom I could see a corridor leading towards the rear of the property. Stumbling a couple of times, I made my way to the floor below.

Richard ran off in front of me, there were several rooms leading off to both sides of the corridor. He was busily moving into each one, emerging a few seconds later. At the end of the corridor there was an old door, as soon as I sore it my heart sank. It was a possible escape route, had they taken it, were they now outside?

"Mister Hunter, in here, it's a studio, camera and lights, this is where they were going to kill the women"

Next came a scream, off to my left, Stephen pushed passed me and ran towards the sound. There was another scream, this time louder, that was followed by a woman's voice.

"In here, I am in here"

Stephen rushed in, "she's here mister Hunter"

I rushed to the room into which Stephen had disappeared, inside was a young woman, tied to a chair. She was shaking uncontrollably, tears streaking down her dirty cheeks. For the second time in as many minutes my heart sank. This wasn't Victoria, it wasn't my daughter.

Richard burst in, "ok mister Hunter, there is no one else here, she is the only one. Is this your daughter mister Hunter, is this Victoria?"

I couldn't seem to find the words, I just stared at the young woman. I guess Richard realised the truth and took control of the situation.

"Steve, you stay here and see to her, call the police and an ambulance. We are going after those two twats, don't know when we will get back so sit tight"

"Right Lee, let's get outside, they must have left by that door at the end of the corridor. Listen darlin, Steve will look after you, you are safe now, don't panic, he will sort you out"

Without saying another word, he turned and left. I looked back at the young woman, gave her some fairly pointless comforting smile and followed Richard out of the room. We sprinted towards the door, out there somewhere was my daughter, Lennard Post and Olivia Cranfield. We had to find them and find them very quickly.

Richard reached the door a split second in front of me. He turned the handle and pulled the door towards him, just as I arrived. We both forced our way through the opening and into the daylight at the same time. I wasn't aware of anyone standing outside or where the blow came from, but the first thing I remember was hitting the ground in front of me.

The world seemed to rotate for a while, the feelings of nausea welled up inside me. Then the pain began, slowly at first but then bursting like a huge firework display, screaming and whistling in my ears. The taste of blood pervaded in my mouth, I spat out the offending taste onto the ground. It didn't take long before I came to the realisation that we had been attacked. Someone had been standing outside, perhaps to one side of the door, waiting for us to emerge.

As my vision started to clear, I could see movement in front of me, there were sounds as well. It was blurred but it began to make sense, two people were fighting, there was shouting, and the sound of punches being thrown. I felt the sting of dust in my eyes, I blinked them clear, my head throbbing as I did so.

Next came another impact, this time as the two men fell on top of me, forcing the air from my lungs. I pushed back with all my strength, forcing the two combatants away to my left. Still shaken by the whole turn of events, I forced myself to my feet and tried to clear my head. In front of me was

Richard sitting on top of another man, raining punches down onto him. Through the haze of my stunned mind the man looked very familiar. Quite tall, a scruffy appearance and wearing an old raincoat.

I shook what was left of the mist of confusion from my brain and immediately recognised who he was. It was none other than Paul Willow, one of the main players in the original case. I drew a deep breath and shouted at Richard to stop. Whilst I wasn't averse in seeing Willow pummelled to death, I needed to speak to him first.

With surprising quickness Richard ceased his attack. He turned to look at me, with a puzzled look on his face.

"What's up mister Hunter?"

"I need to speak to him before you end his life"

He looked back at Willow, blooded and moaning as he lay beneath his assailant.

"You need to be quick, we have to be off mister Hunter, try and find the others and your daughter"

Those words, 'find your daughter' brought me back to reality with a sharp snap. I looked down at Willow, he turned his head away from me, it took all my willpower not to walk over and kick him.

"I will be back for you Paul Willow and don't doubt it. All those lies you spun, all that pain and terror you caused to others. You are the worst of all, an ex-cop, sworn to uphold the law and to protect. You spat on that promise Willow, you let everyone down who depended on you. I will get to the bottom of all your ill deeds, I will use my last breath to ensure the law punishes you and you pay the price for your crimes"

I looked back at Richard, he had a large gash above his right eye, the blood dripping down onto Willow. He turned, looked down and levelled three more prodigious blows on Willows face. I smiled as I heard the crunching of his skull and felt perversely pleased at the pain he was suffering.

"Right mister Hunter, we need to go, Steve will make sure this piece of shit goes nowhere at all"

I looked all about, there was no sign of anyone else, not even in the fields beyond the house. I stood there, it seemed strangely quiet, had they got away, was my daughter gone for good?

"The car Richard, we need to get to the car"

"Car mister Hunter?"

"Yes, that Red Mercedes Benz parked at the front of the garage, at the top of the drive. That's Lennard Post's car, find that and we find my daughter"

He didn't need to be asked again, he turned and sprinted to the front of the house, I followed best I could even with my knackered knee.

We sped past the side of the house; we certainly couldn't have gone any faster. I rounded the corner, crossed the lawn and turned to look at the garage. It was then that I realised the car was no longer there, they had escaped. My anger flared, all I wanted to do was go back into the house and beat Paul Willow to death. I wanted to explode on him, kick and punch him, use any instrument at hand to disfigure and finally kill him.

I opened my mouth and screamed, the fury and rage enveloped me like some violent whirlwind. I was out of control, way past the red mist stage, I needed revenge, I wanted to kill, and Willow was my only target.

As I turned to run back towards the rear of the property, I felt a strong grip encircle my right arm. It was vice like, powerful and I sensed would not be shaken loose. I pulled at the tether holding me back, but with no success at all. Turning I caught sight of Richard's face, it looked calm and in control.

"Listen mister Hunter, I know how you feel, and I am certain of what you want to do. It won't help though; we need to get out there and find that car"

His controlled manner and calming words quickly cooled at least the extremes of my rage. I pulled one more time but there was no way he was going to let go.

"Come on mister Hunter, let's get to my motor, I know the roads around here, he can't have gone far. The road to Bicester is closed for bridge works, there is no way he has gone to Buckingham, too much traffic and controls, especially at this time of night. The only way he's gone is the main road to Aylesbury. If we are quick, we can catch him before he gets there. He won't be looking for my car, all we need to do is follow him and wait until he stops. There are a million sets of traffic lights on that road, all we need is patients"

It made sense of course, and I was glad of his help, but that rising tide of panic was beginning to overwhelm me. My daughter was in his evil grip, and I couldn't help her. All he needed to do was find a quiet lane, a lay-by somewhere where he couldn't be seen, and that would be it.

"Right Richard, let's go, I have a bad feeling about all of this, I sense that we are already too late"

A red E200 AMG Mercedes Benz.

The car lurched from left to right as it sped through the country lanes. Victoria was bound and blindfolded in the rea of the car. She could feel someone sitting next to her, and judging by the smell of perfume, it was most probably female. The vehicle engine roared, she could sense the speed increasing and then decreasing, any moment now she was certain they would crash.

"Just stop and let me go, my father will be here soon, and he will most certainly catch you. Just stop and throw me out of the car, I won't say a word about you, I have not seen your faces"

There was no reply, just the howl of the car engine and the occasional screeching of the tyres. Soon the swaying from side to side stopped as the car accelerated and seemed to maintain a steady course. Victoria assumed they were on a straight road, perhaps the main road to a large town or city. She heard a couple of sirens race past going in the other direction. Maybe they were an ambulance and police car speeding to an incident somewhere nearby.

The woman sitting next to her pushed closer, pinning her against the door, Victoria could feel the woman take hold of her arm.

"Keep quiet you slut, it's going to be over for you very soon, and you will be glad when it is. Your father will never rescue you, there's no fucking chance of that, he is useless, just a washed-up ex-cop, so just sit back and shut up"

"I won't shut up, just let me go……."

Victoria didn't get the chance to continue, a sickening blow smashed into the back of her head. It made her feel dizzy, sick to the stomach. She gasped, pushed herself forward in an attempt to get away from any further blows that might land.

"I told you bitch, shut up. It's way too late, you will be dead very soon and no one is coming to help you, no one, so get used to it!"

A man's voice then piped up, "listen, there is a lane about a mile in front of us, it's on the left. We can turn down there, a couple of miles further on there is an old abandoned church. No one is allowed near it, it's full of asbestos and it was built over an old flint mine. Any minute now it's going to disappear into a big black hole. But not yet, it's going to be safe enough for us, great for what we have to do. We can park around the side, drag her inside and do the bitch. You can record it on your phone, we can then upload it onto the internet. I have some tools in the back of the car, a wrench, an axe, we can use them, it won't be quick for her but who the hell cares"

"Great idea Lennard, do it, I am not fucking bothered about her suffering, the longer it takes the better, so long as I can do what you said I could. I can't wait to hear her scream, see the blood all over the floor, just like when you killed your wife, that must have been fun. Not as much fun as those three women you killed all those years ago, I really enjoyed Paul Willows description of their deaths. The level of excitement was wonderful, it got better every time he recalled the events"

"Ok, well keep her quiet, we will be at the turn in a couple of minutes, it's not far from there"

Those words made Victoria's blood run cold, she shivered with terror. Perhaps no one was coming, maybe there would be no rescue, but one thing was for sure, soon she would be dead. The car continued for a short while before Victoria began to feel it decelerate. The indicators started to click and then there was a left-hand turn. Next, they would arrive at the old church.

They were only minutes away now, minute's from feeling the cold steel of that axe, the sickening, bone splintering blows of the wrench and the warm flow of her blood onto the floor. She would die alone, accompanied by strangers laughing at her misery, recording the whole scene for others to watch as she begged for her life.

She pulled again at the cable ties, but there was no give in their soulless plastic grip. They just bit further into her flesh, but the pain didn't mean a thing, she had to escape. Panic began to overwhelm her, her breath and pulse raced, her mind screamed, the pressure in her head was almost unbearable. She was out of control and racing towards her demise and there was nothing she could do about it.

Then she felt it, the car began to slow once again, this was it, the old abandoned church. This is where her life would end, and there was no one here to help, no knight in shining armour, no father to pull her from the grip of these sick lunatics. She opened her mouth to scream but nothing came forth, no sound, no hope and no more tomorrows.

The Chase.

We rounded the corner and parked just a few feet away was Richard's stunning, electric blue BMW 8 series coupe. It was £82,000 worth of power and luxury, whatever happened next was going to occur quickly with it's 530 horsepower engine.

We slid inside the car and exploded out of the village at a rate of knots I had never experienced before. It felt like we would take off at any moment, thrust into the sky by the rapid acceleration. Only moments passed before we reached the back road that would lead us towards the main route to Aylesbury.

"What if they haven't gone to Aylesbury Richard, what if they did go to Buckingham?"

"Trust me mister Hunter, they will have gone to Aylesbury. In any case, we can't go in more than one direction, so we have to make a choice. Put it this way, if I were Post and his girlfriend, I would go to Aylesbury, ro doubt about it. It's a large city. I could easily lose myself there, you would never find me, not a chance"

I was somewhat comforted to know that Richard was certain about Post's movements. My daughter's life was about to end, if he had gone in another direction, I would never see her alive again.

Soon we joined the main road and the car accelerated to unimaginable speed. We seemed to flash past everyone with consummate ease, nothing would be able to keep up with us, not even the fastest police car. I had to speak, the feeling of impending doom began to invade my mind. If we crashed now there would be nothing to drag from whatever wreckage remained.

"Why have they gone to Aylesbury Richard, it's a major city, they wouldn't get the privacy they need to carry out their murderous fantasies. Why not just find an old cottage somewhere or an abandoned farm building? They need to take their time recording what they do, they need to be away from everyone, away from prying eyes or nosy neighbours"

This seemed to catch Richard's attention, I could see his mind turning over, I just hoped it wouldn't distract him from his driving.

"You are right mister Hunter, but where the hell would they go? This is a very expensive part of the world, not far from London and the main motorways and international airports. Nothing is abandoned around here, it's all too valuable to leave it like that. Everything is used, farmhouses are renovated, cottages re vamped, old pubs converted into modern places to live. Trust me, there is nothing out here, nothing at all. If it's possible to rebuild, renovate or convert it, someone has already done so.

Maybe they have a safe house in the main town, somewhere they can go, secure and out of the way. They might have an old industrial building, plenty of them in the city, nice thick walls, if that's the case, I know where they might be"

"Right, well let's get there, and make it quick"

"Don't worry mister Hunter, I know exactly where they are, and it's right in the centre of Aylesbury"

It didn't seem possible, but Richards BMW 8 series coupe accelerated. Everything seemed to disappear into a blur. I wanted to look over to the speedometer, but I was terrified at what I might see. I took a deep breath and hoped he was right, and we would find Victoria in that industrial unit in town and most importantly, find her before it was too late.

We raced towards Aylesbury, not caring about any speed limits or other road users, going around roundabouts in the wrong direction, speeding through red lights. In just a few more minutes we would arrive in the city and save my daughter from her killers. There was something wrong though, I could tell Richard had something on his mind. The speed of the car dropped; a frown pasted across his face.

"Richard, what is it?"

"I know I said there is nothing abandoned out here, but I do know of somewhere mister Hunter. It's a place where no one would interrupt them, it's a risk, but we need to check it out"

"Yes, but didn't you say it will be in the industrial estate in Aylesbury"

"I did mister Hunter, but there is somewhere, an old building out here in the countryside. I know what I said, but there is one. We used to call business meetings there, check in deliveries from abroad, unload lorries in the night, it's miles away from anyone, no one would ever know you were there. We don't use it anymore, it's too dangerous to be inside the old place. I can't stop thinking about it. I know it's going to take time mister Hunter, but I think it's worth having a look, we can quickly ascertain if anyone is about, it won't take a few more minutes"

The Abandoned Chapel.

They pulled up outside the old building. It was evident that time and nature had taken their toll on the place. A dilapidated sign hung above the main door, mostly obliterated with age, but the words 'Methodist Chapel' could still be seen.

The roof sagged alarmingly in the middle, and all of the windows had been smashed. Several large cracks made their way up and down the plastered walls, like dirty fingers enveloping the whole building. It was clear to any onlooker that the structure was close to failure. Today however it was still standing and made an ideal hideout to anyone not wishing to be found.

"Right Olivia, get her out of the car. Use the back door to the chapel, it's always open. Keep her tied up and get inside quickly. I will bring the wrench and the axe, we will do her quickly, get the video out there for everyone to see"

Olivia Cranfield didn't need to be asked a second time. She opened the rear door to the car and dragged Victoria out and across the overgrown car park. The rear door to the building was broken and jammed closed but a swift kick opened it with ease.

Inside smelt of damp and decay, cobwebs abounded, rot and damp proliferated. There were several old pews to the right-hand side and a smashed pulpit lay in pieces, like the rotten stump of a long dead tree. The rest of the floor was empty of everything except shards of glass from the broken windows. The glass crunched underfoot as she dragged Victoria inside.

"Right bitch, lay down here and don't move, right!"

Victoria Hunter obeyed, any thoughts of resistance had long since disappeared. Terror and disorientation had clouded her mind, turning her into a zombie like empty shell.

Olivia Cranfield levelled a kick into her ribs, causing Victoria to shout out aloud in pain. She curled up into a tight ball, trying to turn away from the assault and the agony.

"Like I said, don't move or there will be plenty more where that came from"

The rear door sprung open once again, this time Lennard Post strolled confidently inside. He had a huge smile on his face, and in his hands, he carried a rusty old wrench and a small axe. He walked over to where Victoria was laying, looking down at her he laughed.

"I wonder what her big shot father is going to make of our little movie. That stupid twat couldn't tell a lie from the truth if his life depended on it. How the hell he ever got to be a senior cop defies belief, his brains must be full of shit I swear.

Anyway, we have his daughter now and I am going to enjoy every minute of it"

"Pity he couldn't clear your name for the murders, that would have been so funny"

"I think he almost did Olivia, imagine that, the devil killer cleared of all charges"

The two laughed at what might have been.

"This place looks like crap Lennard, are you sure it's not going to collapse anytime soon. The floor is rotten, I am not sure it's going to support our weight"

"Don't worry, it will do and there is no chance that anyone will ever find us here. They will be charging off to Bicester, Buckingham or more likely Aylesbury. By the time they realise we aren't there, we will be long gone, and she will be long dead"

"OK, so what do we do?"

"Right Olivia. Get your phone out, I want you to record every second of this, don't miss a thing. I am going to drive some nails into the floor, we can tie her hands and feet to them. This will make the cutting easier, keep her from stopping us"

Post reached into his jeans pocket and pulled out a hand full of large nails. With the axe he began to hammer them into the floor. This set of several unsettling events, firstly an amount of plaster fell from the ceiling and several creaking and cracking noises emanated from under the floor.

Next three floorboards sprung up near to where he was working, throwing grey dust into the air. Shortly after, there was a sickening sound from a few feet behind them. The wooden floor on which they were standing lurched and settled several inches lower.

"Lennard, for goodness sakes stop bloody hammering. This place is about to collapse around us. If you aren't careful, she won't be the only person dying tonight. Can't we just hold her down and get the job done?"

"If I am doing the cutting and you are filming, who is supposed to hold her down. No, one more nail and I am done. We can stretch her out and make a start"

He gently knocked the final nail into the rotten wooden floor, they were ready.

"Right, you tie her hands to the top two and I will do her legs. Make the rope nice and tight, we don't want her to move"

They pulled Victoria straight, stretching her arms and legs out to the large nails hammered into the floor. Like before, she didn't resist, shock had now taken control of her mind. She was paralysed by the situation, perversely waiting to die. Shaking uncontrollably, she was eventually stretched and tied to the nails by her hands and feet. The rope cut into her flesh, causing blood to ooze forth, but she felt no pain.

"Right Olivia, pull up her jumper and bra, and pull down her jeans. I want to see everything from her pubic bone to her throat. This axe isn't that sharp so it's going to take a while to open her up, but once we do there will be blood and innards everywhere. You need to be ready, get that mobile on-line and do it now"

Nervously she obeyed, pulling their victims clothing up to her throat and down to her knees. She lay like a white tailor's dummy, tied down on the wooden floor. Lennard and Olivia felt a rising tide of excitement and arousal. It had been many years since last he sacrificed a victim. Back then there was no practical mobile phones, no internet to broadcast what they were doing. It had been purely for their own pleasure, watching those women writhe in agony, listening to their screams, watching their blood flow all over the floor.

Now things were different, yes, the plan had been to murder three women tonight but that had changed. This one would have to do, but they would lavish all their attention upon her.

"Right Olivia, is your mobile on?"

"Yes, I am recording now. As soon as you finish the sacrifice I will upload it onto the net, don't worry"

"Ok, point it down at the victim, I want to say a few words.

This pitiful wretch, the daughter of a joke of a detective by the name of Lee Hunter, will be sacrificed tonight. I am the devil incarnate and I will cut her flesh, pull out her entrails and eat them. I will drink her blood; her agony will be a joy to behold. It will give me strength and power, I am the Devil Killer, and you will all fear me"

He then bent down and picked up the axe and held it above his head, ready to strike.

"I will bring this blade down onto her, she will cry out in pain, her blood will flow, and I will be made powerful again. Too long have I been in hibernation, for many a year the devil killer has been imprisoned for doing his work. Not any longer, I am free again and I will do what is right"

He spread his legs and swung the axe behind his head ready to strike. Before he did so he took one last look over to Olivia Cranfield. She had a huge smile on her face as she held her mobile phone, pointing it directly at Victoria Hunter.

She nodded, "strike devil killer, do your work"

We pulled up slowly, killing the engine some distance from the building. Quietly, we got out of the car, not bothering to close the doors behind us.

I could hear talking from within, we needed to get into the chapel and get in now!

"Mister Hunter, we need to do this together. We have the element of surprise; they don't know we've found them. We need to act quickly, kick that door in and rush them. We can't hold back, we certainly cannot hesitate. We smash it open, and go and subdue those two, understood?"

I didn't speak, I just glanced over at Richard and nodded. We approached the door, I could feel the tension in my brain, ready to explode, like a huge bomb on a timer. This had to be right, the voices needed to be that of Post and Cranfield. The grinding thought in my mind was that they were just a couple on a clandestine meeting or someone doing a drugs deal.

I took a huge breath and looked across at Richard one last time. We kicked in the rear door, fortunately our collective effort burst it open, and we rushed straight in. The first to enter was Richard and I quickly followed. The whole scene was one of horror, something out of a very nasty movie.

We didn't speak, we sprinted forward towards Post. Richard was the first to get to the devil killer, launching himself across the remaining distance between himself and that deranged lunatic. He caught him around the shoulders, causing the axe to fly off behind him. There was no mercy from Richard, as they crashed to the floor, he rained several blows into the face of Post. His blood showered off in all direction, he screamed in pain, but Richard did not relent.

Meanwhile, I tackled Olivia Cranfield, sending the woman sprawling across the dirty wooden floor. We both rolled out of control, unfortunately, I banged my head on one of the old rotten pews. For a second this stunned me, giving Olivia Cranfield just enough time to get to her feet. Looking about, she spied the axe laying to her right, without hesitation she picked it up and made her way to where I was laying, still trying to clear my head.

She swung the weapon down at me, missing by inches, only to swing once again. This time the axe grazed my right shoulder sending a flash of pain through the whole of my body. I reacted, but just in time to prevent the third blow, pushing my assailant backwards and back onto the floor. The axe sprung out of her hand, skipping across the floor and out of harm's way.

By now, Lennard Post had been completely subdued by Richard and lay half unconscious on the floor. Responding to the other melee, Richard ran and picked up the axe before going over to Olivia Cranfield and dragging her upright.

"Now Ms Cranfield, I really think you need to consider your next move, I am holding the axe and I will not hesitate in using it, that's not a threat, that's a solemn promise"

"Then use it, I don't care, the devil killer will come to my rescue, you will not live to see tomorrow"

Richard laughed, "Listen, the only people who will die around here are you and that Post laying on the floor. Now settle down and do as you are told"

With a strange rush of silence, the whole scene came to a shuddering stop. A few seconds ago, I was fighting for my life, now all that was over. Post was half unconscious on the floor, Richard had a firm hold on Cranfield, this was it, our job was done.

I looked to my left, strung out on the floor was my daughter, half naked. It seemed surreal, something from a nightmare, it took me a few seconds to gather my thoughts and act. I stumbled to my feet and made my way over to her. I called out her name, but she didn't respond, she just lay there shaking and crying. Grabbing the axe from Richard I hacked away at her bonds, soon she was free, I made good her clothing and held her closer to me than I had ever done before.

As I held my beautiful daughter, Richard called for the ambulance and the Police. Post and Cranfield had been tied to one of the old pew's, all we had to do now was wait. This tragic horror story was over, now we could all go home and start on the long road to recovery.

It wasn't long before the sound of sirens could be heard, soon Victoria would be taken to hospital and Post and Cranfield to the local police station. At lease this time Post would never get out of jail and the rest of woman kind could breathe a sigh of relief.

As for Olivia Cranfield, well time would tell. Was she brainwashed by Post, could she have taken a different course. The courts would have to sort that one out, the psychologists and the criminologists would examine her and determine if she was merely a passenger or an active participant.

Eventually the sound of tyres on the gravel outside the chapel could be heard. Richard came in and announced the arrival of the ambulance, I asked him to take Victoria outside and to the paramedics. I needed to talk to Post, find out why he did what he did. Why start again after his release and what part did Paul Willow actually play.

They sat there on the old rotten pew looking defiant and arrogant. Perhaps the two most dangerous people not currently in jail. Post stared directly at me; I approached him and tried to look confident. Where to start, that was the first thing, I had so many questions to ask, perhaps diving straight in might be the best approach.

"Well, I must admit Lennard, you had me fooled. I suspected you at first but by the end I was certain of your innocence"

"Then you are as stupid as you look Hunter. Why would you ever believe a convicted killer, the evidence at my trial was accurate and conclusive. I managed to convince you of my innocence or at least I cast some doubt into your mind. You really need to ask yourself whether you are best suited to the detective game"

"Well, that's what I am and so far, I seem to have made the right decisions, at least in the end. I need to clarify a couple of things with you before the cops take you away.

Can I assume the person responsible for the latest couple of murders in Aylesbury was Paul Willow?"

Post laughed, looked over at Olivia Cranfield and then back at me.

"That's the first bit of detective work you have got right so far. Yes, Willow acted on my instructions, I figured it would put an end to the finger of suspicion pointing in my direction. It seemed to have worked, or at least it did for a while. He did enjoy killing those two women, to be honest, the photos he sent me suggest he was very good at it. If you pull the phone from my top pocket, I can show them to you. Willow really has a talent for killing, seems to enjoy the blood thing, oh yes and cutting into living flesh.

Anyway, it allowed me to get things organised for the resumption of my work. He went and collected your daughter and that other thing we left in the house. Oh yes, and he got a kicking from some bitch in Aylesbury he tried to capture, that was really funny. It was like days gone by, he would collect my victims and I would enjoy myself killing them, wonderful, what a fucking team"

"So, Peter Dexter was right all along, you are the devil killer"

"I guess so, he never worked out what Willow was doing for me though, another bloody pisshead idiot, is he dead yet? The funny thing was Willows suicide, it was just a ruse so he and Olivia could make plans for my release"

"So why make such a mess when you killed your wife. You left so much evidence behind, something you didn't do with the first victims"

"I know what you mean. It was just a spur of the moment thing, I guess I got carried away. You see, she was only ever going to be a sacrifice, the lady sitting next to me is my one and only love"

"Dexter said they could never charge you with the original killings because you always had an alibi, even being in the police cells on one night"

"It's surprising where bribery can get you, and of course Willow being a cop at the time helped when changes or falsifications to police documents were needed. That included placing me in police cells when I was in fact out enjoying myself with my second victim. Oh, by the way, how the hell did you know we were here, please don't tell me it was a lucky guess"

"To be honest Lennard it was. We were heading to Aylesbury, Richard was convinced you would be hiding there. It was as we passed the turning that he remembered this old place. His organisation used to hide things, in the basement, unload shipments and the like.

He said it was ok for many years, the 'keep off' signs certainly worked. But as time went by, the building really became unsafe, so they stopped using it. It was just a hunch on his part, it's just the kind of place he would have taken someone, no one would hear you scream out here, seems no one did Lennard"

He started to laugh again, but this time he didn't get to reply. The whole building began to shake, slowly at first but then with increasing ferocity. The floor on which I was standing creaked, lurched upwards and then seemed to disappear under me, everything became disorientated. My balance whirled out of control; my conscious mind attempted to comprehend what was happening. I instinctively looked down but all I could see was a boiling mass of grey dust, splintered wood and a black void. I think I called out; I remember putting my arms out in front of me and then blackness.

I had absolutely no idea how long unconsciousness had overcome me, or indeed where I actually was. Total blackness now filled every part of my world, my back and head throbbed uncontrollably, and my mouth and eyes were clogged with dust. I pushed some masonry off my legs, more dust stung my eyes, there was a smell of rot and decay. I felt unsafe and in a dangerous place, it was certain that any minute death would come and take me.

Nothing seemed to make sense, one moment I was talking to Lennard Post, the next, well here I was. Eventually however my mind began to come together, and I started to realise exactly what had happened and where I now found myself. The floor to the chapel must have collapsed or worse, the whole building had come down around me. I tried to sit up, or at least what I thought was up, in the total darkness it was difficult to discern anything at all.

Then a chink of light, somewhere behind me, a thin pencil of white piercing down from above. I must admit that it seemed rather appropriate for a chapel, rather God like. It wasn't long before the dust began to thin, not by much but just enough to allow me to see. Off to my right was a large pile of masonry and smashed timber boards. To my left were several mangled pews mixed with a quantity of roofing tiles, there was a pipe to my front spewing water.

I tried to stand, slowly at first but eventually I gained my full height. There was a sense of claustrophobia, it seemed the wreckage of the building was close to me on all side. Still with pain in my back and head I slowly turned around. Apart from the shaft of light I could see nothing more than a few feet around me, the rest was just a black empty void.

I shouted out, perhaps not the best thing to do in a partly collapsed and extremely unstable building, but it was more reflex than a considered action. The sound was muffled, it reinforced the feeling of being enclosed on all sides. I listened intently but nothing came back, or at least nothing that I could hear.

"Ok Hunter, you need to get yourself out of here because no one is going to help you"

There didn't seem any preferable direction to start, so I made my mind up to go towards the pipe. At lease the dust might be a little clearer in that direction due to the gushing water. I slipped and fell several times but eventually realised that this avenue was completely blocked. So, there was no other alternative, it was back towards the shaft of light, perhaps someone up there was trying to send me a message after all!

The darkness and grime were overwhelming but once I remembered my mobile phone and its built-in torch, things started to become clearer. The shaft of light was coming from a hole in what was left of the floor above. Through it I could see the sky, the gable end of the building and the door through which we had entered the chapel. It seemed that the whole building had collapsed, only leaving one end, a couple of roof beams and the back door.

I shouted again, and to my great relief someone responded, it was Richard.

"Mister Hunter, are you ok?"

"Yep, just a bit knocked about, but I am fine. Is Victoria with you, is she ok?"

"Your daughter is fine, the ambulance left just after the collapse mister Hunter, she will be in the hospital in a few minutes. The whole area out here disappeared into a grey cloud of dust and busted plaster. It was like a foggy day in the middle of winter, I wandered about in the haze for what seemed like and age. I have phone the fire brigade, they are on their way. The police will be here in moments. Stay put, don't move, things look really bad up here, so just relax, the fire and rescue people will have you out in minutes"

"You put her in the ambulance yourself?"

"No, the paramedics came and took her to the front of the building where they had parked. It was a good job they did, just as they disappeared around the corner the whole place collapsed. I heard the siren mister Hunter; they have left I am certain of that"

I had that odd feeling that something was wrong. I knew what Richard had said was right, why wouldn't it be. So, what was it, why did I feel the way I did, maybe the shock had gotten to me, maybe the adrenalin had stopped flowing.

"Can you see Post or his girlfriend Cranfield? They can't be far from me; I was standing right next to them when the walls came in"

"I can't see anyone apart from you mister Hunter, it's just this little hole here where the sun is shining through"

"Right, I think I can scramble high enough for you to grab my hand. Keep your eyes on me, I am on my way up"

I clambered up through smashed bricks, large pieces of broken plaster and splintered wood. To be honest it was somewhat easier than I first thought, and it wasn't long before I could see Richard's hand sticking through the large hole in the now broken floor.

The feeling of relief as I moved back into the world above was immense. The warm sunshine, clear air and feeling of freedom was almost overwhelming.

"You were lucky there mister Hunter, I hate to think of how much weight came down around you. A foot in any other direction and you would be dead for sure, just like those two in there with you"

It was then that I realised, "those other two" as Richard had put it. They were only a foot or two away from me when the building collapsed, so they should have been in that space with me. I cast my mind back to when I had regained consciousness. The pews were there, I could see the space around me, but there was no sign of Post or Cranfield and there should have been!

"Richard, are you sure there are no other ways out of this mess?"

"Don't know mister Hunter. I had hold of your daughter, handed her over to the paramedics, then the whole place just fucking collapsed. I spent a couple of minutes coughing my lungs up and trying to clear the dust from my eyes. I guess the paramedics did the same before they left. It was only seconds later I heard you shouting, you were only down there for a few minutes"

"Listen Richard, we need to scout around this place, where the hell are Post and Cranfield? They weren't in that space with me, if they escaped from another opening, we need to find them"

The two of us raced to the other end of the building but there was nothing to see, other than rubble and dust. We split up and took two more areas of collapse, it wasn't long before Richard shouted out.

I climbed over a small pile of bricks and roof tiles to see Richard standing by what looked like a dusty bundle of rags, half buried in the rubble. As I approached it soon became clear this dirty bundle were the remains of Olivia Cranfield. I could see she was dead; she had that pallor about her skin, lifeless eyes, reflecting the clouds and blue sky above her. There was a large chunk of wood sticking out of her back, like some kind of rough medieval lance.

"She's a goner mister Hunter, that's for sure. Thing is, if she managed to get this far out, even with that thing stuck in her back, perhaps Post did also, so where is he?"

We both looked around, we checked about the whole sorry site, there was nothing, except a possible trail in the dirt towards a set of vehicle tracks.

"Mister Hunter, I really want to be wrong about this, but are these Post's tracks? Perhaps he is injured, broken by the collapse. Maybe he stumbled towards the vehicle that was parked here, maybe he was picked up"

"So, what the hell was parked here?"

"Not sure mister Hunter, it could have been anything. Perhaps these tracks have been here for days. My car is parked on the other side of the rubble, I can see Post's car from here, so he hasn't taken off in that"

I walked around in circles trying to think of what the tracks and the vehicle tyre marks could mean. If Post had got out, maybe someone had picked him up, but who? Willow was still in Steeple Claydon, that's for sure, and no one else would have known they were here. The police were yet to arrive, as were the fire and rescue people.

"I can't think Richard, the only other vehicle that came here was........."

"The paramedics mister Hunter, has that fucker got in the back of that ambulance?"

I didn't want to contemplate what Richard had just said. If he was in the back of that vehicle, then he would be with Victoria. Not only that, but Post was also capable of just about anything. The paramedics, my daughter, everyone in that vehicle could already be dead at the hands of that lunatic.

"Come on mister Hunter, let's get into my car, that ambulance has gone to Stoke Mandeville hospital, it's ten minutes from here, lest go"

Again, we rushed off towards Aylesbury, this time it wasn't just my daughter's life in danger, it was the crew of that ambulance. Post was a deranged killer, goodness knows just how many people he had actually killed. I was determined that he wouldn't be adding any more innocent lives to that total.

We were no more than minutes from the outskirts of Aylesbury when Richard noticed an ambulance parked someway down a farm track, just off the main road. There were trees on one side and open fields on the other. It was almost hidden from the main road, but the bright colours of the vehicle gave away its location.

Goodness knows how Richard managed to spot the vehicle, but it was the miracle break that we needed. He turned off the main road and down the track. There was no way to hide our approach, so we rushed towards the ambulance as fast as we could.

As we advanced, I could see the rear doors of the ambulance were open, and someone was laying on the dusty ground. It was one of the two paramedics, they seemed lifeless, sprawled on their back, legs and arms splayed out.

"What do you want to do mister Hunter. Be cautious, but it seems we are too late for that, or just dive straight in"

I didn't reply, as we stopped some ten yards from the vehicle I jumped out and started to run towards the person laying on the ground. If Post sprang out on me, I would have to deal with that as it happened.

Arriving at the body on the ground I could see it was a woman, perhaps fifty years of age. She had a large gash to the side of her head, blood oozed out and stained the light brown earth. I knelt by her side, the was no pulse, no signs of life at all, she had clearly fallen victim to Lennard Post. There was more, something that chilled me to the bone. Wrapped around her throat was a bright red silk scarf, exactly the same as those found on Posts earlier victims.

I heard something to my rear, I turned in fright but was relieved to see Richard approaching me.

"Is she dead mister Hunter, I don't like the look of all that blood, it's way too much to lose"

"She's dead alright, and Post did this, look at this silk scarf, it's his trademark. We have to find out where he is Richard before anyone else dies"

"I don't think we have far to look mister Hunter"

Richard was staring to one side of the ambulance, clearly there was someone standing at the front of the vehicle. I jumped to my feet and joined him, and right there, no more than a yard from the front of the ambulance was Lennard Post.

He was holding my daughter around the throat with his left arm, and in his right hand was a scalpel, sharp surgical steel glistening in the afternoon sun. He held the blade to her throat, already a small trickle of blood ran down her neck.

"Well, detective Lee Hunter, we meet again. Before you ask, the other paramedic is also dead. I sliced his throat with this very blade, you should have seen the blood, it gushed like a broken water pipe. He ran across that field in a blind panic, he must be dead by now, there is no way he survived that injury. You know, his screams were wonderful, it really turns me on to listen to that noise.

Now it's your daughters turn, I can't wait to feel her warm blood running down my arm. Oh, by the way, did you notice the red silk scarf on the other woman's neck, nice touch hey. Trouble was I hit her too hard, bloody killed her straight away, dam schoolboy error. Please don't tell anyone I fucked up like that, I wouldn't want anyone getting the wrong idea about my skills"

"Listen Post, just let her go, take me instead, she hasn't done you any harm"

"Why do I want you Hunter, I kill women not men. Anyway, I won't get any satisfaction from killing you, I want to kill your daughter and watch the look on your face, magnificent. You can hear her scream and the gurgles as she chokes on her own blood, wow I can't wait"

I wanted to run over to him, grab the scalpel from his hand and thrust it into him, rip him open, tear him apart. I looked around, Richard stood to my right, that late afternoon sun illuminating his features. He looked at me, I could see what he was thinking but my daughter would be dead by the time he got to Post.

"There is no point in looking at your friend Hunter, she is going to die and there is absolutely nothing you can do about it. There is no one here to save you, no plan that will work. Even if both of you rush me, she will be dead long before you can stop me cutting her throat"

Are you not frightened of death Post, if you let her go, I will let you go, that way we both win"

"To be honest Hunter, I am tired, I have spent years in jail, I don't want to go there again. Even if you do let me go someone will catch me eventually. No, this is the end for me, I will slice her open and do the same to my own throat. I will leave it just long enough so I can see that look on your face"

There didn't seem to be a way out, eventually Post would act and I couldn't think of what to do to stop him. I looked at Victoria, her eyes were full of fear, she stared at me, questioning what I might do to save her. I wanted to cry out, reassure her everything would be ok, but it wasn't going to be. Post was going to win, my daughter would die, and I will have to live with the consequences for the rest of my life.

This time I was going to lose. I had beaten the odds so many times during my life and patted myself on the back for my ingenuity. This time was different though, this time there was no way out, this time I had run out of luck.

"Ok Hunter, here we go, get ready to see your daughters blood spirting out, it's a wonderful sight you know. I won't let go of her until she's dead, that way you can watch as her strength fails, and she becomes limp and lifeless.

This was it, I had to move now. In all probability I wouldn't get to her in time, Post would be ready for any move I might make, but I had to try. I slowly pushed my weight forward and prepared myself to run. I hoped Richard would sense this and ready himself likewise.

I was just about to move, make that one last ditched effort to save my daughter when I spotted something in the ditch that ran alongside the track we were standing on. Whatever was there was just behind where Post was holding my daughter. The ditch itself was no more than three feet deep but something or someone was moving up it and towards Post. I looked again, trying not to alert Post to whatever was behind him.

Then I caught sight of a yellow and green high visibility jacket, like the one on the dead paramedic laying at the rear of the ambulance. Could this be the other paramedic, the one Post had seen running away across the fields. I thought he had said he would be dead by now, but perhaps he had been wrong, very wrong indeed.

I tried to think of something to say, in an attempt to keep Post's attention away from his surroundings. I couldn't think of anything meaningful, but luckily Richard came to my assistance.

"Listen Post, my organisation can get you out of the country. You don't have to worry about being caught, no one will know where you went, they will never find you"

"Good try, whoever you are, but trust me, they will. I am too fucking dangerous to let go. They will search everywhere, they will never give up, I don't want to live like that, looking over my shoulder day after day"

It was just enough of a distraction, as the paramedic emerged undetected out of the ditch, carrying a large stone in one hand. I could see he was covered in blood and moved slowly and very awkwardly, but he was here and ready to act. Stumbling once but remaining silent, he approached Post. My heart missed a beat, I was certain he would be detected, and Post would turn and finish the job. He got closer and closer, time seemed to stand still, every step he took felt like hours.

He was almost there, no more than a couple of feet from my daughter and Post when he made a mistake. I am not sure whether he stumbled again or tripped on the trackway, but Post heard him and turned.

Post didn't hesitate, he launched himself at the man, stabbing him several times in the stomach. They fell to the dusty earth, but despite his injuries, the paramedic managed to put up a fight.

I caught site of Richard to my left, he sprinted towards the two, I followed his path with my eyes, and it was then I realised Victoria was standing there, like a statue, alone. I set off, now stung into action, running as fast as my aching body would allow. I shouted her name, she responded, looked at me, smiled and held out her arms. Seconds later I had her, holding onto her as tightly as my arms would allow. She was sobbing against my chest, I turned, took her by the hand and ran.

We stumbled a couple of times, all the while wondering if Lennard Post was just about to stab me in the back. I dared not look back, I just wanted to get away, far away. It wasn't long before I began to tire, as did Victoria. I needed to stop, look back, assess the situation. Richard was still behind us, as was the injured paramedic. I had my daughter, she was safe, but those other two, maybe they needed my help.

Some distance from the ambulance we finally came to a stop.

"Listen Victoria, down there is Richard's car, it's a flash BMW Coupe. Go and get into it, lock the doors, I will be back shortly"

"No dad, come with me please"

"I need to help Richard and that poor guy. I can't just leave them, I owe both of them so much, you owe them your life"

"Dad please....."

"No, go, get in the car, I will be back, don't worry"

I didn't wait, I had to help. I let go of her and started to run back to the ambulance. Before I reached the area where the man had attacked Post it was clear that things had come to a head. Richard was standing over Post, who in turn was laying over the paramedic.

Richard looked over to me as I approached, a look of calmness on his face.

"Don't worry mister Hunter, it's all over. I think the ambulance guy is a goner though, that's a shame, we owe him a lot. Odd thing though, I think Post is too, it seems like the scalpel ended up in Posts neck, cutting is carotid artery, several times, must have been an accident hey"

As I slowed, I wondered about Richards last statement, how the hell could that blade have cut Post's neck several times, especially if the paramedic was already dead? Arriving at the scene it became obvious from the blood on

Richards clothes that perhaps he had more to do with Post's death than he was ever going to admit.

The scene in front of me was one of both sadness and relief. The innocent paramedic, doing his job, saving lives, now he had bled out on a dusty track just outside Aylesbury and no one was here to say thank you for saving my daughter's life. Then there was Post, a psychopathic maniac, killer, torturer, and bringer of death. I was glad to see his blood, still slick and warm, running out of his torn throat and neck.

I wondered how many people, innocent souls that had been taken by Post. I guess we will never know, only Post, Cranfield and perhaps Paul Willow would know the answer to that question. Post and Cranfield were dead, and I was certain that Willow would never confess to anything, so we will never find out.

I looked up into Richards eyes. He seemed oddly unperturbed by the scene, he seemed relaxed, perhaps just another day's work.

"Listen Richard, I need to thank you and Stephen for your help. Without you two my daughter would certainly be dead of that there is no doubt at all!"

"Mister Hunter, no need to thank me, what Post was doing was out of order. Don't get me wrong, I am no pillar of society, but he was some sick fuck and needed to be put down. Me and Steve will go back to doing what we do best, and I guess you will do the same. Go and hug your daughter, let this be a lesson to both of us, you never know what's around the corner, so never take family for granted"

It seemed a very wise statement from a local gangster, but he was more than a hired hard man, that was for certain. I guess I owed him and Stephen my life and the life of Victoria, and I would always be grateful for that.

Two months later.

After the incident, I spent a whole month with my two daughters. It was fantastic, lots of days out, even went over to France on the ferry, oh boy was I sick! Never mind, I will add 'never travel by sea' to my lists of things not to do, ever, ever again!

Richard was right of course, don't take family for granted. Maybe it's just a consequence of living, work and making your way through the maze of life, you just end up doing exactly that. Then something happens which reminds you just what is important, that's the people around you, your family and friends.

Anyway, the business is going well, Chris managed all the new cases, and my lovely PA Jan Talbot is back, great news. Tony Bianchi has set up his new whiskey importing business, he brought me a couple of bottles. It took me all weekend to drink them, apparently together they cost over five hundred pounds. To be honest, they were wonderful, but it didn't stop me feeling like shit for the rest of the week.

So, where do I go from here? Well firstly stay out of the way of the police. Marcus Cook and Deborah Smith are somewhat pissed off with my meddling and using the criminal fraternity to help solve cases. My point was, we got the job done, so where is the harm. There point was, 'do that again Hunter and your nicked', ok, point taken!

I received a text from Richard and Stephen, they invited me for a drink at the Tiger Inn. They said the local police returned to normal, whatever normal is in their world. I will visit them again one day, I know they are on the wrong side of the law, but they are on the right side of humanity, and I can't help but have a fondness for them. After all, I owe them more then they can ever imagine, and I will always be grateful for that.

I guess I will tell Jan to filter out anything that looks to be more exciting than watching some errant husband. I don't want anything to do with psychopaths, evil cults or bent cops. Let's have a couple of years of boring stuff, boring is good and that's the way I like it. Oh yes, I have booked a holiday, work comes second from now on, yet another consequence of this case. I have been contacted by an old friend of mine; he is setting up a walking holiday in Italy. Looks great so I am off for a couple of weeks, nice and quiet, relaxing days in the mountains, what could possibly go wrong!

In loving memory of
Peter Dexter.
Detective Chief Inspector (Retired).
O3/04/1946 – 01/02/2024.
R.I.P.